TOGETHER THEY FLY

Beryl Chapman

Cover design by Jim Wilkie taken from a watercolour by the author.
Opening chapter illustrations are from pen drawings by the author and Jennie Hooper.
The author thanks those who have helped and inspired her to write this book.

TOGETHER THEY FLY

Beryl Chapman

BARNWORKS PUBLISHING
PULBOROUGH, ENGLAND

First published 1995 in Great Britain by
Barnworks Publishing
St. Annes Cottage, Bury, Pulborough, West Sussex
RH20 1PA

British Library Cataloguing in Publication Data.
A catalogue record for this book is available from the British Library.

ISBN: 1 899174 00 1

Typeset by Rosetec of Worthing, Sussex, England.

Covers printed by Chichester Press, Chichester, West Sussex, England.
Printed and bound by Hartnolls of Bodmin, Cornwall, England.

To all who care for wildlife

THE ENGLISH LAKE DISTRICT

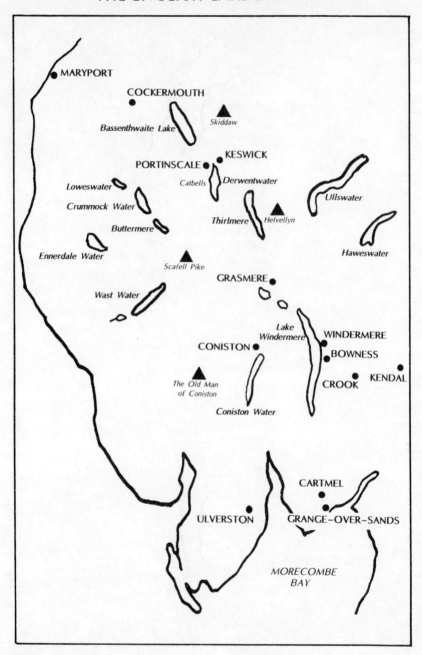

LAKE WINDERMERE

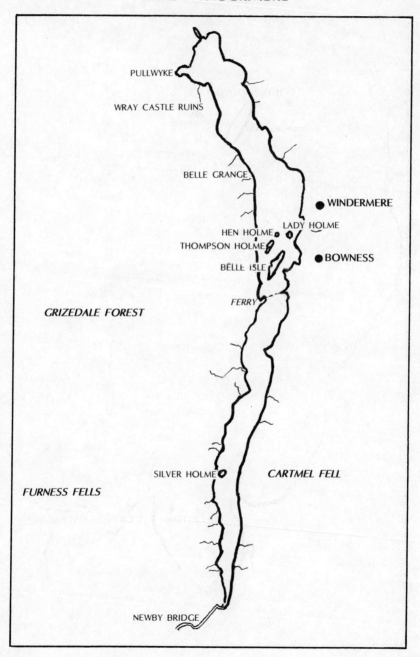

CHAPTER 1
THE WINGS OF CHANGE

He glanced anxiously over his shoulder at his sister, who was hurrying to his side, and called encouragingly to her. The other three were ahead and he was keen to catch them up. Suddenly, the leader's wings opened and his eager feet slapped the water causing his body to rise into the air and almost simultaneously his two companions rose with him. The brother and sister left the water and all five flew in low formation towards the expectant group of swans further along the river.

The musical sound of their flight reached the ears of Jackie and Steve Brough watching from the bank. They felt a mixture of pleasure and anxiety for the departing cygnets; anxiety, purely for their safety and pleasure because they had succeeded in rearing them from babies into healthy young adults.

The sun glinted sharply through a chink in the grey clouds, causing wet grass to sparkle and its light to reflect from the dancing ripples into the couple's eyes. Bare branches of the nearby silver birches swayed gracefully in one of March's sudden breezes.

The blue-grey water, which had been churned up by the five pairs of webbed feet released from their imprisoning swan carriers, was beginning to settle and allow the broken reflections of the surrounding trees and fields to reform .

With a last lingering look at the birds, Steve bent to pick up the untidy pile of carriers which looked like open plumbers' tool bags. Jackie brushed some splattered mud from her jeans.

"Patch looked very worried when you let her brother go before I could release her. They've always been so close, haven't they?" she said. "It's a shame that when she grows her adult feathers they will disguise the white splodge on her forehead and then we won't be able to recognise her so easily."

Steve agreed and set off towards the waiting car but Jackie lingered a few moments longer for a last look at the birds before following her husband. She felt the motherly twinge of loss as she watched her borrowed children going out into the world and out of her care.

The old Ford Cortina estate bumped over the rutted track which wound between the fields, leaving the river behind. Buds on the trees were swelling, creating little knobs on the twigs which, not long before, had looked so smooth. Here and there evergreen trees and bushes helped to fill in the still sparse scenery. A squirrel, surprised by the vehicle, hurried with a looping gait until it reached the safety of a gnarled oak when it seemed to flow up the tree and vanish.

Upon reaching the road Steve turned left and, moving quickly through his gears to reach top, soon had the scenery rushing past the windows as he raced home for lunch. He glanced at Jackie who was sitting quietly beside him, her eyes on the view ahead but he knew by her vacant expression that her mind was back with the cygnets.

She was remembering people bringing the tiny bundles of grey fluff to them in ones and twos. The RSPCA[†] had brought the brother and sister because their mother had been killed. Two of the others had been found wandering and lost, whilst the third single baby had been brought by people whose dog had carried it home. It was fortunate the dog had not injured the cygnet but the people were unable to say from where it had come.

---

† Royal Society for the Prevention of Cruelty to Animals

Soon the gables of an old house came into view and Steve slowed ready to turn into the drive. The house belonged to Jackie's father, Ken Mason, with whom the young couple lived.

Most of that morning Ken had been busy in the garden tidying up some overgrown climbers, although his heart was not in it. He shook his head with mixed feelings as he thought of his once quiet life. Now, there was so much coming and going of people bringing injured birds. How nice it would be to have peace with someone of his own generation to love and who would care for him, too. But he could not imagine trusting anyone again.

A wet nose thrust itself into his hand. "Ah Bess, m'lovely, there's nothin' insincere about the love of a dog." The black and tan German shepherd sat down beside him with her dark brown eyes fixed intently upon his face. Her big tongue lolled over shining white teeth as she dusted the floor with her happy tail.

Just then she heard Steve and Jackie's car turning in at the gate so she jumped up and, with a welcoming bark, rushed across the garden to greet them.

Ken, noting the time, picked up his tools and followed her.

"We're home, Dad," called Jackie, guessing from the way Bess kept looking behind her that he would be outdoors.

"Hi, Dad," Steve called, momentarily catching sight of his unruly grey hair.

" 'Ello there, yer two. Alright then?" He did not wait for any further conversation but went towards his tool shed.

Jackie quickly got to work in the house preparing lunch while Steve put away the swan carriers and looked around to check that the remaining birds were settled.

About twenty minutes later they were all in the homely kitchen eating sandwiches. Three mugs of steaming tea stood on the table together with a bowl of fruit salad, a jug of fresh cream from the nearby farm, and a plate of homemade cakes.

"Well, it seems yer've actually left the five be'ind, as yer've come back with an empty car," teased Ken.

"Yes, Dad. There's five pairs of webbed feet less to flatten your grass. You know you really should find a lady friend and then you'd have something else to think about other than being a fuss-pot." She smiled at him to soften her words, as they were as close as different generations could be.

"No fear, m' lass. I don't trust people no longer, dogs are a much better bet."

"Oh, Dad, you are incorrigible."

11

"Changin' the subject Steve, there's some letters for yer by this mornin's post. A couple look to be from estate agents and bein' Sat'day yer might want to see som'at or other."

"Thanks, I'll take a look." Steve went into the hall and, picking up his letters, returned to the kitchen.

"Isn't it time yer let that kestrel go, Jackie? She was screamin' at another that was 'overin' over'ead this mornin'."

"Yes, perhaps it is, 'tho we're still not sure her wing muscles are strong enough, after being immobilised in plaster, to enable her to hover and hunt."

"Fair enough lass, but if yer keep 'er too long she'll become too dependent on yer and it'll be worse for 'er. Feed 'er well, and leave the aviary door open with food put in an obvious place. Yer must take some risks."

Bess gave a long drawn out groan and flopped down across her master's feet, as though she really did not agree with any of this conversation and, why 'was no-one taking any notice of her?' A big weather-beaten hand offered half a sandwich to his complaining friend.

"Dad, you spoil her. You'll utterly ruin her."

"So? I spoilt yer and it's not done yer no 'arm, 'cept yer boss me about som'at dreadful. Any'ow yer keep tellin' me to find another woman, well she's lyin' at m' feet, where women ought to be."

Steve interrupted the banter by waving a house detail sheet at them. "This sounds interesting, listen — 'Cottage in one acre, low price for quick sale. Some renovation needed, including land drains'. "

"That means, cottage fallin' to bits and garden like bog-land. So, by 'cheap' it means that by the time yer've spent out on it to make it 'abitable it 'll be expensive."

"Dad, you really are a pessimistic old cynic."

"No dear, just a bloke what's learnt the 'ard way that life's not 'anded out on a platter. Suspicion's a safeguard 'gainst those that's out to do yer. Go and see it by all means, but look with real eyes, not thro' rose tinted specs. Look for dry and wet rot. Look for tiles off the roof, or damaged tiles or a dented roof that could 'ave 'ad a tree fall on it and maybe's damaged the interior structure. Look at room ceilin's for patches caused by damp, then find what caused 'em. If yer decide it 'as possibilities go through all the things yer'll 'ave to do to make 'em right, price 'em in yer mind and work out 'ow long yer'll need to do the work. Remember if yer're goin' to do it yersel's, yer'll need a lot of know-'ow and if yer 'aven't got it, it

12

costs more money. That's 'ow yer arrive at the offer price. G'on, off yer go and enjoy yersel's. Bess and I want some peace and then no doubt she'll be after a walk."

Steve rang the estate agents and made an appointment to view whilst Jackie cleared away the crockery. Then, calling 'goodbye', they went out and got in the car.

Jackie was excited and smiled at her husband as they turned out of the gateway. The young couple had been hunting for their own home for some time, but nothing had come anywhere near the kind of property they needed or could afford. This time the price made it possible but what condition would it be in? Naturally they were full of cautious expectancy.

Taking the A590 they headed north "We're to make a right turn after Haverthwaite, probably sign-posted Grange-over-sands, which'll be the B5278, then once we're on it there should be a left to Barber Green, after that we follow the estate agent's directions. It sounds as though it is in a reasonable position for people to reach us with birds. So let's hope we like the cottage and it's in a reasonable state of repair."

"It wouldn't be easy for me to continue giving piano lessons though, Steve, would it?"

"No, my love, that it wouldn't. You'd have to find new students if we feel that we can't rely on my earnings from writing. You remember that lady who brought us the lesser black backed gull with the broken wing? She suggested we should form a charity if we planned to do more bird rescue work. We must find out more about it."

"The idea certainly sounds interesting, but I don't see how it can take the place of income."

"I see it as an additional form of income. We would have to find volunteer helpers who could organise various fund-raising functions and, as those takings are not subject to tax, that helps too. Of course there'd be donations, and if these are given under a Deed of Covenant we reclaim the tax that people have paid to the government. The money I'm earning wouldn't be enough to keep us and all our increasing bird patients, especially if vets' bills have to be included. So, if we're really going to do this work as we've been discussing, we'll need a great deal of help in all ways."

"It sounds rather daunting. Do you think we should forget the whole project before we commit ourselves completely?"

"That depends, my love, if we're thinking only of life from our point of view, then yes, let's forget it. But what will you do when someone brings an injured bird — tell them to take it away? We know full well if they troubled to bring it in the first place, they haven't a clue what to do with it and may just leave it under a bush somewhere, or 'put it out-of-its-misery'."

"I couldn't do that."

"No, neither could I. We must go on somehow."

"There's the turning, B5278." Jackie pointed to the partly hidden entrance.

"Good girl." He swung the car to the right, into the narrow road.

After a few more turns they felt they must be getting nearer.

"Keep your eyes open for a "For Sale" board."

At last they found it. Steve turned in through a dilapidated gateway, stopping on the weedy gravel path. He got out of the car and stood looking about him. His father-in-law was right, it looked a forlorn and neglected place. The gate rested at a drunken angle, hanging by one hinge. The windows, patterned with spiders' webs, were lost behind a jungle of overgrown shrubs and weeds. Paint was flaking off the woodwork and a broken roof-tile lay at their feet.

"It looks such a sad, lonely house. Amazing isn't it, how even a house can seem to be begging for someone to care for it."

"Now then Jackie, remember what your Dad said. He's a wise old bird, you know. Look with your eyes open, and work out whether it will do and whether we can afford to make it habitable, and forget your heart."

"Yes, I know. You're both right, but ... ."

The sound of tyres crunching over the gravel broke into their conversation and heralded the arrival of the estate agent.

"Good afternoon Mr and Mrs Brough. A bit overgrown isn't it?" he said, as he fought his way to the front door and inserted the key.

The door swung open with a little groan to reveal a hallway with a patterned tiled floor and three rooms leading off it. Their echoing footsteps followed them through the first doorway into the main living-room, which was quite big and airy. Jackie walked across to one of the latticed windows to look at the view, but found it to be mostly hidden by the overgrown climbers outside which were threatening to force their way indoors.

After they had been shown the other rooms, the agent went to sit in his car leaving them to wander where they wanted and discuss matters in private.

The upstairs ceilings sloped down to join the walls as the rooms were built high up into the roof space. "So these are skeilings — I wondered what they were," commented Steve as he looked around the main bedroom. He carefully opened a window and they leaned out between the thick, lakeland stone walls. Outside was utter peace and all that could be heard was a thrush singing.

"Do you think we could make it right? It's so lovely here, I really feel at home."

"Let's go outside and see what the garden is like. Don't forget if we're to start a charitable bird hospital the outside possibilities are more important than the house."

They pushed their way through the jungle of weeds to find the out-buildings which were in suprisingly good condition. Then they wandered on to find the wet area.

"You know, there must be a natural spring somewhere round here for so much water to be lying, which could be a god-send to us for our pond."

By this time they were both feeling eager as, at last, they had found a place that appeared to be right. They looked back at the neglected cottage, which seemed to be frowning at them under its low roof.

"Apart from the odd tile, that roof looks in quite good nick, in spite of the invading creepers. Which is lucky, as that would be expensive to replace."

The estate agent walked towards them, stopping any further conversation.

*

Bess yawned her special yawn which always ended with a squeak, then sat up and looked at her master. Ken heard the yawn and pretended to be asleep but watched her through slitted eyes disguised by his eye-lashes. Bess stared at him but getting no response got up and, placing one heavy paw on his knee, poked his chest with her nose.

Ken had to respond, he laughed and hugged the big dog. "OK, gal. Yer win. Walkies!" The three-year-old dog who weighed just on ninety pounds, bounded into the centre of the room and joyfully whirled round twice with thunderous barking. "Com'on, let's go up to the beck."

A cabinet-maker by trade but, having taken early retirement, he now only did "specials". He enjoyed the work and it brought him useful extra income when needed. A meticulous craftsman, he had a name for the excellent quality of his work. Throughout his working life he always had more customers than he could satisfy.

He preferred to finish his furniture in either French polish or wax. If he used varnish he created a silk finish rather than a high gloss.

Since his divorce twelve years ago Ken, naturally a friendly and helpful man, had carefully avoided any situation that might leave him at the 'mercy of a scheming woman'. He was a man who had put his whole being into loving and trusting his wife. When Jennie fell in love with another man and left him it shocked him greatly and completely shattered his confidence in the female sex. He made an exception of his fourteen-year-old daughter who had chosen to stay with him when the break came.

There had always been a deep understanding between father and daughter. In the intervening years Jackie had cared for him and kept house, this strengthened the bond between them.

When she married Steve five years later she refused to leave Ken, so he split the house to give them independence. Knowing how important it was for a newly married couple to be alone, he did not wish to be an interfering parent breathing down their necks. He had always liked Steve and believed the pair of them had every chance of making a good marriage. Still, he had not bargained for his garden being given over to so many birds, several aviaries and even a small pond. The latter, being at the bottom, was threatening to engulf his vegetable patch.

Ken and Bess walked on across pasture land, at that moment empty of cattle, heading for the track which would lead them to the beck. It was a favourite walk, where he could 'lose' himself in the surrounding hills and Bess could run free without coming to any harm. In the distance could be seen the mass of Furness Fells, which acted as a purple-grey back-drop to the soft greens of the country around them.

Ken stopped and, leaning against a dry stone wall, idly fingered a patch of lush moss growing in a crevice between the stones.

He was a solidly built man with proud, straight shoulders. His hair was grey-to-white with a balding patch at the back of his head. These days his expression was usually serious. When something made him laugh, his whole face would light up and laughter lines would betray his now-hidden character.

He gazed into the distance to the place where he had proposed to his wife all those years ago. He had thought her so bonny. She had a small, nicely shaped body, which used to tuck well into his arm as they walked. Jackie was very much like her. "Women. Can't trust 'em. I was a fool to 'ave fallen for 'er, let alone married the wench.

But then, I suppose, there'd 'ave bin no Jackie and life would 'ave bin pretty pointless without my little lass."

Bess drew his attention to herself by bringing him a stick and pushing it into his hand. She knew when he became introspective and always found some way to cheer him up. He grabbed the stick and, hurling it away, admired his dog's rhythmic gait and powerful, muscular body as she raced after it.

A skein of Canada geese honked as they flew overhead, making Ken think of his daughter and wonder how she and Steve were getting on at the cottage. He would be sad when they went, but he knew it was high time they lived their own life. He would look around for the perfect retirement home for himself. After all, being in his early fifties, he could take his time to get it right. A workshop would be useful as he would still want to use all his tools.

Man and dog continued their walk, following familiar paths and eventually circling back home. As they came within sight of it they saw the old estate car returning from the opposite direction.

Stopping on the driveway of their Ulverston home, Jackie stepped out of the car and looked at the familiar house. Her old bedroom window was glinting in the sunlight. It was from there that she used to look out towards Hoad Hill with its famous Barrow Monument, a replica of the Eddystone lighthouse, built in memory of Sir John Barrow. When she and Steve married, she had turned the big double room at the back, which overlooked the garden, into a bedroom for them both, decorating it in blue and beige. The other bedroom had been made into a bathroom.

She had been brought up in this house and her inside gave a lurch at the thought of leaving it. However, she had fallen for the old stone cottage and Steve felt the grounds were perfect for their proposed bird hospital. She thought about leaving her father alone. It was his own fault that he was alone as she had tried hard to find him a lady-friend, and had suggested he join associations for companionship, but he would not do so. She knew she could not push him any more, neither could she live his life for him. She had a duty, also, to her beloved Steve. To have a home of their own was important but she could not help her divided loyalties. Never, in all her life, had she been able to hurt anyone without hurting herself more in doing so.

Steve's hand clasped hers, and she looked up into his dear face. He smiled at his neat little wife, admiring her pretty oval face framed by light brown hair which topped her five foot six inches of stamina and strength. 'Also, ins-and-outs all in the right places and

17

to the right amount,' he thought to himself. "Come on dreamer, our dinner wants cooking and the birds need feeding."

She pressed herself to him and snuggled her head onto his shoulder as they began to walk to the house. There was no need for words as, being so in love they often knew what the other was thinking. Steve placed a light kiss on her forehead, she turned her face up with a smile and kissed him mischievously on the nose.

"So that's the game is it, my girl?" Swiftly, he bent down and, with one arm still round her shoulders, he scooped up her legs with the other, lifting her slight person into the air. She let out a happy shriek as she clung to him, which brought Bess bounding in from the road barking at them to behave.

With her tail waving, the dog took Steve's hand carefully in her mouth, telling him firmly to put Jackie down. He did so and turned his attention to Bess, patting her and pushing her about, in rough play. She growled in mock ferocity as she leapt around then, spotting the house details that Jackie was holding, she reached up and grabbed them. Shaking them vigorously she raced off towards Ken, who had just come through the gate.

"Hey, you torment, bring them back and in one piece, too," shouted Steve but at the same time Jackie called, "Bessie, Bessie bring them to me, good girl."

The dog swerved to avoid Steve's grabbing hand and, circling back to Jackie, gave her the papers.

"What a good girl. Thank you, Bess. See, Steve, we girls react better to politeness."

Bess was looking for something else to do and, seeing Jackie's handbag on her arm, gently took hold of the strap turning her eyes up to the girl's face, clearly asking to be allowed to carry it. "Alright, Bess, take it into the house for me." The big dog held the bag proudly and trotted off with it.

"I suppose you'll be telling me that even a dog can ask politely," he teased "Go on treasure, you go after her and see to the meal and I'll do the birds."

Ken smiled happily as he followed his dog and daughter indoors.

Down at the river the five cygnets had become part of the existing group consisting of four adults in white plumage, the rest juveniles, in various shades of grey according their ages. The brother and sister from the new five, stayed fairly close together but the other three mixed readily with the main group.

It was not long before one of the young cobs became attracted to the sister, Patch, and kept coming up to her and going through some of the courtship movements. She responded to his advances and they both swam up to each other, raising their long necks and gracefully turning their heads first to one side then to the other. They did this in unison several times, before dipping their bills for a ceremonial sip of water and raising their heads high letting it slip down inside their long necks.

The brother did not like all this and hissed at them, rather ineffectually, as they were too preoccupied with each other to take any notice of him.

The young cob stayed with the brother and sister until, gradually, the sibling bond between the pair weakened. Early one morning, the suitor cob ran across the water with his wings beating strongly for take-off. Calling excitedly to his chosen one he flew round her in low circles, inviting her to join him, whilst the brother sat on the water a little distance away, watching.

His sister whickered to him, then looked up at the calling bird. Unable to resist the urge, she opened her wings, ran on the water and flew to his side. The brother watched as his sister became a distant speck before slowly he turned and paddled after the main flock.

Several weeks later a lone female cygnet came gliding in to land on the water a short distance away from them all. She was rather timid and remained amongst some reeds. Although she needed company, she had recently been attacked by a resident mated cob swan when she had, inadvertently, landed on his territory.

The brother, still feeling the loss of his sister, was intrigued by the new-comer and swam slowly towards her. She, sensing his attitude, came out to meet him. He turned his head away as she arrived, denoting non-aggression and she did likewise, then they turned their heads the opposite way. By this time, they had stopped so close that their feathers were all but touching. They continued to sway and turn their necks, like the evocative arms of an oriental dancer, before taking that ceremonial sip of water.

The new pen swam close behind the now proud young cob and joined the group. She was confident that, as his newly accepted mate, he would protect her.

19

The purchase of the stone cottage went remarkably smoothly and Steve and Ken had got on well with the restoration work. They had repaired the rotten woodwork, scraped off the old flaky paint and were repainting it. The drunken gate had already been repaired and re-hung on new hinges. The creeper was pulled off the roof and the tiles and the stonework cleaned and repaired.

Aviaries and a general enclosure for swans and other water-birds were built. Also temporary facilities to take the hospital cages had been constructed in one of the outbuildings.

There was an old Aga in the kitchen which, apart from soap and water had not needed any more attention. Steve loaded in some coke and struck a match. "We'll help the cottage dry out by leaving this on low whilst we are coming backwards and forwards. By the time we move in everywhere will be warm, dry and welcoming." The fire caught on and smoke billowed out into the kitchen causing Jackie to rush to open the back door and close the hall door. "It's only because of the cold damp chimney, Jackie, it'll soon clear."

Jackie started "beavering away" in the garden; chopping down brambles, digging up nettles, ivy roots and everything else that had taken such a hold. She cleared one huge spot and piled all burnable stuff onto it. Very soon the pile was enormous.

"Hey there kiddo, what are you about to do, burn the house down just when we're getting it respectable?" Steve's voice floated down from the top of the ladder where he was painting the guttering.

"No dear, I'll let you do it later, you know fires won't start for me."

"Then make another pile further away, there's a good lass. It'll save me having to move it all again before I set light to it. But first, how about a cuppa?"

After weeks of work the cottage was ready for them to move into. The outside was bright and tidy having lost that sad, uncared-for, appearance. The inside was clean and shining too with scrubbed floors and fresh paint on walls, ceilings and woodwork.

At last removal day dawned. Ken, driving a borrowed van, pulled onto the cleaned-up driveway. Jackie and Steve were following and parked the Ford, the roofrack piled high with carpets, by the front door.

They were lucky, as the sun chose to shine for them they could stand things outside, enabling them to get carpets down first, before putting the furniture in its place.

Jackie thought it was going to be easy and that they would be straight before nightfall. She did not allow for all the contents of the cardboard boxes and plastic bags which had to be emptied into their new places. Soon, they could barely move for all the stuff cluttering the floor.

"Right, I'll leave you and Dad to unpack and go back in the van for more things. We must keep moving. After the house stuff, we have to bring as many birds as possible today or poor Dad will be left with feeding and cleaning them out."

"Too right, son. Too right," boomed a voice from another room.

*

By the time winter came Jackie and Steve had happily settled into their new routine. A pond had been dug, filled by the convenient spring that had been keeping the lower ground wet, and the water-birds were thoroughly enjoying themselves. Further aviaries were erected, each with their own housing. There was a hospital with warm cages for the sick and open-topped enclosures for the bigger birds. These had all been created within the larger of the existing outbuildings. Later, using another outbuilding, they would construct a convalescent house with a variety of cages and enclosures to suit all types and sizes of birds.

One day a solicitor, who specialised in charity work, came to see them. When they took him round the premises they were happy to find that he was very impressed with what he saw. He listened intently to their plans for the future and said, "It's very refreshing to hear that you have your own means of support, and are looking for money for caring for the birds and not yourselves. Unfortunately, many people see charity as a means of an easy existence for themselves, and their work takes second place. However, there's no reason why you can't reclaim expenses, petrol for the car, clothes for working in and, of course, pay yourselves a wage."

"That certainly takes the pressure off us as I was beginning to wonder, if the bird intake got high, how I was going to deal with them as well as earn a living," said Steve.

21

"You must take it a day at a time and balance the income from your work for the charity with that from your own work. In that way you should tick over quite nicely. It's the people that milk the charity money and are always screaming for more that finally go under: their supporters soon get wise to them!"

After the solicitor left they went indoors. Jackie made some coffee, which she took with some sandwiches into the living room where Steve was busy studying the charity rules.

"It seems that we have to find some people to act as Trustees, and then we have to form a committee to run the Trust and organise fund-raising," explained Steve.

"It sounds very interesting," commented Jackie

"Yes, but there's a lot involved. Do you agree that we should go ahead and sign up the paperwork to get our charity status through?"

"Yes, Steve, I think we must do it!"

The next two and a half years went past quickly. The hospital obtained its charity status, and became known as Birdholme Wild Bird Hospital Trust.

Jackie, busy teaching several youngsters from Cartmel to play the piano found the regular money very useful. She was a patient and sensitive teacher and, as she was becoming known, there were many enquiries from eager parents wanting her to teach their children. The steadily increasing birdwork was demanding more and more of her time and she had to limit her pupils accordingly.

Steve had taken over one of the bedrooms for his study and wrote articles on a regular basis for several journals interested in nature. Over the past years he had studied bird welfare, conservation and their disappearing habitats together with environmental issues in his deeply loved Lake District. Born and bred in Ulverston, he had travelled Cumbria, Lancashire and Yorkshire studying in such detail that he could write with authority and insight.

Thanks to the donations from many well-wishers, they were able to purchase much needed hospital equipment.

One day a man had brought in a badly injured seagull which needed immediate surgery. Steve had had to use injection anaesthetic and, although he carefully assessed the dosage, the bird was too weak to stand it and died. Very upset and rather embarrassed, he left the surgery to tell the waiting man what had happened. However, far from blaming Steve, the man said he knew where he could get an old anaesthetic machine which was still working. If Steve would like it, the man said he would donate it to the hospital.

Jackie and Steve made a lot of enthusiastic new friends, who worked with them, both in raising the all-important working capital, and running collection services for injured birds when the finders themselves were unable to deliver them. There was always the twice-a-day cleaning, feeding and medicating of the sick and injured and, of course, new patients could arrive at any time, instantly requiring attention. During nesting time they hardly had a moment to themselves as nestlings had to be fed at least hourly throughout the daylight hours. There were many joys and many sorrows in the work but it was always worthwhile.

Ken, meanwhile, had stayed at the old house with Bess and visited his daughter and son-in-law from time to time, both socially and to help with the birds and garden. Jackie kept urging him to find a lady-friend but he remained stubbornly determined not to allow himself to be hurt again.

Whilst sorting out a cupboard that was well overdue for such treatment he found a crumpled photograph of Jackie as a youngster playing with Steve and his sister Emma. It had been taken at Steve's parents' home. Tom and Jill Brough lived at the south end of Ulverston in a rambling farmhouse with about five acres of land, where they kept a herd of goats and sold milk and home-made cheese. Emma had married Jeff, a lad whose mother was Australian. After his father had died his mother had returned to her homeland. Soon afterwards, Emma and Jeff followed as he was needed to manage the family sheep-farm near Perth in Western Australia. It was strange to think that she was now living in the homeland of the black swan and her brother was working with the white swan.

Ken remembered the happy days when the two families were very close friends and often visited each other. He enjoyed helping Tom with his racing pigeons, cleaning out their loft and studying the birds and their individual qualities. There was no doubt in his mind that it was from his father Steve got his love of birds and also his affinity with them. Birds and animals know instinctively the people whom they can trust and those whom they must avoid, and Tom's birds never flinched when he picked them up to examine them. He was well-known for his breeding of quality racers and people would come from all over the North of England to buy stock to improve their own lofts.

Rummaging amongst more stuff in the cupboard Ken discovered another photograph where Steve was proudly carrying an injured swan after he had helped the RSPCA inspector to catch it. His young Jackie was walking at the boy's side with such a happy carefree smile on her face. The two youngsters had been firm friends from early school days and never once lost touch with each other, so it was no wonder that they eventually married. As Ken's mind wandered through the happy scenes around the farmhouse and land he saw the youngsters playing with the lovely black and white border collie, Shep. Jill had bought the dog from a farmer who had decided that the animal, then eighteen months old, was not good enough for herding work and wanted to sell him to a good home. Steve had said quite recently that old Shep was getting near his end and his mother, in particular, was dreading the day when he would no longer be with them.

Ken regretted losing contact with his old friends. It was his own fault, he knew, but after his wife left him he felt so bitter and humiliated that he became quite a recluse and, apart from his shopping and work, saw very few people. After so many years it was difficult to change his ways. He pulled his mind back to the present and viewed the pile of things surrounding him on the floor.

Bess chose that moment to come bounding upstairs to find her beloved master. She charged straight into the room and snuffled in his ear before washing his face with her ample pink tongue.

"Get off with yer. Don't take advantage of an ol'man surrounded by things 'e doesn't know what to do with."

Bess dropped her front down amongst the paper and clothing leaving her rear end in standing position and waved her tail, causing a draught which lifted various sheets of paper into the air.

"I did 'ave this stuff in some semblance of order and now look what yer've gone an' done."

Bess thought it all highly amusing and grabbed an old jumper in her mouth before whirling round the room with it and tossing it away into a corner. She then came back to Ken and stood looking at him with laughing eyes and waving tail.

"I understand. I've got to put it all back or throw it away. OK, gal, then go and get that jumper and bring it t'me."

Bess bounded after the article and grabbing it she hurled it across at Ken. With a new lease of life he piled everything back in the cupboard and shut the door on it all. "Com'on, tease, let's go in the garden."

The five cygnets had grown to maturity. The sister had lost her white patch as it had merged with her beautiful, new, white feathers and she lived happily with the same cob who had enticed her away from the river. They had selected their special area on the western shore of Windermere. Like a newly married couple with their first home they fussed over the furnishing of their nest.

The brother remained constant to the young female who had arrived soon after his sister had left. She had joined the river group at the right time, just as he was feeling so alone. They too had chosen their first nesting place; a reedy patch in a quiet area at the southern end of Lake Windermere.

CHAPTER 2
LIFE ON THE LAKE

DAY SHIFT

The grass, dressed in its new spring colours, shone untainted by dust and age. The surface of the lake glistened, mirroring the surrounding trees and banks, their images broken here and there by mischievous ripples. The warm morning air was filled with bird song; little voices coming from trees and bushes, either greeting each other or warning off rivals from their nests and feeding sites.

A cock blackbird flew down to the water's edge and began to bathe. Dipping his front and flapping his wings, throwing silvery droplets into the air, he sent little ripples running out into the lake.

A graceful, white cob swan, his neck held in a gentle curve, glided out from the reeds. After a few moments of looking about, he also began to bathe. Opening one wing, he beat the water powerfully, using this to roll his body over to get it wet. He then reversed the procedure to wet the other side. Neck outstretched and using both wings he sent up great sprays of water. Then, after circling quickly to wet his plumage thoroughly, he settled back to preen.

A sudden sound and his head shot up abruptly. He listened and looked intently all around. Satisfied that there was nothing to concern him, he resumed his preening. He deliberately took each primary feather in turn and, drawing it through his bill, knitted together all the little hooks, closing any hole that had formed. He kept wiping his bill across the oil gland at the base of his tail in order to waterproof each feather in turn. He attended to his main body feathers in bunches, closing up ragged barbs and oiling them to keep his entire plumage warm and waterproof.

This continuous attention is very necessary to keep the water from penetrating to the skin. Failure to do this would not only cause him to get cold but also become waterlogged and sink.

Finishing his morning feather-care he raised his head and body, opened his wings and seemed to stand on the water as he shook his feathers into place. Then he settled back again with a satisfied look on his face. The stillness of the scene was disturbed only by the movement of the bouncing surface that he had created. His head turned this way and that watching and listening. Suddenly he heard something. His neck shot up straight and he arched his wings into a high display, showing anxiety and possible aggression. He set off quickly for the reed bed.

The swan was the matured brother. The towering vegetation opened up inside to a small area of water surrounding a tiny island which was completely covered in nesting material. His pen called softly and he answered, dipping his head in greeting.

She was sitting in the middle of a heap of dried grass and water weed, about six feet in diameter, with a look of contentment on her face. Little 'pipping' noises were coming from somewhere, the cob swimming up to her, poked about in her plumage. She hissed a gentle warning at him, then from under her wing appeared a tiny, fluffy, grey head with black shining eyes and a little black bill. The newly hatched cygnet stretched up, 'pip-pip-pipping', and the cob softly grunted to his baby son. Another fluffy head struggled out from behind, then two more bills poked out from within her breast feathers; all were calling.

The pen still sat with the peace and contentment of motherhood in her eyes, which contrasted with the surprised look of the cob.

Suddenly, a fifth head appeared between the wings on her back and 'pipped' louder and more demandingly than the others, as

27

though trying to make up for being last. He struggled right out to stand, wobbling and waving his little wing appendages about for balance. Placing one of his flat, webbed feet on top of the other he toppled off his mother's back, bouncing to the edge of the nest and plopping into the water.

The cob hissed in alarm and the pen immediately alert, reached over to try and help her little son but he floated out of reach. In her hurry she stood up, spilling babies out of her plumage, who all fell down into the water — from peace to chaos.

The newly-hatched babies bobbed around their parents like little fluffy corks, tossed about by the choppy water. The cygnet who had caused the rumpus, paddled across to the cob and tugged a white feather which was sticking out. He stretched his little head up high to gaze at his huge father. The proud cob bent his long neck down and grunted a welcome.

The adult birds began pulling up bits of soft vegetation from below water, satisfying their own hunger and tearing up some more to leave floating on the surface. The babies excitedly rushed amongst it snatching bits but dropping them again, not knowing what to do with them. They did not need food at that time, as they were still living off the remains of the yolk sacs in their bodies, but it was a useful lesson. The cygnets soon tired and one, a little female, scrambled up onto her mother's back. Calling to the others, the pen carefully clambered back onto her nest, then both parents pushed the little-ones up so they could disappear into their mother's plumage, to dry off and get warm again.

The cob turned away, swimming through the narrow entrance back to the lake to keep guard over his family.

A while later, the cob's sharp eyes caught sight of a movement across the water. Reeds were disturbed as a mallard drake swam out and began bathing and splashing about. Quickly jumping into the air with a whirr of fast beating wings, he flew off, leaving glistening water droplets falling back into the lake like a draught-blown, beaded curtain. The cob watched the drake fly low over the water before turning inland to swoop up and over a hedge.

The drake flew across the field to an untidy hedgerow at the far end. Here he dropped to the ground and stood looking about him for a few moments before walking quietly through the long grass and into the hedge bottom.

Sitting on her nest, completely camouflaged by her colouring, was his mate. The nest was scraped out of the soil and lined with her own gloriously soft down plucked from her breast. This action has a dual purpose, not only to line the nest but to expose her brood patch, allowing warmth to be directed straight to her eggs. The thick foliage above and around hid her from prying eyes and she sat there dozing; contentedly brooding her twelve eggs.

The drake had come to escort her to the lake for her bathe and feed. She stood up and carefully covered her eggs with feathers, dead leaves and grass, to keep them warm and safely hidden. She went to her mate and they greeted each other, bobbing their heads up and down.

He walked off quietly with her following closely behind, until they were at a safe enough distance from the nest not to give away its position. They flew straight up, levelling out to head back to the lake.

The duck bathed quickly, forcing her buoyant, little body under water to wet her plumage before racing round, splashing with her beating wings. Suddenly stopping, she began preening her more important feathers, then hurriedly snatched a few bill-fuls of weed and drank a little water. Finally, with a loud 'qua-a-a-ck' she took to her wings and shot up into the air. It was not long to hatching time and she was very anxious to return. Replying in his husky voice, the drake speeded after her to escort her back to their nest.

The pair, who were excellent parents, had been nesting together for several years and were devoted to each other. As before, they landed away from the nest and looked around carefully before stealthily walking the same route into the hedge bottom.

On arrival, she pulled back the feathers and inspected the eggs, but did not turn them as she had been doing previously. They were too near hatching. She settled herself down over them and contentedly put her head beneath her wing to doze. Nature makes her mothers lazy at nesting time, inducing them to be content to sit and brood. The drake walked off again to their chosen 'safe distance spot' before flying back to the lake.

The cob saw the drake return, just as he had witnessed the pair's recent actions. He knew their daily pattern, as well as everything else that happened on 'his' lake. He followed the routine of the moorhens who had chicks in another part of the hedge, not far from the ducks.

These very self-assured little water-birds were always flicking their tails, emphasizing their conspicuous white rumps. Small red eyes glowed like jewels in their black faces, the bright red of the fleshy shields on their foreheads continuing into short thin bills, ending in 'dagger-like' tips the colour of daffodils; a warning to others to be wary of these quick-tempered little 'time-bombs'.

The cob watched the cock moorhen searching in the muddy water's edge for grubs to take back to his newly hatched family.

When the chicks are first hatched the hen bird feeds them from food brought by the cock but once they are a few days old the pair take it in turns to hunt and feed, so the babies always have one parent in attendance.

The two-day-old chicks had snuggled down in their nest, high up in a thorn bush, where they were to remain for three or four more days. The parent birds had made the nest of sticks, twigs and leaves and lined it with moss, feathers and dried grass. Here the chicks were warm and comfortable, especially as they were covered by their mother's body. They dozed contentedly to her rhythmic breathing.

The cock bird arrived with his bill full of small wriggling worms, and using his clawed toes and long legs, he began climbing up the bush; walking and jumping.

He called as he approached and his mate returned his greeting, 'Tickic, tickic, tickic.' Four tiny balls of black fluff, each waving little wing stubs, excitedly called for food. They stood up, or rather wobbled, on their black legs with disproportionately long toes. The hen bird accepted the worms from her mate, taking a small piece at a time, she poked it inside an open bill. When all was gone she sat down again and very gently preened the nearest little head.

The cock bird stayed for a few minutes exchanging little noises with his family, then took himself off to find more food. The following day the hen would work with him, as the chicks' appetites were growing fast, but would brood them at night time, both for safety and warmth, whilst he perched high up in the thorn hedge; keeping guard.

Suddenly, the cob's attention was drawn to sounds from his own nest area and he hurried in through the reedy entrance where he found his mate and young afloat. She greeted him, dipping her head and muttering softly, then paddled sedately up to him. The babies milled around them calling in thin voices.

The paired birds met, breast feathers practically touching, necks held high with downward pointing bills as they proceeded with their graceful neck-turning movements. Ignoring the cygnets, they turned their heads first one way then the other, with slow deliberation, repeating this several times before finalising their pair-bonding with a sip of water. Raising their heads slowly with bills pointing upwards, they let the water run down inside their necks, finally with a waggle of the tails they ended their greeting and turned their attention to their babies.

Just as though they had discussed the matter, they swam off with the cob leading, the pen urging the cygnets ahead of her so that she could follow, keeping them in view. The beautiful flotilla proceeded out of their secret place and onto the lake; continuing in formation. The little-ones were 'calling' most of the time and bobbing about over the ripples caused by the cob's wake.

Crossing to the other side of the water where there was some succulent vegetation the cob pushed his head and neck deep under the water several times, pulling up great quantities of water-weed. The adults ate some and the pen tore off lots of pieces which she left floating for the cygnets.

Five grey 'powder puffs' dived into the weed and whirled it about, snatching bits here and there and tossing more over their backs or flinging it away. Accidentally, they swallowed some and liked it, so began their first important lesson in life; eating.

It happened to be one of those blissful days in late spring where everything seems perfect. After a good feed, the adult birds began to bathe in quite a crazy manner. They rushed around, turning quickly, with their huge white wings outspread. Beating the water in exhilaration and dipping their necks under the surface, with whale-type movements sent waves over their backs wetting their plumage. They rolled to one side using the opposite wing to aid them, repeating the performance for the other side, before pushing themselves upright with both wings outstretched and beating. Standing on the water, they shook themselves to settle their plumage and return the myriad of diamond-like water droplets they had borrowed from the lake.

Rocked and tossed about by the turbulent water the cygnets, like all young things, tried to copy their parents without success.

A solitary mallard duck, watching from amongst a nearby clump of reeds, was mesmerised by the commotion and swam towards the family in curiosity.

The cob saw her immediately and lowered his head to 'duck level', puffed out his feathers, arched his wings, and charged — hissing loudly. As he reached her he darted his head forward and tried to grab her but she was too quick. With a loud quack she dodged him and took to the air. She was lucky to escape as many ducks are killed by cobs guarding their families: they are grabbed by their necks and pushed under water to drown.

Still tense, he looked around him for any more danger that might threaten his family. There was a group of mallards about fifty yards away swimming with some coots, whose white foreheads and bills stood out in the sunlight.

He was just relaxing, having assessed these birds to be far enough away not to bother him when he spotted a lone male great crested grebe, swimming low in the water. His head and about two inches of his neck were gliding along rather like the periscope of a submarine leaving a narrow wake.

The swan was wary of this bird, as he knew he was capable of swimming long distances under water and surfacing again, unexpectedly. He had done this before, appearing right by the cob's side giving him quite a fright, before vanishing again to cause him more concern as he searched frantically for the grebe.

The head moved further away before sinking beneath the surface, leaving just the dissipating wake. The cob stiffened and looked anxiously about him, wondering where it would reappear. A loud chorus of 'quacks' distracted him as a group of mallards took off in unison.

They flew to a wide, open area of grassland which often became flooded in winter and was good, not only for its grass, but for finding worms and other succulent morsels.

The day slowly passed and the cygnets were getting tired. One little female managed to climb up onto her mother's back, snuggling down in her feathers, the rest paddling quietly along, between their parents, as they slowly made their way home. Nearing the entrance of their 'secret place' a moorhen flew low out of the reeds with a loud 'Kurruk', just missing the cob's head. He stopped in surprise, hissing his annoyance; but it was too late; the moorhen had gone.

The family turned in through the reedy entrance and paddled to their little island where the pen clambered up, laboriously, to settle for what would be the last time on her nest. From now on they would not need its protection. The cygnets struggled up after her and crept into her plumage. The parents exchanged a few snorts, as the pen tucked her head under her wing leaving the cob to sail slowly out onto the lake.

Away across the field the mallard duck was dozing on her nest, her head also under her wing. Her mate was standing in the shallows of the lake, idly watching the other birds. The moorhens had returned to their nest site and the hen bird was stepping carefully over her tiny fluffy, black chicks, 'chip, chipping' quietly to them. The cock bird had perched high above the nest, ready to doze with alert ears. She snuggled down and the little 'tip,tip,tippings' of the sleepy chicks subsided.

The sun, like a red, fiery ball resting on a purple blanket of cloud, paused above the horizon. Beaming its last, the sun too, prepared for bed and finally sank beneath its bed-clothes, leaving a rosy glow.

The sounds of the day-birds died away and a stillness seemed to cover the earth like a soft, warm cloak. The fading light lulled nature's day creatures to sleep; some however, not too deeply. A little owl, a bird of the early dusk, called sharply from a nearby tree and its mate answered from further away.

The day shift was ending — the night shift just beginning.

Night Shift

The moon which was a little over half full – slipped out from behind a cloud. It was enough to illuminate, in a soft grey, the shoreline and companionable trees standing in silent groups. In contrast, the velvety black of the lake was bisected by a brilliant pathway of shining silver.

The cob sat motionless on the water. His neck was laid over his back in a soft curve and his head, with closed eyes, was tucked into his feathers. He dozed lightly, needing his sleep, but nevertheless ready to protect his family.

At that moment, several miles away to the north, his sister was welcoming her own cygnets into the world. The first one to hatch was a female and as the soft grey down dried, her little head showed a tiny white star on her forehead, a perfect replica of her mother.

Something swished passed the cob and he awoke instantly. His head shot up and his neck feathers spread out with tension, making it look twice as thick and, intimidating to any adversary. His head flicked this way and that, as his eyes searched for the reason for the sound. He listened intently and, when he heard it again, tilted his head enabling him to locate its source.

There it was — a water bat — flying about twelve inches above the lake, repeatedly dipping down as it hunted for insects. It was about two inches long with an eight-and-a-half-inch wingspan. The brownish fur on its back contrasted with its light underparts, so that, as it twisted and turned it seemed to change colour: sometimes merging with the background and at other times standing out against it. There one moment and gone the next, he would reappear in a different place. Presently, the cob noticed another, and another, all flitting about above the water or, diving to catch water boatmen or water skaters.

The swan was just closing his eyes again; his head drooping and his long neck sagging until it was nearly at rest on the white downy back, when he was jerked awake again. A tawny owl called from near the water's edge, to be answered by his mate about a quarter-of-a-mile away. Again, he heard the 'Kee-wick' but this time there was no answer.

Once more he began to relax but a movement in the reeds, between himself and his family, made him alert yet again. Turning quickly to go to their defence he immediately recognised the dark grey head with tiny ears surmounting a whiskery face, which appeared from under the water. He knew this little chap. It was a water vole who had a hole further along in the bank. Being mainly a vegetarian he posed no threat to the cygnets. The pen heard the rustle of the reeds too and called anxiously to her mate. He answered reassuringly.

The night continued in this way, with the day-birds partly sleeping, partly listening, and idly moving about. The owls hunted like ghosts, flying swiftly on softly feathered, silent wings, calling occasionally. At dusk and again at dawn, bats flew to and fro' over the lake, over the land and between the trees, snatching insects from the air. They called continually with high-pitched voices which bounced back to them from objects enabling them to fly, swiftly and safely, in the dark. This also helped them to locate their prey accurately. Moths stood little chance if 'bat-radar' found them.

Throwing her beautiful, mystic light over the birds and animals of the lake and countryside, the moon slowly climbed higher into the sky to scribe its own arc from east to west across the heavens.

The bark of a dog fox rang out, to be answered by his vixen on the opposite side of the lake. The cob stared hard at the place from where the sounds had come, and saw the fox slip off through the trees. The vixen was by her den looking about her and sniffing the air as, from amongst the grass near her, little heads peered out.

Four cubs threw away all caution and began to play. Their little tails, held upright with a slight curve over their round, podgy bodies, waved from side to side. They snarled and yapped as they grabbed each other in mock battle, rolling over and over. The vixen sat and watched.

The cob was not worried by them as he knew the vixen would not leave her cubs. However , the dog fox had vanished into the trees and the swan wanted to know where he had gone, foxes can swim and his cygnets were very small. Suddenly, there was a piercing scream, then utter silence, as life on and around the lake momentarily froze.

The dog fox had caught and killed an unsuspecting rabbit and was trotting off to join his family to present his kill. They had heard the sounds and, in eager silence, were waiting, expectantly. When he appeared the cubs rushed to meet him and, squealing with excitement, jumped up trying to grab the meal. Their father held it as high he could and kept trotting until he reached the vixen, where he dropped it in front of her. The cubs leapt onto it snarling and snapping at each other, tearing pieces off the warm flesh. Two of the cubs only had mouthfuls of fur and shook their heads to free it from around their teeth.

The parent foxes sat watching until the little ones had eaten enough before they went in to finish it off. The dog, having let his vixen have most, sat and waited until she took the cubs back to their den. Standing up, he sniffed the air and looked around before purposefully trotting off again into the night. The bright moon made him restless, so he began a much longer trip which would encompass a farm. After all, he had not had much of that rabbit.

The moon had crossed the lake and was sinking behind the trees on the western bank. It was not long before the mysterious soft glow of dawn began to colour the sky.

A silent shadow separated itself from the trees moving cautiously down to the water's edge. It was a young roe deer; a doe born the previous year. She moved into the shallows for a drink, looking up frequently, so that water fell from her lips as her anxious eyes searched for danger. The bats reappeared, speedily flitting about as before, their high-pitched squeaks being carried on a light breeze which had sprung up with the dawn.

The dog fox was returning with the remains of a kill. He had found a hen asleep under a tree in a garden and, with a quick shake, had killed her. Having eaten as much as he needed, he was taking the rest to his family.

A cock crowed from the same garden that the fox had visited. Before long a blackbird started to call, then other blackbirds joined in so that the song spread as the challenge was taken up. The lovely repetitive phrases of the song thrush followed punctuated by the 'coos' of wood pigeons. Robins warbled their liquid songs, contrasting with the sharp calls of pheasants. Sedge warblers daintily trilled and tiny wrens, with their powerful voices, brought the Dawn Chorus to an exhilarating crescendo. Water-birds called too, so that the entire area was one mass of song as the sky lightened, foretelling the sun's arrival.

The cob turned on hearing sounds coming from his nest area and waited expectantly. The pen came into view with the cygnets swimming very close beside her. He called and, with excited 'pippings', the little-ones rushed to meet him. He lowered his head to their level and snorted his welcome. The pen came up to him and they greeted each other with their graceful neck movements, muttering softly in contentment. A little male cygnet snapped at one his father's feathers to draw attention to himself so insistently that the cob put his bill beneath the little-one and tossed him a short way off. The cygnet landed up-side-down but righted himself immediately and began to bathe to cover his loss of dignity.

The large buttermilk sun peeped through the trees on the eastern bank illuminating the clouds, giving them the appearance of floating cotton wool. Gradually the clouds changed to more sombre hues as the sun began its journey across the pale turquoise sky. A new day had begun.

CHAPTER 3
CATBELLS

It was a beautiful, warm, spring day and Ken was idly wandering in his garden with Bess, who was ambling beside him occasionally stopping to sniff at any interesting smells. He looked back at the old house with sadness. Once there had been sounds of happy voices, laughter and music when his wife was there and his daughter, still a child, played with her young friends. The remains of the old swing that he had made still hung in the oak tree. The house had an air of tiredness about it for, although he had kept it in reasonable condition, he had lost interest in the perfection he once demanded. The garden was neglected and his shrubs, roses and herbaceous border all fought with an invading tangle of weeds.

Jackie often chided him but he no longer cared. He missed his daughter, although he would not admit it, and did not regret urging her and Steve to find their own place. He felt a wet nose in his hand and Ken fondled the big furry head.

"Ay! lass, we got our peace, didn't we? And a bit more than we could do with. Tell yer what, let's pack a bite t'eat and take the car to the foot of Catbells. Yer'd like a nice climb wouldn't yer? And we'd forget oursel's. Eh, Bess, lass?"

With a new spring in his step he led the way indoors and began making some sandwiches, pushing them unceremoniously into a plastic bag. He found a couple of tins of beer and some chocolate biscuits, which he stuffed in too. Then he took another plastic bag and piled in some bonios.

Upstairs, he found his rucksack and, on his knees at the front of his wardrobe, he began pulling piles of things out onto the floor as he searched for his fell-walking boots and thick socks. He had bought himself some new boots only last year from Keswick and it was high time he gave them an airing. They were under some old jumpers that he had thrown in some time ago. Looking guiltily at the mess, he thought how Jackie would have scolded him if she had been there to see it. 'Later'll do, to sort it out', he thought as he bundled it back.

He returned downstairs and collected his parka, cap and scarf, adding the last two items to the rucksack.

"We can't trust weather on th'ills, can we Bess?"

The dog wagged her tail in agreement; mouth open showing her white teeth and generous, pink tongue, which hung out to one side; she was happy that they were obviously going somewhere differzxent.

They went into the kitchen where Ken put the food and drink into the rucksack and fastened the straps. Picking up his parka, he pulled it on over his sweater and corduroy trousers then, hooking one strap of his rucksack over his shoulder, he stood for a moment looking round and thinking.

"Keys," he said out aloud, and felt in his pockets.

"Woof," commented Bess looking at her lead and towel.

"Well done, ol' gal." Ken picked them up and, reopening a corner of the rucksack, put them in and swung it back onto his shoulder. Satisfied, Bess pushed through the door as it was opened.

Ken's feet scrunched on the gravel drive as he walked to the rather dilapidated garage. It had certainly seen better days, at one time it had been a handsome wooden building but now the roof dipped a bit in the middle. The woodwork under the eaves was rotten here and there, allowing nest-building birds to move in. The doors had to be half lifted to open fully. Inside, however, stood his shining Rover car.

Ken unlocked the car and opened the boot to put in the rucksack. Bess stood near, eagerly watching and waiting. Opening the back door, Ken straightened the plastic cover beneath a rug, carefully tucking the edges of the rug down around the seat and up over the back. His car meant a lot to him and was immaculate. Satisfied, he beckoned to Bess to jump in. Finally, he moved to the driver's door, flicked off a present from a roosting bird, opened it and got in.

He ran his hands lovingly over the steering wheel, and glanced at the rich mahogony dashboard before switching on the ignition. This was his own little world where he never felt lonely and, backing out into the sunlight he felt his spirits rising. He began to whistle as he turned into the lane.

Driving north he took the left fork for Coniston, and after passing Lowick Bridge and Water Yeat, he looked out for the first glimpse of the lake. The road ran along beside it for a little way before swinging left for Torver, Bowmanstead and finally Coniston village. As he drove on through the narrow winding roads he noticed little Tarn Hows on the right, before travelling onwards to Skelwith Bridge and into Ambleside.

As usual, there was a queue of traffic slowly wending its way through the town and Ken felt relieved when he was out on the other side, heading for Rydal and Grasmere. Again, he had to join a queue and wait as visitors wandered off the pavements either to get round other people or to cross the road.

Many were obviously on holiday, enjoying themselves looking in shop windows, visiting the graveyard of the local church to see Dorothy and William Wordsworth's grave, and also Dove Cottage, where they had lived.

Free of traffic once more he drove on for Thirlmere. The deep forbidding water lay below on his left, backed by the great mass of Cumbrian Mountains, whilst on the right-hand side of the road were the frowning screes of Helvellyn. He motored on, taking the left fork at the head of the lake for Keswick. Once more he had to queue, as traffic wound its way through the narrow streets with pedestrians overflowing onto the road from the crowded pavements.

"The Lakes are gettin' very popular, Bess. It seems like yest'day that these towns belonged just to us. Only at certain 'oliday times, did we see visitors. It's a pleasure t' see 'em enjoyin' the area, but a pity they all come at the same time."

The dog gave a grunt and sigh in reply. She usually responded to her master as they were such close friends.

"Ah! That's it Bess... Portinscale. We'll drive thru' there, alongside Swinside and park above Haws End in the car park." Ken drove along the narrow roads and into the car park where he switched off the engine. Bess whined in anticipation.

He opened the door, stood out and stretched, then opened the rear door for Bess, who bounded out with a joyful 'woof'. He went to the back of the car to get his rucksack, which he took back to his driver's seat. He sat down sideways, leaving his feet outside and took off his shoes and socks, pulling on his thick socks and new boots, zig-zagging the laces round the studs before tying them. Standing up, he moved his toes about and decided one boot was too tight, so sat down again to slacken the laces.

Bess went to him and peered at what he was doing with her nose about two inches away.

"Yer short-sighted or som'at, dog?" he chided.

Bess whirled round in a complete circle and dropped her front end onto the floor, leaving her rear in the air with its long tail waving. She jumped up again, barked and prodded him in the shoulder before bouncing away out of reach.

"G'on with yer, yer daft bitch." He collected his rucksack, struggled into the straps then closed the car doors and locked up. " 'Ere gal, mind that cattle grid."

There were several walkers already making their way up the track ahead of them. Ken turned left instead and walked round the base of the mountain until he came to another narrow track where there was no-one at all.

Man and dog walked on, up and up, with a little rest here and there. The path became a mere sheep track but that did not deter them. About a third of the way up Ken sat down and looked below at Derwent Water, which appeared like a model lake bordered by tiny trees. He could see the houses of Keswick and Portinscale and the narrow road, like an undulating ribbon with tiny "Dinky" cars moving along it.

The deep rich blue of the lake which, surrounded as it was by the spring green of the fields and trees, presented a breaktaking view. The lakeside ferry was plying its way past Friar's Crag leaving behind a long wake in the otherwise still water.

A sheep came along the track from below them and stood staring in surprise as she was not expecting to find company other than fellow sheep. She bounded away along another track to avoid having to pass them.

Bess thrust her nose in Ken's neck urging him to get up and move on. "Alright then, pest, yer win. A poor ol' man can't even rest, not when there's women about."

He stood up, brought his hand down with a whack on his dog's rump, sending her off amongst the bracken before circling round and charging back.

" 'Ey! watch out, yer vandal, yer'll have m'rollin' down on m'backside. Com'ere and pull me up, yer've got four legs — I've only got two." He took hold of the tail and told her to move on. Bess leapt from tussock to tussock, round the winding track, pulling her beloved master behind her.

It was the last third of the way when he called to her to stop. Thankfully, he sat down with Bess sitting so close that she leant against him.

"Yer've got all this 'illside and yer 'ave to sit on *my* tussock," he grumbled. Bess snuffled his ear, giving it a quick lick.

"Give over, yer daft bitch," he retorted but put his arm round her shoulders and hugged her.

Way down below them the sun shone on the lake sending back a dazzling light. It seemed to Ken that the life down there belonged to another world. As he looked towards Keswick and Portinscale he noticed some swans fly into view. Even from that distance he could see them send up a spray of water as they landed on the lake.

"Right gal, let's make the ridge."

The last climb was even steeper and, although he had done a great deal of fell-walking in years gone by, he was rather out of practice.

"Years are tellin', gal, give yer ol'dad a pull up." Bess turned back to him, immediately. He grabbed her tail, so that she could tow him up again.

At last they reached the ridge and turned to walk to the summit. "Nearly fifteen 'undred feet, Bess and time for a biscuit. Do yer agree?"

Suddenly, ahead of them, Ken caught sight of a lady sitting on a rock, her hair blowing about her smiling face. She was wearing a pale blue sweater, grey trousers and hiking boots. She was watching their approach with fascination. Ken felt a little irritated at seeing her, as he thought he was alone up there. Here was a woman, actually smiling at him, invading his privacy.

She clicked her fingers to the dog, who normally ignored strangers. For some unknown reason Bess trotted across to her with a waving tail. She held out her arms to the big German shepherd, just as though the dog was her own long, lost friend. Bess greeted her too, giving her face a lick. The lady wrapped her arms around Bess's neck and buried her face into the rough shaggy fur.

"Oh, you darling, darling dog," she said and tears began to pour down her face.

Momentarily, Ken was transfixed and so amazed that he was not sure how to deal with the situation. There she was, cuddling his Bess, and weeping too. What an irritation! His curiosity, however, was getting the better of him. It was Bess who had muddled his thoughts. Why was she so friendly? He stood nearby in silence wondering what to do.

"Oh, I'm so sorry, what must you think of me," she said, letting go of Bess and searching for a handkerchief. "It was just that I was watching you coming up the hillside, displaying such a wonderful comradeship between you and your lovely dog. Then, when I called to her, I was so amazed that she came to me; it was as though she knew me. German shepherd dogs are not usually so free with their friendship. You see, I lost my beautiful Dusky last year. I miss her so much and, feeling your lovely girl in my arms ... just sort of ... broke me. Please pardon a silly woman."

Ken, completely disarmed, sat down on a boulder quite near her. "Don't worry yersel', lass," he heard himself saying "I understand now. I agree about these dogs not givin' their friendship easily. I must admit at bein' amazed at 'er be'aviour m'sel'."

They sat still and in silence for a little while looking at the peaceful valley — surrounded by hills. Bess was between them enjoying being stroked by both. Neither of them realised this until their hands accidently brushed against each other and they, apologising hastily, withdrew them.

Bess wondered why she had suddenly become unpopular. Turning her head to each of them she moaned, making them laugh, relieving the embarrassment of the situation.

"I've got some sandwiches and beer in m'rucksack," said Ken impulsively. "Would yer like to join me? Oh! By the way, m'name's Ken Mason and this is Bess."

"How do you do, Ken, and you too Bess. I'm Becky Granger."

She held out her hand to him. He took it, a little shyly, then dropped it and dived into his rucksack which, by this time, was on the ground. Taking out a plastic bag of rather squashed sandwiches he pulled it open and said "Would yer like ....? Oh, dear! They look a little worse for wear."

They looked at each other, laughing, as she took a handful of sandwich crumbs.

"I'm sure they will be delightful. It's very kind of you to share them with me."

42

Bess sighed. She lay down with her head on her paws and lowered her ears, which gave her a dejected air.

"Bess..... Biscuits...." The dog's head jerked up. Her ears shot back to their elevated position and she eagerly waited whilst her master put some bonios under her nose. She crunched her way through them, put her head back on her paws and closed her eyes.

Becky and Ken finished the sandwiches, drank a can of beer each, and leant back contentedly. It did not seem to matter that they were complete strangers. They just sat in silence on either side of Bess. It seemed quite natural.

Ken stole a sideways glance at his companion. She was of small stature, neat and tidy, except for her greying hair that was rather wind-blown but that gave her a down-to-earth appearance. At first sight, he thought she was rather 'county' but whether she was or not did not matter, as she was definitely a country woman at heart. Bess loved her, so she must be alright. Her fingers were idly twiddling the hairs on Bess's neck. Ken looked straight at her.

"What 'appened to yer Dusky? Did yer 'ave 'er a long time?"

"Yes, she was my husband's dog and we had her from a puppy. Charles died some five years ago and Dusky and I consoled each other. She died last year at thirteen. I've missed her terribly. I kept wondering whether to get another but I've been moving about between various rented accommodation and it's not easy to do that with an animal. When Dusky died it was the last straw, so to speak. I sold up our old house and most of my furniture and put the rest into store. I found various places that seemed interesting and stayed for a month at a time, always hoping to find somewhere I felt I'd like to put down new roots. I'm staying in Portinscale at the oment. I must say I like it but I'm not sure if I'll be too lonely there when the winter comes. Being a country person, the thought of going to live in a town doesn't appeal so I don't really know what to do."

Ken sat still, listening. He was a good listener and in the past he often heard people's life stories simply by sitting quietly. He was stirred by Becky's story and, to his surprise, found himself telling her about his divorce and Jackie and then her marriage and finally of his own loneliness. "Dogs are more to be trusted than people, I always think."

"I know what you mean, Ken, but sometimes we really need people too. As long as we don't panic into a friendship, we can usually sort out those we can trust from those we can't. At our age I think we're more discerning, less likely to be fooled. I don't usually

43

talk to strangers, certainly not in the way I did with you," she qualified with an embarrassed little laugh. "It was Bess who caused that to happen, I just couldn't help myself."

Ken smiled at her and patted his dog. "She's a good dog and knows someone that's to be trusted. I've not faulted 'er yet. Will yer be walkin' back down the ridge?"

"Yes, I think it's time I wandered back." After a moment, she looked at him, hesitantly, and said "I've shared your sandwiches and beer, now would you do me the favour of having a cup of tea in my little rented home?" She looked him straight in the eyes. Her almost turquoise blue eyes pleaded with him to say 'yes'.

"Thank yer, Becky. Bess an' I'd be very pleased."

He stood up and held out his hand to help her up too. He found he was no longer shy of her, in fact, he felt he knew her. He pulled on his rucksack and she straightened a twisted strap behind his shoulder, then they set off together down the ridge.

They laughed and chattered as they went, climbing up boulders and jumping down the other side. They hardly noticed the beautiful views on either side of them as they were so happy in each other's company. At the lower end of the mountain was a rocky descent and she sat down on a rock so as to slide down to the lower rock more easily. Ken's hand was always ready to steady her, whilst Bess bounded around them frisking about like a puppy having caught their happy mood. They had negotiated the rough descent and were walking along the track which lead towards the car park which they could see between the trees, when Ken said "I 'ave m' car 'ere, it's that two-toned green Rover there."

Becky followed his pointing finger to where the sun was picking out its paintwork and, as they got close enough for her to see it properly, she said "It's a lovely car, you keep it beautifully."

Ken smiled as he opened the passenger door for Becky. Bess stood for her paws to be wiped before jumping in and lying down. After throwing his rucksack into the boot he got into the driver's seat and they moved smoothly away.

The car felt so complete with Becky beside him and Bess resting in the back. He was surprised at himself and kept glancing sideways at Becky, not really believing it was happening.

CHAPTER 4
SUMMER TIME

MALLARDS

At first glance the hedge bottom seemed quite empty of life but there, beautifully camouflaged, sat the mallard duck. Her mottled brown plumage blended perfectly with the dead leaves and twigs which still lay on the ground. Long grasses hung over her back in graceful curves and the low branches of a thorn bush gave her shelter from both the weather and prying eyes.

She had been brooding on her precious eggs for twenty-eight days, partly sleeping, partly watching, but today she awoke with a feeling that something was about to happen. It was very early morning and already her mate had visited the nest site to escort her to the lake for her usual morning bathe. She had merely answered his call, without moving.

All around the fields and lakeside, birds were singing in the trees, welcoming the new day. Nearby, some rabbits were hopping about nibbling grass. One stopped quite near to the mallard and sat up to wash his face and ears. The duck flattened herself level with the edge of her nest listening intently, her head tipped to one side. She was relieved when the rabbit moved away as she could hear sounds from beneath her.

She had laid her eggs daily and only started to incubate them after the complete clutch had been laid. In this way the young would hatch within twenty-four hours, so that when she left the nest the following day, she would not leave any behind.

She listened to the little chipping sounds which were beginning to come from the eggs and replied with a soft whisper in her throat. It was that special mother-contact so necessary to the unhatched babies, which would not only give them encouragement, but also help them recognise her call quickly after they hatched. This could be of vital importance to them in the face of danger.

Soon little voices began to answer her, only to be silenced again as chipping sounds resumed. Their little bodies squirmed as tiny egg teeth tapped inside the shells, trying to break out from their cramped quarters.

The morning progressed with the usual activity around her. Nesting song birds flew about searching for food for their own chicks, some from nests along the same hedgerow. The mallard watched as a cock moorhen flew towards her across the field from the lake. His brilliant red bill was filled to capacity with a bulging bunch of wriggling worms. He was bringing these for his mate, who was sitting high up inside the hedge.

The duck tucked her bill back under her wing and dozed lightly. Now and then she lifted her head to listen, calling softly to give encouragement to her ducklings. Some were tapping away at their shells, some calling in thin little voices and others resting from their efforts. The mother sat placidly without any desire to move. The drake visited her several times throughout the day but she always sent him away again not wanting to run the risk of attracting attention to herself at that critical time.

Feeling a movement beneath her, she pushed at the egg with her bill. The duckling called loudly this time and, kicking and struggling hard, managed to break the shell. Soon a head and neck appeared but immediately laid back exhausted. He breathed air into his lungs, closed his eyes and rested. More and more sounds were coming from others and the little mother quietly answered each of her babies, building for them that important safety line.

The first duckling, after renewed struggles, emerged completely and again lay still to rest. He was wet and bedraggled but a perfect little creature. The duck reached beneath her, took hold of the broken shell and tossed it as far away as she could, then covered her baby carefully with her body.

She had eleven more eggs to hatch, each occupant would have its own private battle to break out of its imprisonment. If a duckling did not have enough strength to break out at this stage, it would soon use up the limited air within the shell and die.

One by one the tiny, wet ducklings emerged, leaving the duck to toss away each empty shell. By late afternoon eleven babies and one egg lay beneath the duck, now dry and warm. This period of rest, after their fight for freedom, enabled them to regain their strength.

The drake was swimming around and bathing with two other males when he suddenly thought of his mate on her nest. Without hesitating he opened his colourful wings, each bearing a broad, blue band across it and launched himself into the air calling excitedly in his soft husky voice. As he left, he showered the other birds below him with water, causing them to shake their heads and look up at the departing culprit.

Flying swiftly across the field his shadow crossed a fieldmouse causing it to 'freeze' instantly, in the fear it was to become prey to something but, as the shadow passed, it hurried on again.

The drake landed quite a long way from its nest then walked stealthily, looking about constantly as he had no intention of giving away his secret place. Every now and then he stopped to listen before walking to the hedge, zig-zagging in and out of it to confuse any observer, until at last he arrived at his mate.

The pair nodded their heads up and down in duck greeting and spoke quietly. Feeling welcome, he sat down beside her and listened to the little sounds coming from under her plumage. He answered them and, in doing so, taught them to recognise his husky voice, too.

Tiny brown and fawn heads popped out and stared at their father. The family group was complete for the first time. It was an important step for him to see them, as much as it was for them to recognise him. Their safety could well depend on this for, if they went up to the wrong parents, it is quite likely that they would be attacked or even killed. This is nature's way of ensuring that parents give maximum food and protection to their own offspring by not allowing competition from another family.

The little heads had withdrawn again into the warmth and comfort under their mother, while the adult pair sat and enjoyed the peace of the new family. The duck, still feeling broody, had tucked her head beneath her wing to doze.

Evening was approaching before the drake stood up, shook himself, and began his walk back along the length of the hedgerow. Again, weaving his body in and out as though gathering an invisible thread that he laid earlier. When he was at a safe distance he opened his wings and flew back to the lake.

As his feet touched the water he seemed to burst like a balloon and, quacking continually, he rushed around in fast irregular circles, still flapping his wings and paddling at the same time. He circled time and time again, stirring up the water until a sequence of ripples ran away from him, these in their turn disturbed groups of birds, a patch of reeds and various other water-plants. Where, a moment ago, there had been peace, suddenly there was pandamonium as others joined in the fun; seemingly ignited by the exhilaration of the drake.

Very early the following morning, just as the dawn sky was sending a creamy light over the distant blue-grey hills, the drake flew to his family. As he was approaching the nest site a movement in the long grass made him circle to take a better look. Realising what it was, he landed and hurried forward to greet his mate. He quacked huskily, his head bobbing and shaking from side to side. The duck was walking slowly and proudly amidst her fluffy ducklings.

Some of them seemed to roll rather that walk and one kept tripping over its own feet. On seeing their father and having recognised his voice the little-ones rushed to his side. Some were calling to him and jumping up to try and reach him. He lowered his head and spoke to them but their mother called and they rushed back to her. The first lesson in obedience being successful, the family took up formation, walking slowly around the edge of the field towards the lakeside.

Suddenly, a shadow came over them from behind and, with an urgent quack, the duck spread her wings and her frightened babies rushed beneath them. The drake immediately took to the air to chase a black crow away. Only after he considered his adversary was far enough away did he return to his family, to lead the little procession once again on its journey. The drake always walked in front followed by eleven ducklings in a huddle with the duck close behind. The twelfth duckling had died in its attempt to get out of its shell.

As this was the third year the pair had nested they were experienced parents. They gave the little-ones many rests so it took a long time to reach the lake. Those tiny legs had to hurry to keep pace with the slow moving big ones and therefore soon became tired. Their mother had to be especially watchful as, like all curious youngsters, they were easily distracted by a leaf blowing about or a passing butterfly. Each one was in danger of becoming separated from the family.

At last the procession reached its destination and the ducks were soon all afloat. The babies called to each other as they bobbed about on the wake caused by their parents. Other mallards came to see what was happening but the drake lowered his head and charged, sending them away. The duck, quacking loudly, brought the babies to her protective wings. They had learnt that lesson well.

MOORHENS

The paired moorhens were both swimming about searching for insects to take back to their family, when a coot appeared from amongst the reeds; immediately their respective battle cries split the air. The croaky calls of the moorhens competed with the higher-pitched coot-call being a prelude to a fierce battle. Although the coot was the larger and stronger bird, the moorhens were a two-some and defensive because they were nesting.

The cock moorhen rushed at the coot throwing his body backwards onto his tail to elevate his long powerful legs and sharp-clawed toes, which acted like a boxer's fists. The coot did likewise and each bird struck and restruck trying to get through each other's guard. The hen moorhen watched for a few moments, before anger drove her to help her mate to get rid of this potential enemy.

Without a sound, she charged the coot from behind and gave a loud shriek as she jabbed him hard with her powerful, stubby bill. The coot turned on her, which gave the cock moorhen his chance and he dived at his enemy. The battle was over. The coot fled, chased noisily by both moorhens, until he was a safe distance away.

The pair stopped and turned to face one another with their feathers raised, tails up and flicking showing their white rumps.

They arched their necks as they met face to face and, pointing their bills downwards, turned their heads away losing their aggression in this submissive behaviour. Separating a little, they begun bathing and preening until the hen bird remembered her young. She rushed to the edge of the water and delved in the mud for some grubs, before hurriedly flying off in the direction of her nest.

Once on the ground near the hedge, she ran and hopped up inside her bush where she was quite invisible to any who might have been watching. Using her long toes with their sharp claws she gripped each twig firmly, then strode up from one foot-hold to the next. Finally, as she neared her nest, she hesitated and looked about her, just to be sure that she was unobserved.

The chicks were waiting hungrily for food and called noisily, flapping their little wing stubs when they saw her. One was so keen to be first to reach his mother that he overbalanced and fell out of the nest, bouncing from twig to twig until he landed, shocked but unhurt, on the ground. He picked himself up and, terrified at finding himself in strange surroundings, ran about making agitated cries.

Up in the nest the hen bird stuffed grubs into the begging mouths. She then fluttered down to the ground frantically calling, "Kittic kittic". The chick tried to run to her, but became entangled in some goose grass. The more he struggled the more he became ensnared.

His mother saw him and hurried to his side, calling urgently to him. By accident she trod on the tangle of goose grass, holding it down as she poked at him with her bill. Somehow she managed to help him out, whereupon they were able to go to the foot of their bush together.

She looked up at her nest and saw three black fluffy faces with red bills, each tipped with yellow, looking over the edge. She did not know what to do as she could not get the chick beside her back into the nest, neither did she want to leave him alone as he would be too much at risk from predators.

Just then there was a rustle above her. Another chick which had leaned over too far, was bouncing down. He too, was unhurt because of his thick down and featherweight body. Two up and two down — now what?

The chicks on the ground began to wander about investigating their new surroundings. The second arrival experienced great difficulty in negotiating one out-of-proportion long leg with its extra long toes, past the other one. He continually hooked one toe round his other leg as he tried to walk and fell over.

His mother glared at him in frustration and rebuked him firmly, "Kittic, kittic". She looked up at the other two and called to them to come down but they only waved their little 'arms' about and called. Their mother was getting more and more agitated, when out fell a third baby. She grouped them together and tried to get the last one down but it was too afraid and hid down in the nest.

With a sharp "Kittic" to the three beside her, she flew up into the bush and hurried to the nest. Desperately, she tried to push the baby out but it cried in terror and rolled away from her bill. The hen looked down to see what the others were doing. Oh dear! They were wandering about and not even together. She hurried down and scolded them loudly. They ran to her with their wing stubs waving and their heads outstretched in begging attitude. What was she to do? Suddenly, she gave a very loud call to her mate who was out on the lake.

He was swimming lazily when the call reached his ears and without a moment's delay he leaped into the air and flew swiftly over the field to the nest-site. As he approached he shouted "Kaak kaak" to ward off any enemy that might be present. He landed by his disorderly family and, with a voice of authority, ordered them to his side. Relieved, the hen bird went back to the remaining chick. Being more relaxed, she sat down a moment with it and spoke quietly. The chick relaxed and snuggled down beside her.

The chicks on the ground began to wander again, so the cock bird started to walk them slowly towards the lake.

Watching her departing family, the hen bird renewed her attempt to hook her last little-one out of the nest. This took the baby by surprise and out it fell, bouncing down, watched by mother from the nest. She flew down after it calling reassuringly and gently preened its head before slowly walking after the others. This chick also had difficulty with its feet and its many 'trip-ups' slowed them down even more. The mother's quiet "Kittic, kittic" gave encouragement to her little-one.

After walking part of the way across the field the cock moorhen stopped to rest his brood and wait for the rest of the family to catch up. They sat by a tall dock plant, the chicks snuggled close to him, dozing and resting their tired legs. The hen with her last chick arrived and the parents greeted each other. She sat down close beside her mate, pushing the chick between them. They rested for quite a long time relieved to be together again.

51

The warm colours of the low sun which heralded the early evening found the moorhens still journeying. A little owl watched the approaching family from a nearby tree with great interest. He called and left his perch to fly low over them trying to scatter the little-ones. However, the adult moorhens saw him and gave a sharp warning call to the babies, who closed in quickly to their mother. The little owl circled and swooped down low again but the cock bird was ready and took off at speed. Flying straight at the intruder with a loud cry, he flipped over in the air onto his back and lashed out with his long legs. He missed. The owl dodged and flew off, having no intention of arguing with those long toes armed with 'daggers' — also the moorhen was the bigger bird!

Danger over, the family once more set off towards the lake, the parents being anxious to find a safe place for the night where the hen could brood the chicks.

THE SWANS

The swans were on the other side of the lake with their heads under water investigating the mud for insects or small fish. They were at the place where a channel led away from the lake, winding through tall reeds, towards a narrow stream. Below the grassy banks the clear, sparkling water bubbled over the stony bed and trickled around scattered rocks. The cob was heading for this area for his family's first long swim.

He slowed down as he reached the reeds and drifted to a stop allowing the young ones to rest. He looked around him with quiet interest, then turned as his pen drew level, dipped his head and whickered to her.

As the parents lazily watched the various activities of creatures on and around the bank the cygnets, inquisitive as ever, began exploring under the water stirring up mud and insect larvae. Water-boatmen came scurrying by, their tiny 'oars' working hard to propel them over the surface. The cygnets hesitated a few moments in fascination before charging after their quarry, causing the water to slop about and splash their parents.

As the cob's dreamy state was disturbed he turned and paddled into the channel. The pen urged her babies to hurry after him leaving her to bring up the rear. Gliding sedately between the reeds she completed a procession of dignity and impudence. Reaching deeper water, the cob noticed a patch of luscious grass on the bank. He snatched some as he paddled along.

Further on, the sun glinted on the lively water as it hurried over the stones and the cygnets excitedly tried to catch the sparkle. The bank continually changed so that in some places it was high with steep sides and in others it sloped smoothly down into the water. Bushes and trees lined the river. At one point a spreading weeping willow leaned over the water sheltering a little bay within its embrace.

The cob led his family through this green curtain into the hidden bay, where they enjoyed themselves searching for interesting things to eat. A kingfisher, perching over their heads on his favourite twig, was well hidden from any searching eyes of either predator or prey; his own black, beady eyes scrutinised the water for small fish. The swans disturbed some minnows and, like a colourful dart, the little bird dived into the water to come up again with a wriggling fish in his sharp bill. He took it back to his twig, tossed it into the air and expertly caught it again head first. In this way the fins and tail were folded when he swallowed it so the bones did not stick in his throat.

Feeling restless, the cob led the way out of the secluded bay and paddled on until he came to the river. Here, the deeper water, which flowed over mud instead of the sparkling stones, took on quite different characteristics; the stream had seemed playful but this river was steady and purposeful.

The swans were swimming beside a narrow track on the bank made by the feet of people and animals. Several colourful groups of people were strolling along enjoying the sunshine and children were racing about, laughing and shouting. Some people had dogs who were happily occupied following the many varied smells.

The cob looked across the river to open fields. In the far distance the hills were veiled in a blue-grey haze. With a great longing he began paddling hard and opened his wings but, realising their uselessness due to his missing flight feathers, he waggled his tail and settled back again onto the water.

Mother Nature cleverly arranges it that nesting swans lose all their primary wing feathers at once so they are grounded during the period when they are needed to care for their young. Most birds, where it is dangerous for them to be grounded, moult out one primary feather at a time and their young are able to fly very quickly. The swans' habitat is water which gives them a certain protection without the necessity of flight, so they remain with their relatively slow-growing youngsters.

Gradually, the river became wider and deeper. Some fishermen were sitting on the bank with their fishing lines out, patiently waiting and hoping for a bite.

The cob gave the bobbing floats a wide berth and hissed sharply to his inquisitive son, who had moved out of line to look at the strange orange and white object. The other two males tried to immitate their father and also hissed, but nervously kept well clear of the 'thing' about which their father had so sternly warned. The two apprehensive females huddled close to their mother.

Around a long, sweeping bend in the river the current was making swirling patterns. These were due to some weed that had become entangled in a broken branch which was jammed against a tree root. Just a little further on was a quiet bay where the bank was bare of vegetation. The sienna-coloured dried earth sloped gently down into the water, inviting both entry and exit. The calm air and warm sun made the cob feel lazy. He lowered his feet and felt for the ground. Standing up with a snort he let the water run off his plumage before slowly placing one flat, webbed foot onto dry ground. He lumbered out to stand looking about him. Moving forward again, he stretched out his neck to pull at some grass and clover growing a couple of yards higher up.

The little grey cygnets, 'pipping' happily, pottered about at the edge of the water. Their jet black eyes occasionally twinkled in the sunlight giving them a mischievous air.

The pen dipped her head for a drink, lifted it high to let the cool liquid flow down her throat, before shaking herself and clambering out to join her mate. The babies hurried after her with anxious calls, appearing to be blown around her like litter in a breeze. Finally, all the family settled down for a rest .

Later in the day, a group of people came walking upstream towards the swans, their mongrel dog racing around enjoying himself. When the dog ran too far ahead his owner, half-heartedly, called him back. Apart from flicking an ear towards the sound, the dog took no further notice and raced on, obviously quite used to being disobedient. The man did not bother to call again, ignoring the fact that there were ducks under the nearby bank.

Barking loudly, the dog bounded towards them and stopped amongst long grass on the bank, his nose twitching in excitement as he leaned down peering at them. Luckily, it was a high part of the bank and he could not reach them. He turned and ran on, his voice reverberating in the otherwise quiet air. In between yapping, his tongue lolled out of the side of his mouth and flapped up and down as he ran.

The noise alerted the cob immediately and he stood up. Stepping from amongst his family who hurried back onto the water, he waited tensely, listening to the disturbance. He saw the dog as it burst out from some bushes and, at the same time, the animal saw him.

The swan opened his wings fully and stretched his head up so that he stood nearly five feet high and walked forward, hissing angrily. The dog hesitated but raced on. The cob, lowering his head and neck, charged, beating his wings angrily which sounded very menacing. The dog skidded to a stop with amazement on his face and surveyed the large, formidable creature which had seemed to grow before his eyes. The huge bird was almost on top of him but the dog, who was still full of excitement, barked defiantly and leapt forward to try to grab some feathers.

That was his greatest mistake for the cob delivered one powerful blow with his right wing-butt, knocking the dog clean off his feet. With a yelp of pain, he scrambled up and fled until the blow, which he had taken mostly on his shoulder, soon had him limping badly. The swan lowered his wings to an arched tent-like position over his back, with the backward curve of his neck between them bringing his head nearly down to his chest. There he stood, like a 'white knight' ready to do battle for his lady.

A whicker from his mate, who was waiting on the water with the babies, eased his tension. Turning, he walked quietly to the water's edge, pushed off with his webs and joined his family on the water. The little male cygnet who had missed nothing, left his mother's side and paddled to his father. Together they moved off once more in quiet formation but this time in the homeward direction.

The summer days were slipping by with adult birds and animals busily tending their young and the youngsters occupied with the business of growing up; learning to feed themselves, then to search for their food and, finally, the general art of self-preservation.

The trees, bushes and other plant-life each had their own pattern to follow with a whole world of friends, foes and dependants.

Friends are those who prey on foes or help to pollinate the flowers. The jay is special to the oak as he plants acorns. Unlike the grey squirrel he does not first nip off the growing tip. Thus any that escape his later search have a good chance of growth.

Foes, apart from man, are usually the insects that eat or otherwise damage leaves, as well as the grey squirrel who rips the bark from trees and joins various birds to eat the fruits.

Dependants are creatures who rely on the plant kingdom for food and shelter.

Each year fallen leaves give nutriment back to the parent plant and also offer winter hiding places and warmth to various creatures.

Eventually a tree must die and, even whilst still standing, the bark becomes riddled with beetles and other insects making a huge larder for insectivous birds. Holes in the trees provide nesting sites for woodpeckers. When a tree actually falls it becomes a haven for land animals, until fungi help to break down the wood so that, eventually, nothing remains.

One morning a few weeks later, after the swans had had their bathe and were busy preening, the cob spotted a new bird flying low over the water. It was coming straight towards them. His head shot up high to get a better view. The stranger came in fairly close and landed, turning its head to look at them.

The cob hissed, lifted his wings a little and charged but the bird vanished, leaving the cob looking all round in anxiety. He recognised it as one of those divers who had the unnerving habit of vanishing under water, only to reappear somewhere else. It was a female great crested grebe.

Just as the cob was relaxing the grebe bobbed up beside him with a fish in her bill, but on seeing his great bulk she promptly vanished again. The agitated cob opened his huge wings wide and, beating the lake with them, sent up great columns of water which cascaded back again. He paddled angrily around in erratic circles, trying to protect his family from the unseen enemy.

The cob's reaction had caused a further commotion as he had accidently hit his pen when he opened his wings. She opened her wings too and hissed at his carelessness. Somehow, one of the female cygnets had been hooked out of the water and tossed a few feet away and she, righting herself, looked around in bewilderment then, 'pip-pipping', hurried back to her mother. The grebe's head materialised at a distance and the family were able to relax once more.

Remaining vigilant, the cob watched as something in the distance was moving towards the new female grebe. It was the head and a short portion of neck belonging to the resident male grebe. As he drew closer it was 'up periscope' and the neck grew longer. A short distance from it an oval object surfaced which, as the two parts joined, became his body; the bird was complete. Finally, he was riding quite high on the water and, tilting his head to one side, showed off his crest as he observed the new-comer. He seemed quite fascinated by the amusing little female that had caused such havoc amongst the swans.

There he sat in his full glory, bill pointing slightly down and crest fully erect as he moved closer in order to get to know her. He called in his croaky voice and dived in a shallow dive to come up again beyond her.

She immediately spread her wings and drew her head down onto her back and they met face to face to enact a head-shaking ritual. Parting again they returned with lowered heads, raising them slowly and simultaneously erecting their crests. After shaking them from side to side with bills pointing downwards, they waggled and swayed them alternately.

The female preened a feather or two, both birds dived, coming up again holding some weed in their bills. Paddling hard they pushed themselves upright and, breast to breast and practically touching each other — still holding the weed in their bills — they swayed from side to side. Abruptly, the female turned and ran away with feet pattering over the water and wings flapping. A short distance away she stopped and, with outstretched wings, displayed with her head pulled down over her back. The male dived to reappear within seconds with a fish which he offered to her. She accepted the fish and at the same time accepted the male as her future mate.

As dusk approached, the pen settled herself with the cygnets on another little island out on the lake whilst the cob sat on the water nearby.

Water bats were out, darting and swooping over the surface, snatching at insects which were flying low due to the warm weather and low cloud.

The mallard family were bobbing about in a group. The ducklings had grown their proper feathers but still had some tufts of fluff showing between them. Soon they would be able to fly as their wings were nearly fully grown. There were only eight left however, as the other three had become victim of another creature's need for food. The family had integrated with other mallards, being safer in a larger group.

A sudden bark of the dog fox instantly silenced the chatter on the lake. The vixen looked towards the sound from across the other side of the water and the 'yips' of the cubs added another

57

dimension. Mother and youngsters were going hunting, not only for food but as an essential lesson. The dog was going off on a long trip as is the way of this animal when no longer needed as provider.

The moorhen chicks were full size. They had lost their yellow-tipped, red bills which had now turned black; they would remain like this until they reached maturity, when the bright colours would return. Although still a family unit their confidence was such that they spread out on the water, spending more and more time on their own.

The clouds slowly moved over, letting the moon throw her soft glow across the lake and countryside. The pen slept with her head under her wing with four sleeping cygnets close beside her. The more precocious male, forever 'pipping' in his enquiring little voice, was sitting on the water next to the cob. Father and son were both looking out across the water when the clouds once again covered the moon as though closing the curtains for the night.

CHAPTER 5
"KESSY"

Becky Granger, driving her silver-grey Hillman Super Minx, was on her way back to the flat she rented in Portinscale.

She had been staying at Maryport on the coast for a few weeks enjoying the atmosphere created by its maritime past. Before making a decision on one of the most suitable flats she had seen recently, she thought it best to stay for a while to see if she really liked the area. She looked forward to returning to Portinscale as it was the nearest thing she had to a home.

She had left Cockermouth and was travelling in a south-easterly direction towards Lorton.

A kestrel hovering high in the sky spotted a movement on the road and, closing its wings behind it, dived. Like a high-speed dart it shot out of the sky towards a mouse that was scuttling away from the vibrations on the road caused by the car. Becky saw the bird within seconds of hitting it and was braking hard. She glanced frantically in her mirror but, luckily, there was no other vehicle in sight.

She stopped and, jumping out of the car, ran back to the bird which was lying face down, wings spread out wide. Very carefully she picked up the little road casualty, holding the bird in such a way that the tallons could not close on her fingers, in case it was still capable of trying self-defence. Opening the boot with her free hand, she took out a cardboard box and tipping out the contents, placed the kestrel inside and closed the box flap. Shutting the boot again she took the boxed bird into the car and placed it on the passenger seat. She sat for a moment or two, feeling upset and shaken before driving gently and smoothly away.

Twenty minutes later she arrived home. Before opening the car door she cautiously lifted a corner of the box flap and saw two fierce, black eyes staring, fixedly, up at her.

"It's alright pretty one, I won't hurt you," she murmured, closing the flap again. She opened the door to her flat before collecting the kestrel, which she carried into the kitchen and placed on the table.

Becky put the kettle on and began searching in the freezer for some minced beef. The cup of tea was very welcome. She was sitting quietly drinking it, deciding what to do with the kestrel, when she remembered that Ken had told her about a wild bird hospital.

She had met Ken several times since that day on Catbells and thought what a nice man he was. She wondered what had happened to make his wife desert him. She thought about her dear husband with whom she had spent twenty-five happy years of married life.

A scratching in the box drew her wandering thoughts back to her present problem. "Firstly, I must feed you," she said to the bird and went across the room to see if the meat had thawed. It had, so she dropped a lump into the box, making the bird jump. Draping a net curtain over the opened flap to let in some light, she hoped to encourage the bird to find the food and eat.

The next thing, she decided, was to contact Ken and ask his advice. She found some coins and walked to the nearby telephone box. Unfortunately there was no reply so she returned to the flat. She repeated the procedure at hourly intervals until, eventually, he answered. It surprised her when her heart jumped with pleasure at the sound of his deep voice.

"Ken, it's me, Becky."

" 'Ello, m'dear, this is a nice surprise. 'Ow long 'ave yer bin back?"

"Only four hours but I have a problem. I hope you don't mind me ringing you at this hour but I need some advice."

"Time is unimportant. Any'ow, eight o'clock isn't late. What's wrong, lass? 'Ow can I 'elp?"

Becky explained about the kestrel and said, "It's so beautiful, all dressed in rich reddy-brown with black flecks and a pale, creamy colour underneath. It was tragic, another second or two and it would have been safe as there was nothing on the road but me. I feel awful that I hit it."

"Don't be silly. 'Ow on earth could yer be to blame for that? Does the bird 'ave a blue–grey 'ead?"

"No, it's the same rich brown as its back. Why?"

"Just interest, lass, just interest. It sounds as though it's a female, from yer description. Well, it's a bit late t'do anythin' now. Yer 've no 'phone and there's quite a journey involved to get the bird to m'daughter's, so give 'er some food and close 'er down so that she sleeps. That'll 'elp to rest 'er from shock. First thing tomorra', I'll come for yer and take yer to Jackie's."

"Oh, don't bother coming up here - tell me where you live and I'll come to you, there's no point in you doing a double journey when I have my own car."

"Alright, then, we'll go on in m' Rover, leavin' yours 'ere."

She told him about her time away and how pleased she was to return to Portinscale and asked him what he had been doing. She felt she wanted to keep him talking as the sound of his voice was so comforting. When her money ran out she put down the receiver and walked back, deep in thought.

She wondered if he found pleasure in talking to her, too. Knowing his distrust of women she was anxious to know whether their friendship meant more to him. "What would Charles think of me, behaving like a silly young girl instead of a widow of fifty?" Suddenly, she had a distinct impression of him smiling as though he approved and Becky smiled back, saying, "I'll always love you darling, but I'm still here and you've moved on." She felt remarkably peaceful as she opened the door and walked into her home amongst the hills.

The following morning Becky got up early and made a cup of coffee and a couple of slices of toast, but resisted the temptation to peep into the kestrel's box. Instead, she talked to the bird, hoping to give it confidence.

61

It was not until after she had finished her breakfast and washed up that she went to the box and, still talking in her quiet soothing voice, carefully lifted the cover to see those piercing black eyes watching her. "Good, you're alive, pretty girl, so that's a start anyway. Would you like some meat?" There was still a small lump of minced beef left from the previous night, so she carefully dropped it in front of the bird and backed away.

Observing from her note pad, which hung by the kitchen doorway, that she needed some sugar and flour, she decided to pop along to the shop down the road before going off to Ken's house. She had no idea how long she would be away as Ken was the sort of person who would suddenly say "Let's do this" or "Let's do that" and, as he was fun to be with, she was unlikely to refuse.

Returning from the shop she put away her purchases then, going to the kestrel's box, saw with satisfaction that the food had gone. Closing the box firmly, she took it outside and placed it carefully on the front seat of her car. She collected her handbag and closed the front door.

Momentarily, she stood watching the white cummulus clouds scurrying across the blue sky. High above her head the tree tops swayed about. "The wind must be quite high today so it would be a blowy day to climb Catbells," she mused.

She took the Keswick road, turning right at the junction with the A591. It was a lovely morning and she noticed the dazzling sunlight on the hills contrasting with the dark Thirlmere waters as she passed its shoreline on her approach to Wythburn.

Driving through Grasmere she had to follow the traffic as it wound its way, like a slow moving serpent, past the shops. She was able to speed up as she headed for Rydal, on to Ambleside, then along the shoreline of the friendly-looking Lake Windermere towards Bowness. At last she crossed the head of Morecambe Bay and looked for the signs for Ulverston. Turning into Ken's drive, she sat for a few moments looking at the old house where he had lived all his life.

Bess heard the strange car and barked thunderously, bringing Ken's face to the window. He waved, then disappeared, to reappear a few moments later from his back door holding Bess's collar.

Becky, meanwhile, had got out of her car and eagerly called out, "Bessy, my lovely, it's only me."

The German shepherd's expression changed from the who's-that-in-my-garden look to the oh-that's-my-friend look, so Ken let go of her collar and she bounced up to Becky with a welcoming bark. She waltzed round twice, wagging her tail, pushing up against her new friend's hip and nuzzling her arm.

Becky dropped to her knees and hugged the dog rubbing her own face in the soft fur of the animal's neck, to have it washed in return by its owner's wet tongue.

"Yer must be a bit of alright Becky, as my Bess never be'aves like this with people outside fam'ly."

The man and woman gazed at each other in silence. It was a look which says far more than words. Ken, unable to stand the intensity of feeling any longer said, "Com'on, let's see to that kestrel. My car's over there so I'll take the bird while yer drive yer car into my garage and we'll go."

Ken and Bess were waiting in the Rover, as Becky approached he leaned across to open the passenger door for her. Getting in, she closed it and was met by a big nose which came from the back seat and snuffled in her ear.

"Lie down now, Bess, yer can talk to 'er later." Ken slipped into first gear and scrunched slowly over the gravel drive and onto the road.

"You surprised me then, I didn't realise the engine was running, she's so quiet and smooth. I thought mine was quiet but this one! Well, what can I say?"

Ken was pleased and he beamed with pleasure. "Yes. She's a great car but the lakeland roads aren't the best for 'er as she's made for the open ones where she can move. She's smooth as she's a six-cylinder ... yer used to a four. But yer 've got a nice car too, and yer keep 'er nice."

Leaving the A590 and turning onto the B5278 he said, "Shortly we'll turn left into a very narrow, windin' road which runs sharply up a steep 'ill. It's grand scenery. I think yer'll appreciate it."

Ken was right. Becky did like it and sat in silence staring in wonderment at the passing glory, before commenting how lovely it would be to go for a walk there. Ken smiled to himself and made a mental note of her sentiments.

"Your daughter certainly lives in a lovely part of Lakeland and it's perfect for a wild bird hospital — so quiet."

"Yes, that's very true but it's not all that easy for people to reach, 'cept for locals."

"Oh I don't know, look at me, now, with the kestrel. If you find an injured bird and feel enough to care and don't know what to do yourself, then you are prepared to travel."

As they reached the top of a rise they saw in the distance the sign, Birdholme Wild Bird Hospital. Very soon Ken stopped the car to open the gate, drove in and up to the front door. He opened the rear door for Bess and commanded, "Go and find Jackie and Steve."

The dog streaked off, whilst Ken collected the kestrel in her box and waited with Becky for someone to arrive. Excited barking sounded from behind the hospital building, proving that she had found one of her quarries. Soon, Jackie appeared playing with Bess.

"Dad! Hello." She came hurrying towards him with a happy smile on her face, Bess trotting along beside her. Suddenly the dog stopped and looked around, with a single bark she raced off again into the distance, to return a little later with Steve.

Ken turned to Becky and said, "This is my daughter." Then, turning to Jackie, he said, "Meet my friend, Mrs. Becky Granger."

The two shook hands and Jackie looked back enquiringly to her father, rather taken aback by the situation.

"Mrs. Granger 'ad an unfortunate 'appenin' yest'day when drivin' towards Lorton, as a kestrel chose that moment to swoop down and fly in front of 'er car."

"Oh dear, shall we have a look?" she said, recovering quickly and smiling at Becky.

"Hi there, Dad." Steve strode up to them.

" 'Ello lad."

"Mrs. Granger, this is my husband, Steve," introduced Jackie.

"Hello Steve. Oh, do call me Becky. Mrs. Granger sounds so stiff."

There were polite smiles all round, no-one knowing quite what to say, being so surprised to see Ken with his new friend. Jackie broke the embarrassed silence by taking the box and leading the way to the hospital reception area, where they could take a look at the bird without the risk of it giving them the slip.

She pulled a thin glove onto her left hand and whilst talking to the bird she gently slipped her hand underneath it. Carefully threading her fingers between and around the bird's legs, she held them firmly to prevent the tallons sinking through the glove into her hand. Putting her bare hand over the kestrel's back and wings, she lifted her out.

"She's got a bright eye, so the shock's not got her. Let me see that wing." Steve gently extended the suspect wing. "Thank you Kess, that's my finger, can I have it back?" He extricated it from the hooked beak. "Come on Jackie, you're not doing your stuff."

"Sorry, love." She extended two fingers of her right hand forward, one on either side of the bird's head to hold it.

Gently, Steve felt along the wing bones and found the site of the break. "She's lucky, the break's in an easy place. It's away from the joints so I can tape it to the closed part of her own wing and it will be set in three weeks."

"Will she fly again?"

"Yes Mrs. - I mean Becky. She should be flying within a few weeks of it mending, after the stiffness goes and the muscles have repaired."

"Oh, I am relieved. Do I leave her in your care?"

"Yes, that's right. I'll set it and then she'll go into a cage in the hospital and stay there, being spoilt by Jackie, until the binds can come off. After that she'll go into an outside aviary until she's flying strongly enough to be able to hunt and hover."

"The work you do is really wonderful. How do you support yourselves financially, may I ask?"

Steve explained about the Trust and was very pleased when she gave him some money.

"It's for Kessy, and if you need any more you must tell me."

They watched as Steve skilfully bound the wing to itself and then Jackie took her to a cage.

"I thought you would bind it round her body."

"No, not if it can be avoided, as that upsets their stability and also causes them a lot of stress as it can interfere with their movements and even their breathing."

"Dad, I'm sure you want a cup of tea?"

"I thought yer'd never ask." He put his arm affectionately round his daughter and gave her a squeeze.

They were sitting round the kitchen table drinking tea when Jackie, no longer able to contain her curiosity, asked, "Are you from these parts Becky?"

"No, I'm staying in rented accommodation in Portinscale. Since my husband died, I've been travelling around trying to find somewhere to settle. I needed to get away from the very sad memories in our home and so I thought it was best to sell our old house and move around 'til I found somewhere. Finding a new life and a new place is not easy, so before I feel able to buy a home I know I must be sure. I have sold most of the furniture, just keeping some in storage. I have only stayed a few months at a time in most places but have kept on the flat at Portinscale for, although I wanted to look around the coast, I needed a base for the time being. I've found one in Maryport that I like very much but it may be rather blustery in winter. Portinscale would be better, as far as weather is concerned. However, it is quite remote and, being on my own, I could find it lonely."

"How did you two meet?" Jackie risked asking, glancing at her father.

"I was sitting on top of Catbells, watching a man and his dog. They were climbing up the steep slopes which are really no more than sheep tracks. As my hubby and I used to have a German shepherd which died of old age a year ago, my attention was riveted by this man chatting to such a beautiful one, so obviously in complete harmony with him. The man was stopping to rest more and more as the climb got steeper, then he grabbed the dog's tail and got towed up. I was laughing as I'd not laughed for a long time, when your father and lovely Bess reached the top."

"Believe it or not," Ken continued "Bess bounded up to Becky as though they were ol' friends and, to my astonishment, Becky got to 'er knees and began cuddlin' Bess. As I reached 'em, the ol'dog was lickin' 'er face. As yer know she's not one for makin' friends with strangers."

They sat talking for about an hour. Jackie and Steve told her about the hospital and the accidents and treatments of some of the birds. Steve looked at the clock, remembering that he had to go and buy food for the birds. Ken stood up and said they, too, had better be going so he kissed his daughter and they parted company.

They were driving back along the hilly route home, when Ken found a place to pull off the road. Parking there, he switched off the engine and Becky looked at him in surprise.

"It's alright lass, I'm not about to ravish yer," he laughed "Yer wanted a walk didn't yer?"

"Oh, Ken, you don't forget anything, do you?" She smiled happily at him and got out of the car.

They walked for about half-an-hour, admiring the shapes and colours of the hills and the way the light made its own patterns accentuating some parts and throwing others into shadow. They came to a dry stone wall and stood leaning on it, both lost in their own thoughts. What they did not know was that they were both thinking along the same lines, but neither dared to mention it.

Ken put his hand in his pocket and pulled out a bar of chocolate which he broke up and offered to Becky then, after taking what he wanted, he put the rest back in his pocket. Leaning his arms again on the wall, his hand found Becky's for the first time. They stayed still, not saying a word, neither wanting to break the spell of that moment and wary that speaking or moving would do so.

Suddenly, they both looked at each other and Ken released her to cup her face gently in his hands and leaned down to place a light kiss on her forehead. She turned her face enough to kiss his fingers in return.

As they slowly began to retrace their footsteps, they walked in companionable silence, with Ken's arm resting across her shoulders.

Bess, who had been following rabbit tracks trotted on ahead, leading the way back to the car.

" 'Ow about 'avin' a bite t'eat with me, food tastes a lot better with company, specially undemandin' company."

"I'd love it Ken, thanks. I agree about the company bit, it doesn't seem worthwhile cooking just for one. There's no-one to smile and say, "That's good," or, "I feel better after that"."

As they turned into the gravel drive Becky asked, "Shall I bring my car out so you can drive straight in?"

"No, don't yer bother, it'll do later."

They went indoors and Bess trotted into her corner and collected a large well-chewed chew, which she presented to Becky.

"Thank you Bess, is this for me?" She took the chew and pretended to gnaw it then held it out to the dog. Gently taking it back, Bess walked to her corner again where she flopped down with a contented sigh.

Meanwhile, Ken had gone to put the kettle on, getting out two mugs he placed a spoonful of coffee in each. "It's no sugar, that right?"

"That's right, thank you." She wandered across to the window and stood looking out over the garden. "You've got a big garden and it looks really peaceful out there."

"That's tactful, lass. Yes, it's peaceful but rather overgrown. Let's say I'm fond of weeds." He picked up the coffee and took it to the table.

"I know. There has to be a reason to be busy, or someone to please." She looked round at him as she spoke, he nodded in agreement. Their eyes met and the look that passed between them confirmed that they understood each other.

"Let's go into the sittin' room," he suggested.

They sat down in easy chairs with their coffee. Bess joined them and lay spread out on the hearth rug. They discussed their morning together, the walk and the visit to Jackie and Steve.

"Your daughter seems a sweetie and she certainly is very fond of her father."

"Yes, she is that. Yer see, when 'er mother left she was rather disgusted with 'ow she'd been be'avin' and she chose to stay with me. We consoled each other and she's been 'er dad's girl ever since. Steve's a good lad, too. They've known each other most of their lives. I knew 'is fam'ly and we got on well. So I'm 'opin' that things'll go right for 'em. Now! 'Ow about food, would yer like som'at 'ot, like chicken steaks in bread crumbs with mashed 'taters, or som'at cold like quiche and salad?"

"Let's make it easy and have something cold, if that's alright with you?"

"Right ma'am, quiche and salad, and 'elp yersel' to some sherry or som'at off the side table when yer ready."

Ken took himself off to the kitchen and began collecting plates and putting them on the table. The meal preparation did not take him long as he had assembled the salad the previous evening and left it in the fridge. He had bought the quiche early that morning before Becky arrived, as he thought he might like to ask her back. "Yer don't mind eatin' in the kitchen do yer?" he called.

"No, 'course not, that'll be fine."

She picked up the empty coffee mugs and took them through into the kitchen and rinsed them. "Can I do anything?"

"Yes, look decorative. Do yer want another coffee with it or a cold drink?"

"I'd like a glass of water, please."

"Right y'are. Now, if yer'd like to sit 'ere yer can see out into my weedy jungle," he smiled, as he pulled back a chair for her.

They ate their meal and chattered as though they had known each other for years. After they had cleared away they wandered out in the garden to admire the plants and listen to the birds.

"I hope the kestrel will be alright. I certainly feel she couldn't be in better hands."

"She's got a good chance, Becky, so don't yer go a-worryin' y'rsel'."

"Ken, I really must be thinking of going home. I've had such a lovely time that I don't really want to, I must admit, but I've got a reasonably long drive and would like to be back before evening."

"Yes m'dear, that's very wise. This time, we'll keep in touch, yer 'ave my 'phone number and know where I live now. I 'ave yer address and I shall use it. Yer never know, yer might find me on y' door-step when yer least expect me."

She reached out her hand to him and said, "That would be nice."

They walked out to the cars with Bess beside them, swinging her long tail.

"Goodbye Bessy, look after Ken."   Becky stroked the big head before opening her car door to get in.   She felt the weight of Ken's hand on her shoulder and she stopped and turned to face him.   He had a wistful look in his eyes as he took her into his arms and held her tight.   Her arms went round his neck and she pressed her face to him.   He kissed her, gently at first, then more urgently.   Just as suddenly as he began, he stopped and said, "Yer'd better go.   Now take care, drive carefully."

Goodbye Ken, see you soon. Thanks again for a lovely day."

" 'Bye lass, take care."

Ken stood and watched her car disappear down the road before walking slowly back to the Rover.   He drove the car into the garage where moments before the Hillman had stood.

He sat for a little while feeling rather empty, but was roused from his reverie when he heard an impatient whimper outside.   He opened the door and got out.   "Alright Bess, I'm comin', gal."

He closed the garage and wandered into the garden and leaned against the trunk of his favourite silver birch.   "Bess, what's 'appenin'?   Am I bein' a stupid ol' man?   I vowed never to 'ave anythin' more to do with women, 'cept yer and Jackie and 'ere am I goin' soft over Becky.

CHAPTER 6
GROWING UP

Adolescence is a very important time in the animal kingdom as well as for people, it is when they learn about themselves and their capabilities. Their lives depend on discovering how to find food and to recognise and avoid any potential enemy.

The cygnets were almost full-size and had grown their adult feathers although bits of down still poked through here and there. They were not yet white, but a drab brown. Their bills and legs were dark, affording them camouflage in shady spots or amongst vegetation. Their wing feathers were almost complete except that only the tips of their primary flight feathers were showing. The remainder of these were still hidden in their white sheaths making them look like a row of hair curlers. As the young birds' muscles had not developed enough strength to keep up the extra weight of these huge wings they constantly slipped downwards and had to be flicked back into position.

The pen and cob had regrown their primaries and the cob, especially, was eager to fly. Sometimes he would run across the water flapping his wings to lift a little, only to settle back onto the water. He often gazed wistfully up into the sky or away into the distance, longing to go but still feeling the instinct to guard his family.

The young male cygnet who identified with him — let us call him Pip — liked to race across the water flapping his wings, too. Although he could not lift, he imitated his parent and gained satisfaction from doing so. Father and son moved towards each other waggling their tails and speaking softly, after which they turned and swam back to the family where the pen, preening quite contentedly, appeared to take no notice of them.

Not far away, the great crested grebes were swimming with their two chicks darting around them. They were beautiful little creatures with alternate dark and light stripes running from the front to the back of their bodies. Their faces had distinctive red markings. Like all divers, their legs were attached right at the back of their bodies and their feet had a paddle-shaped web on each toe, making them awkward on land but very agile in water. Even at this tender age they could dive for quite long periods for food or safety.

The young moorhens had become independent. The adults, having nested again, were sitting with their new chicks beside them on the bank watching the activities on the lake. The little ones were learning to collect food for themselves and were busily picking over dead leaves and moss. Sometimes one of their parents, seeing something to eat, would pick it up to offer it to them.

On the lake there was a mixed group of juvenile birds including mallards and moorhens. One morning, early in September, a black duck with a white throat flew in to join them. Not only was she a stranger but of unusual colouring. Whereupon she was immediately attacked by the resident mallards. By dodging this way and that she avoided trouble and flew further down the lake to land where it was less populated. Several ducks gave a half-hearted chase but soon returned to the main flock. The black duck wisely allowed them to become used to seeing her at a distance before she would make another attempt to join them.

The cob was growing more restless. His attention was continually drawn in a northerly direction to a spot where Lake Windermere seemed to become swallowed up by trees on the shore. The lake itself was nearly eleven miles long. The width varied from approximately one hundred yards to almost a mile. It was fed by a river north of where the swans lived and by several small tributaries along its shores.

The cob and pen lifted their heads high and whickered to each other. He ran across the water with pattering splashings, his powerful wings beating at the same time. The watching family froze in fascination as he became airborne and circled above them, calling as he looked down, urging them to join him. The pen answered but remained calmly where she was, whilst the cygnets raced about haphazardly flapping their wings but without enough power or co-ordination to lift. They clustered around their mother 'pipping' distressfully, still babies at heart even though their bodies had grown. She whickered reassuringly to them, but gazed longingly at the departing figure.

The cob flew north, keeping low over the lake. His sharp eyes missed nothing; the mixed group of juveniles, a family of mallards, a lone heron, some people with two dogs on the bank and a hovering kestrel high above him. Eventually he was flying level with the ruins of Wray Castle. As he passed, he swung left towards Furness Fells then circled south to fly over Grizedale Forest. Esthwaite Water lay to his left and the bird, following the lower parts of the hills, turned towards it arriving at its most southerly tip. He flew low over the shimmering surface and as it seemed to be deserted he stretched his legs forward to ski in, landing with only a slight disturbance to the water.

The swan sat motionless, with his head held high, listening and looking about him. In the distance he noticed a small flock of Canada geese, with their black heads and white 'chin-straps' topping black necks. As they turned, they showed white rumps which contrasted with their mottled brown backs.

The geese were no threat to the swan so, relaxing his vigil, he bent to take a sip of water, raising his neck again to let it trickle down his throat. His tail began to waggle as a preliminary to bathing and, happily, he bounced his front under the water, rolling to the left beating his right wing joyfully splashing his way round one way and then the other in half circles. His beating wings disturbed the surface, sending up sprays and churning the water. Suddenly, he stopped and sat as still as the choppy water would allow and listened carefully before he began to preen.

Round the corner amongst some reeds was a family of swans who had been dozing. The noise disturbed them and the resident cob gave a tense look to his pen which obviously meant 'stay there with the youngsters while I investigate'. He swam silently out until he could see our cob busily preening. He lowered his head down to his chest laying his neck, like a squashed letter C, over his back and arched his wings over it. With mighty thrusts of both his feet together his body lurched forward through the water, causing a piled up 'bow wave'.

Our cob was still preening with his back to the oncoming adversary. He was paying particular attention to his new primary wing feathers, running them through his bill making sure they were all in perfect condition.

A slight splash reached his ears and he spun round just in time. With an angry hiss he raised his wings and advanced to meet his opponent. They were evenly matched, both mature birds of about twenty-five pounds. The advantage was with the resident swan because he was spurred on by the need to protect his family.

The birds were hissing angrily. Their heads making darting movements, each trying to grasp their opponent's neck, at the same time avoiding the other's bill. Their wings were held high and aiming blows at each other; often hitting water as the other dodged. They circled and surged about, each trying to gain control of the situation. Our cob had grabbed the other bird by his wing but the resident cob, furious at this, managed to twist round and get hold of the intruder's neck, pushing and holding it under water trying to drown him. Our cob kicked hard with his feet and spun his body round delivering several wing blows to his captor. This made the resident cob lose his grip giving our cob the chance he needed and, moving out of immediate reach, he lay his neck out along the water in submission. It was not his territory and he did not want to fight any more. The resident bird gave several victory bites to the prostrated neck but he was satisfied and gave up his attack.

The two birds sat a safe distance apart. The victor, head held rigidly high, stared hard at his adversary in case a further attempt was made on his territory. The vanquished cob, with his neck in a gentle curve, turned his head away showing non-aggression. He paddled steadily away; when he felt at a safe distance, he opened his wings and took off.

He left the lake and landed in a nearby field where he shook himself and began preening in great earnest to rearrange his plumage and rid himself of the sense of defeat. As he calmed down he pulled at some grass before his large body sank to the ground and he looked about him.

The distant honking of Canada geese caught his attention and turning his head towards the sound he watched as small black specks away to the west became larger. They were coming from Coniston Water on the other side of Grizedale Forest and were flying in an uneven 'V' shaped formation, with one side longer than the other.

There were several families, a mixture of adults and juveniles. As he watched, the leader moved out of formation and dropped back to rest, allowing another bird to take over lead position. As they passed over Esthwaite, the small group of geese that our cob had seen on his arrival, noisily took off to join them, moving into formation at the end of one skein.

Back on Windermere, the pen and cygnets had had a quiet day eating water vegetation, drinking and preening but, above all, waiting.

The pen continually gazed up at the sky all around her knowing that, although her mate had flown northwards, he could return from any direction. The light had changed from the yellowish colour of afternoon to a rosy glow as the sun approached the horizon.

There was a distant honking and the pen spun round quickly. The sound was coming from the stillness of the rosy sky and soon she saw the dark skeins of geese which steadily grew until they separated into individuals. They passed noisily overhead to disappear in a north-easterly direction.

The sun was sinking into a strip of purple-grey cloud and a slight chill heralded the September evening. The pen watched and waited patiently whilst the cygnets alternated between dabbling and dozing.

Another sound from the direction of the recent sunset alerted the pen. It was the unmistakable rhythmic swish of swan's wings. Her head jerked up and eagerly she paddled round to face it; every muscle rigid with anticipation.

The speck seemed to grow out of the grey cloud strata. At last the longed-for voice reached her. Eagerly, she called back, her voice waking the cygnets who 'pipped' with excitement. Young Pip began racing about trying to take off and causing turmoil as he collided with his sister.

The chaotic activity stopped abruptly as the majestic figure approached. With wings outspread, webbed feet with slightly elevated toes stretched forward, head and neck held back with bill tucked down level with his chest; he skied in to a perfect landing. He folded his great wings and shook his feathers into place, before he approached his pen and greeted her.

The pair began their courtship movements while the cygnets kept trying to attract his attention by poking him with their bills. He turned crossly and hissed at them to wait, but when his favourite little female approached him in a submissive attitude 'pipping' softly, he relented and turned to face her. She swam close and gently laid her head across his back, he bent his head down to her and whickered softly: just as we might whisper, 'my baby girl'.

Darkness draped the contented family in peace. Their varied emotions of the day were forgotten as they slept beneath a sky bespeckled with stars.

About ten days had elapsed when a large flock of about forty Canada geese flew low down the middle of Lake Windermere preparing to land on the lake. They caused quite a commotion amongst the resident birds. Honking geese vied with quacking ducks and scolding moorhens, as feathered bodies charged about; a swirling mass of black, brown, and white. Bills reached out to grab feathers of the intruders, wings thrashed the water or any bird that was within reach. Feet paddled fast to get their owners out of trouble or into a better position to intimidate others.

The cob placed himself between all this and his family, sitting on the water with his neck within the depths of his arched wings, ready for action if necessary.

The geese stayed for a few hours and then, as though the leader had shouted 'Go', they streamed up into the sky with individual showers of water falling from their bodies. They left in two skeins as noisily and as beautifully as they had arrived.

The cygnets had been exercising their wings constantly since the day of the cob's flight. Now their muscles had developed so much that on several occasions they surprised themselves by flapping their bodies right off the water and having to glide back again.

The arrival and departure of the geese increased the cob's restlessness. So, early the following morning, he looked up into the sky as though considering the weather, then calling to his mate, he began to run over the surface of the still water with strongly beating wings. Airborne, he circled low over his family, looking down at them and calling. This time, without any hesitation, the pen turned into the slight breeze, spread her wings and joined him.

Fearful of being left behind, the cygnets were desparately rushing about with outspread wings. Some collided, hissing in their anxiety. Together, the parents circled lazily, waiting for the youngsters to sort themselves out and take their first flight.

Pip was the first to extricate himself from the muddle, to be closely followed by his sister. The other three became airborne somehow. The cob turned immediately to the south-east, calling to get some order. Pip was soon close on his father's tail and the outstretched neck of his sister, the cob's favourite, was just below him behind his right wing. The other male and two females followed with the pen at the rear where she could keep her eyes on the family.

The youngsters continually 'pipped' with excitement and concern, until they learnt to keep a certain distance from the steadily beating wings. They were used to swimming close to each other but this was different, for they found they had to leave a space of ten feet if they flew side-by-side. Gradually, their wobbly flight settled as their confidence grew and their anxious calling diminished, leaving just the exhilarating flight music that could be heard over a surprising distance.

They were flying high over Cartmel Fell and across a narrow winding road. Tiny cars, their gears whining, laboured up the steep twisty ascents. The cob banked slightly to his right and flew on, thoroughly enjoying the feel of the air rushing over his plumage. He occasionally glanced over his shoulder to make sure all was well. Sometimes, when her eye caught his glance, his mate would call to him and he would answer.

When he saw a glimmer of water ahead, he looked back and noticed that the formation had become spread-out. The youngsters were tiring, so he began to lose height. He went down to circle the water, checking it was safe to land.

There were several small ponds and a much larger one, on which swam a mixed collection of birds. He would have preferred to find a deserted stretch of water but knew he had taken the family far enough, so he led them down to the clearest area.

The cygnets' landing was far from expert. There was a collision as the two females who had been flying at the back, were too close to each other; one skied into the other landing partly on top of her sister. Flapping wings inadvertantly hit each other and made matters worse. They sorted themselves out and, stretching up tall and shaking, began to preen to calm themselves. Pip went to the two sisters and poked his bill into the back of one, as though saying 'silly thing, you made a mess of that'. Immediately, she spun round on him hissing angrily, darting her head at him threatening to grab his neck but making sure he could not grab her first. He 'pip-pipped' in amusement and moved away, whilst she turned her back on him and paddled off behind her mother.

The swans saw many different kinds of ducks and geese, some species that they had never met before. Although there was a little show of 'this is our water, who are you?', there was no real aggression, so the cob relaxed and let his family settle down too.

After a while they swam around to investigate their new surroundings. Rounding a corner, there was a sudden fierce hiss. The cob's wings shot up defensively as he turned to face the sound. He need not have worried because the owner of the hiss was behind some netting separating his area of water from the main pond. He and his mate, who was sitting behind him, were pure white with yellow and black bills; a pair of lovely trumpeter swans. What the cob could not know was that he had landed on the water of Steve and Jackie's bird hospital.

When a pair of brown and white shelducks with pink turned-up bills came swimming along, the drake, being a rather aggressive fellow, foolishly tried to drive off the visiting family. The cob was surprised at this cheeky chap and rushed at him aiming an angry blow with his wing. However, the drake was fast and dived out of trouble, to resurface and swim hurriedly away, leaving the cob to hiss and waggle his tail.

The family swam slowly on, looking about them with interest and on discovering a little bay went in to investigate. As the cob reached for some succulent grass from the bank he noticed two female cygnets, about the same age as his own, sitting on the bank. They 'pipped' a greeting, pleased to see their own kind yet apprehensive of trouble. The cob looked but ignored them, so they slid bravely into the water to join the group.

These two had been sent away early by their father, who was trying to court their mother to re-establish their relationship after nesting. He was quite intolerant of the incessant interruption of his youngsters. Wanting his mate to himself, he had sent them off as soon as they were capable of flying. Luckily for the two sisters they had managed to find Birdholme pond very easily.

Jackie had noticed them one morning and, guessing what had happened, made a special effort to see they had food. She called one

'Star' because of a distinct white mark on her forehead showing up against brown plumage which reminded her of the one they had reared years ago in Ulverston. These two cygnets were indeed the daughters of our cob's sister, the one with whom he had been so close; they were his nieces.

Pip and Star made friends immediately and began swimming around together, calling softly, and even made the beautiful dancing neck movements of courtship. This was quickly spoiled by one of Pip's sisters who chose that moment to come charging through.

The family remained there all that day and by late afternoon noticed the resident birds had began to watch and listen intently. The cob felt something was going to happen and was apprehensive.

Steve and a young helper arrived with buckets of food and the water-birds started to call and crowd around eagerly. The cob kept his family back but his sister's two youngsters went forward fearlessly with the other birds, hungrily snatching at the food as it was thrown to them.

"Jackie, come over here and see what's arrived," called Steve.

She left her bucket by the owl enclosure, which she was just about to enter with their meal, and hurried to the pond. "Oh, aren't they lovely. Did someone bring them in while I was out?"

"No, they've just brought themselves, perhaps it's an early training flight for the youngsters. See how the cob's keeping them all behind him."

Just then Pip swam from behind his father and went to join Star in picking up some grain that had been thrown into the shallows. The cob hissed a warning, but was ignored. Steve threw some bread as hard as he could to the family. The cob hissed again nervously but grabbed a bit that floated near him — it tasted good, so he ate it. He relaxed and the others moved cautiously forward to join in the free meal.

"He doesn't seem to mind having the other two cygnets so close to his own. That's strange isn't it?"

"True, of course, but his are growing up and he knows the others are no threat."

"I know, but he could think of them as a threat to food supply."

"Perhaps he's just a sensible sort of chap, like me." He grinned at his pretty but mud-splattered wife.

"Big head," she retorted and went back to the owls.

The enlarged family stayed together for several days until, one afternoon, the cob called to his family and began running over the

78

water and took off. This time he did not look back. Quickly the cygnets and pen followed, getting themselves into formation as they hurried after him.

Star and her sister looked up in surprise but remained sitting on the water; watching. Pip looked down at Star as he followed his family. This time he flew in the rear position and was getting left behind as he was undecided whether to go or stay.

CHAPTER 7
AUTUMN

The weather conditions had changed from the warm balmy days and chilly nights of early autumn to much harsher ones, preparing nature's children for what was to come. After several days of torrential rain the stream which fed the lake, burst its banks, flooding the neighbouring fields.

This was appreciated by the water-birds who made good use of the new, wide expanse of shallow water where they could easily reach down to dabble for worms in the mud.

Many new birds had arrived, either to spend the winter on Lake Windermere or to use it as a resting place before continuing their migration. More Canada geese had arrived, together with a smaller flock of greylag and pink footed geese.

Another stranger, a goosander, the largest of Britain's saw-billed diving ducks, flew in early one evening but remained aloof from the others. He looked striking with his hook-tipped, slender, red bill — a reflection of his vivid red eyes, which stared out from an elegant, dark green, crested head. His equally dark back contrasted with his white and pinkish underparts. When the sun found a hole in the clouds, its beam focussed like a spotlight, causing those red eyes to glint like jewels.

The rain had eased during the day, as a gusting wind had sprung up and blown the remaining clouds away. The November dusk arrived early and many birds were spread out over the flooded fields searching for their evening meals.

A volley of gun-shot roared out, silencing all creatures and causing them to stand motionless; tensely listening. The wildfowlers remained quiet, lulling the birds into a sense of false security; some birds relaxed and moved about again, others took to their wings. This was the opportunity the shooters wanted and several more shots rang out across the fields, causing instant panic.

One mallard was caught by a glancing shot and a shower of feathers fell from him, but he managed to fly on. The remaining birds rose in a body and headed for the lake. The men had anticipated this. Their guns barked again. Several birds were killed outright and spiralled downwards. Some, shot in one wing, fell out of the sky as their fragile bones were smashed or splintered making the birds helpless. One drake was hit in the leg causing the broken limb to dangle uselessly below his body, but he flew on and out of range of the killers.

Dead birds were floating on the surface with necks and heads hanging under the water; one moment vibrant little personalities the next lifeless bodies. Dogs, sent in to collect them, zig-zagged eagerly about as they searched. Birds that were still alive swam frantically, trying to escape the dogs, but those with injuries were no match for gun dogs. One duck had landed in some rushes and stayed still until the men and dogs went away.

That night there was a half moon which gave the clouds a sufficient glow to enable the water-birds to return when they felt it was safe to do so.

The injured duck came out of hiding. She was so hindered by her painful, broken wing trailing in the water that she moved miserably into a sheltered patch in the shallows to sleep. The flesh was badly torn and the bone splintered: it would not be long before the wound became infected. Eventual death would be a kind release from her suffering. It would come either from starvation, due to her being unable to search for food, or infection.

The rest of the night passed uneventfully with the wind groaning amongst the bare branches and birds sleeping fitfully where they could find the best shelter.

Just as dawn was colouring the sky one of the fox cubs was trotting along the bank, feeling rather hungry as he had not made a successful kill. He stood by the edge of the water watching some mallards out on the lake and licked his lips at the thought of warm flesh. After remaining quite still for several minutes his hopeful expression changed to disappointment with the realisation that they were beyond his reach.

The cub looked around him and was just moving away when a sound from the water, close to the bank, reached his sharp ears. Very carefully he crept forward until, below him, he could see the duck partly hidden in the reeds. He studied the situation and realised that, if he jumped off the bank into the water the resulting splash would alert his potential meal; a mistake he had made sometime earlier! He crept back to where the ground sloped into the water, stealthily moving along close under the bank. The animal moved like a shadow, lifting each paw cleanly from the shallow water so as not to cause a sound.

The duck raised her head, momentarily, from beneath her good wing. Feeling cold she tried to lift her useless wing that lay in the water beside her, to cover her back. The pain and effort was too much for her and, wearily, she closed her eyes again letting her head sink onto her back.

The fox had decided on his route. He walked out until the water was up to his chest then he swam into the reeds and grabbed the unsuspecting duck. Death came mercifully quickly for, with a violent shake, he broke her neck.

The young fox had a struggle to get his victim ashore. The broken wing causing additional problems as he pulled the lifeless form through the entangling reeds and grasses. When he reached the bank he found it difficult to jump up carrying the extra weight. He reached up with his front paws and pushed the duck up onto the ground. Scrambling up the bank he stood panting and looking around, making sure nothing was waiting to steal his meal which had cost him so much effort. With his white tipped tail waving to and fro' he picked up his prize he trotted off into the growing light.

The wind had eased to a pleasant light breeze and the swans were swimming around the edge of the lake, seeking food from beneath the surface. Since their visit to the Bird Hospital, the family had often been out for short flights but each time had returned to the lake for the night.

Pip felt strangely restless with the dawn that followed the shooting. He began running on the water and flapping his wings for take-off but, changing his mind again, returned to his family. He paddled about amongst them repeatedly calling, begging them to accompany him. His parents answered but turned away making it quite clear they had no intention of moving. His brothers and sisters were thrown into a dilemma, wanting to go with him but afraid to do so without their parents. Pip repeated this performance over and over again as he tried in vain to obtain company.

Finally, he gave up. With one last call he pattered over the water with wings soon beating hard. He swept upwards, water falling back from him as, tucking his legs up into his feathers, he circled his family. Impulsively, the sister with whom he was closest, began racing over the water with outspread wings and, within seconds, the music of her flight was harmonising with his own. Relieved to have company he called to her as they flew off together in a south-westerly direction.

The pen and cob watched without a sound as two of their cygnets disappeared on their first lone flight.

They flew over the flooded fields and the shallow river where they had experienced their first swim, then over miles of the countryside they had learned to recognise from recent family explorations.

The wind had dropped completely and it became milder. The clouds, having no driving force, hung about like grey washing on a line. Autumn colours gave melancholy shades to the countryside. Most of the leaves, having been drenched and shaken off the trees, lay in tatters below.

Mile after mile the swans flew. Pip was leading and seemed to know exactly where he was going; over hills, a few houses, fields and woods until they could see a great expanse of the sea in the far distance. As they flew nearer they saw that a wide river joined it as a broad estuary. Birds of all sizes were riding the waves, running about on the shore or flying around in huge, calling flocks.

From their high vantage point they saw a large group of swans and cygnets about a quarter of a mile up the river. These were like a magnet to Pip, who banked and turned towards them. Both made expert landings and the group were soon milling around them, all chattering in happy voices. It was a non-aggressive group of youngsters recently sent off by their parents, last year's birds and a few unpaired adults, hence the easy-going welcome given to the two newcomers.

Thirsty after their long flight Pip and his sister dipped their bills into the water and raised their heads to let it slide down their throats, but stopped abruptly shaking it out again. It was salty and they looked surprised but thirst soon encouraged them to try again.

As the days passed, Pip and his sister gained confidence in their new-found independance and enjoyed being with this large flock of birds of similar age to themselves. Sometimes they all swam lazily up-river to a spot where people often congregated and threw bread for them.

On one occasion, a young boy threw a paper bag and a cygnet grabbed it, but tossed it aside in disappointment. Laughing loudly and feeling pleased with himself, the boy picked up a handful of pebbles and threw these, too, at the birds. One hit Pip on the head and the shock of it made him hiss with fear.

Several days later the birds were once again at that feeding spot and, having climbed out onto the bank, were sitting enjoying some weak sunlight. The same boy, with a friend, came walking along the track. He approached the birds saying, "Watch me frighten this silly lot of birds away, I'm not scared of them."

"I'm not scared either, what can birds do to us?"

The boys picked up stones and began throwing them and laughing with scorn as the frightened cygnets raced for the water, calling in fear.

Pip had been sitting behind a bush and felt trapped as the boys had cut off his retreat. He stood up and hissed, then moved forward to reach the safety of the water but, full of bravado, the boys turned to face him. The leader raised his fist full with stones. Pip, nervous but angry, opened his wings and quickly delivered a powerful blow with his wingbutt onto the boy's chest, which neatly caught the youngster off balance and sent him backwards into the water. Although it was only a little bay it was deeper than it appeared.

The friend backed away quickly, allowing Pip to make for the river but the one who was in the water, splashing about and yelling as he struggled to get out, found himself once again in the cygnet's way. Master of the water, the young swan tucked his head deeply inside his raised wings, gave two strong thrusts with his webbed feet and launched himself at his opponent. Another blow across the head and shoulders of the now terrified boy pushed him momentarily under water. Satisfied, Pip turned and swam after the others, leaving the boy to scramble up the bank with the help of his friend. His teeth chattered with cold and his body and head were sore from the blows. No doubt, he had learnt his lesson!

The following day the leader of the group, who was just over a year old, led them down-river and out to the estuary. The sky above them seemed full of oystercatchers, black and white birds with orange bills, all calling merrily. They spiralled gracefully before landing on the wet sands, where they ran about probing the stones and seaweed for molluscs and crustacea. They were part of the huge flock that, year after year, spent the winter there. The cygnets enjoyed riding the waves which lazily ebbed and flowed over the sands, the sea being in one of its peaceful moods.

Fifteen days had elapsed since Pip and his sister had left the family when, on looking up at the sky with his head on one side, he made his decision. Calling to her, he opened his wings and propelled himself over the river surface to soar up above them all. He looked down calling softly, then more urgently to hurry his sister to join him. Together, on strongly beating wings, they flew north for home.

At last, in the distance, the great lake glinted in the pale sunlight and the cygnets flew straight towards it. Approaching, their eyes searched the water for the familiar figures and they called loudly when they were in sight. Tilting their wings and spreading their primary feathers they lost height in readiness for landing. The siblings rushed to greet each other whilst the pen and cob moved majestically towards them, whickering their greeting.

Emerging from murky, grey clouds, the watery sun sank slowly behind the skeletal branches of a small deciduous wood. Night was about to fall on the family that would remain together now for most of the winter.

The end of the year approached with daylight hours becoming fewer. Bats were hibernating and the water-birds were busy eating as much as they could to build up their body-weight for the time when food would become scarce. Feathers needed careful attention to keep out mud and dirt as it was essential that their bodies remained well-insulated and water-proofed.

Christmas at the hospital was expected to be an extra busy time as the intake of birds did not usually lessen and, if the weather suddenly worsened, it could become quite hectic. Apart from this extra work, Jackie had to organise their own food for the festive season.

85

Sitting at the kitchen table with a cup of steaming coffee, she was listing ideas for gifts and food requirements. She was still uncertain whether to ask her father's new lady friend to join them for Christmas. She had to be careful as she did not want to make him back away, especially when they seemed to be getting along so well.

He used to be so adamant that he would never entertain the idea of getting married again, that Jackie felt she must tread very carefully indeed. She longed to see her father with a companion as she knew how lonely he was, particularly now she had left their old home. He had not said any more about finding a small cottage but she knew the old house was getting beyond him. Every now and then she would go home and give it a good clean. He did his best but most of the time he did not even see the dust. As long as Bess was happy, then he was too.

Nevertheless, she would just have to ask him about Becky. She could always say "Becky must be lonely out there, how about asking her over for Christmas?" Yes, that would do. Jackie was pretty sure her father would not take offence at that. Whilst she was feeling confident, she went and dialled his number.

" 'Ello."

"Hi there Dad, it's me."

"Ah Jackie, I was just thinkin' of ringin' yer. Y'kindly asked me over for Christmas Day, which I'll be pleased to accept as we've always bin together at Christmas and I don't much care for change. But lass, I've bin a-worrin' about Becky as she'll be feelin' lonely. It's always a sad time for 'em 'ats alone."

Jackie was delighted. She did not expect her father to ask, so now her part was easy. "That's fine Dad, supposing we ask her to come to us as well? Do you think she would accept?"

"That's very nice of yer, lass. Shall I ask 'er for yer?"

"Yes please, then you can make all the necessary arrangements."

They chattered on for a while before she put the telephone down and happily carried on with her lists. She would get a present for Becky now that her father had as good as admitted he cared for her. She remembered seeing a book about German shepherd dogs in a shop in Cartmel and would see if it was still available.

She had already got a thick, lovat-coloured jumper for her dad, in a mix of wool and acrylic in the hope that it would be safe from shrinking in the wash. Recently he had spoilt several pure wool jumpers in his eagerness to get them 'nice and clean'. As he walked Bess in all weathers she was concerned that he kept warm. There was no doubt he needed a good wife and it would be a relief to

Jackie if he and Becky made a go of it. There was quite enough for her to do looking after Steve and all the birds. It was a good thing that they had not yet had children. Although, she had to admit, it would be nice and her father kept asking when he was going to be made a grandfather.

The next ten days passed quickly with Christmas shopping, baking, wrapping up presents, planning the meals and, of course, doing her share of work in and around the hospital. There was a lull in the intakes as the weather became unexpectedly mild. Apart from caring for the long-term birds already with them, only two new ones were brought in for treatment.

On Christmas morning Steve and Jackie got up early. After breakfast they went outside to feed the birds and clean the aviaries and cages before going back indoors to begin festive preparations. Both hoped that there would not be a hospital emergency as they needed a break from the continuous work.

Steve went into the hall and switched on the tree lights bending down to pick up a small parcel that had fallen off one of the branches. As he replaced it and stood back looking at the tree, his mind wondered back to his childhood. He remembered how Jackie would come to have tea with him and he, in turn, would go to her house. Thinking about her mother and how kind she had been to him, he was sorry that she had found it necessary to leave the family. He glanced into the kitchen at Jackie whose back was towards him. What a lucky chap he was to have her and their happy, secure home.

He picked up the Christmas card from his sister Emma. It was a photograph of her with her husband Jeff and one-year-old son, Tommy. They looked a lovely family. "Christmas is for children", he mused, "They put the magic into it". He looked at the decorations Jackie had put up and brooded that it was as though they were acting. He wandered back into the kitchen and sat down at the table.

"What's the matter, love?" asked Jackie without turning round.

"Nothing."

"Yes there is, I can feel it. It's like a cold draught of air floating round me."

"I can't keep my feelings from you for a minute." He smiled at her as she turned to look at him.

"Well, sweetheart, what is it? You can't be miserable on Christmas Day."

"Oh, I'm not miserable. I was just thinking ..."

" ... that we should have a baby to make Christmas for."

"You really are amazing, Jackie. Yes, that's exactly what I was thinking. It seems, sort of... empty."

"Well, you never know what can happen at nesting time," she laughed and continued slicing the carrots.

The atmosphere suddenly brightened and Chistmas magic seemed to slip surreptitiously into the air just in time for, at that moment, the sound of tyres on the gravel drive drew them to the door to greet their guests.

"Dad! Becky! – Hello. Happy Christmas. Bessy, come to Jackie."

There were hugs and kisses amidst happy 'woofs' and, with arms full of colourful parcels, they all trouped indoors. After placing the parcels under the tree they followed the aroma of freshly ground coffee into the kitchen.

"It was so kind of you to invite me for Christmas, my dears, I've been looking forward to it ever since Ken passed on your invitation. I must admit the thought of being alone in my little flat at this time was not appealing."

"You are more than welcome, think nothing of it," answered Steve. "We're just hoping that there will not be any emergency to interrupt us."

"Well if there is, you can always give me a job to do." As she spoke Becky looked at them in turn with a genuinely happy smile.

Jackie thought that she really seemed right, as though she already belonged to the family. It was strange, but she and her dad looked as though they had been together for years instead of knowing each other for just seven months. "Shall we open the presents before dinner or afterwards?" she asked.

"I think, before, because by the time we've eaten it'll be time for the Queen's speech, after that we'll pro'bly all fall asleep 'till Bess tells us it's 'walkies' then it'll be eats again."

"You speak for yourself, Dad! You and Steve may well fall asleep but I'll have to clear away and wash up, then you'll want coffee or something and need more waiting on ..."

"Oh, Jackie, my poor 'ard-done-by daughter," he laughed.

"You've got a good point, Dad," commented Steve. "We men must have time for a break after dinner, so I vote for presents before food."

"Woof," came a voice from under the table and the big furry body pushed its way between two chairs and went into the hall. Everyone turned to see what she was doing. They all laughed when she came walking back carrying a parcel, which she gave to Ken.

"It seems as though we've begun. Let's see what she's brought. Yer crafty bitch, it's yer own from Becky," laughed her doting master.

Bess's tail was waving round and round and she moaned with impatience.

"Let her have it Ken, she's such a clever girl. Aren't you my darling," Becky said to the dog and leaned across Ken to fondle the dog's tall ears.

Ken opened the parcel, watched closely by Bess, and revealed a very big chew bone which was prompty removed by the black and tan furry face.

The family went into the hall to the tree which was beautifully decorated with tinsel and fairy lights. From the living room came the sounds of traditional Christmas music and the crackling of the wood fire in the grate. Bess took her chew in there and lay with it on the hearth rug.

"This is all a great credit to y' both and I'm proud of yer. But there's som'at missin'."

"What's that Dad?" asked Jackie puzzled.

"M'grandchild." He grinned mischieviously as he looked down at the parcel in his hands.

"Not you too... I've got enough to do already, without a baby."

"I know that, m'gal, but don't leave it 'til it's too late, that's all."

Jackie blushed and looked sideways at Steve, who was also grinning with pleased embarrassment.

"You have a good point. It's times like Christmas when we think of little-uns, and I was only saying so to Jackie before you came. It's very true though, she really does have her hands full."

"Perhaps I might be around to help a little," ventured Becky a trifle timidly.

Jackie looked up quickly wondering if they were going to be told any interesting news. However, as this was not the case she merely said "Thank you, that's very kind of you. Are you thinking of staying around here more permanently?"

"Maybe, but certainly if I am, I'd be only too glad to help with birds or babies." She gave Jackie an encouraging smile.

Christmas Day ended happily with Ken driving Becky back to Ulverston where she had left her car. It was already ten-thirty and, as Ken stopped the car on the driveway, he took her hand in his and sat in silence for a moment., Although not sure of himself, he said, "Becky, m'love, it's late and I don't like to think of y'driving alone all that way. I've already aired the spare-room bed and it's all made up

89

waitin' for yer. The electric blanket should 'ave switched itself on and made it cosy. Would yer stay, m'dear?"

"Dear Ken, you're a very kind and thoughtful man. How can I refuse. I'd be delighted to stay."

The moon was full and the garden looked quite lovely bathed in its light. They stood in silence for a few moments, seeing it all as though with fresh eyes because of their feelings for each other. Ken's strong arm went round her and she snuggled up to him, resting her head against his shoulder. "I never expected to feel like this again," she whispered.

"Nor did I. I vowed that I'd never give me 'eart to a woman again. But now, 'ere I am in danger of breakin' that vow. Becky, dare I ask yer a special question?"

"Of course, dear one, anything."

They turned to face each other as Ken's arms held her tightly and hers went up and round his neck. His mouth was eager and found hers just as receptive. They were lost to the world. Their spirits became as one and their bodies longed to do likewise. The long, deep, kiss ended and he placed his hand behind her head and clasped it to him. Rubbing his cheek on her hair, he whispered, "Darlin' Becky, would yer marry me?"

"Oh, Ken. Yes, I'd love to. I can't even contemplate life now without you. Anything I've done recently without you being part of it has seemed quite pointless."

"I'm so 'appy yer feel the same way. Y' know, I was goin' to sell this 'ouse and find a cottage quite a time ago, but I just couldn't be bothered. I didn't know what I wanted or where I wanted to go. Now life 'as got back its meanin'. I'll put this ol' place on the market, once the 'oliday is thru', and we'll go cottage 'untin' together."

"That's wonderful, I'll look forward to it. Life has just begun again for me too."

They began to kiss again but a deep moan from down by their feet made them break apart and burst out laughing. Bess really had had enough of lying outside. Bed was calling and she jumped to her feet, whirled round twice with pleasure and bounded to the front door.

Indoors, Ken went to put on the kettle. "Shall we tell Jackie and Steve, or shall we wait a bit?"asked Becky.

Ken thought for a moment or two, then said "They might 've gone to bed, if we ring 'em we'll prob'ly disturb 'em".

"Oh well, that wouldn't be fair."

"Yes, damn it, why not? They'll be delighted. It might even make 'em feel romantic enough to get broody!"

He poured out two mugs of hot chocolate and, hand in hand, they went to the telephone. He put down his mug and dialled their number.

"Steve lad, it's not a bird call-out. We've got some news for yer that won't wait."

"Hello Dad, what's this then?"

They could hear Jackie saying 'what's this, what's happened?'

"I've just asked Becky to marry me and she's agreed."

There was a moment's silence at the other end then they both gave a whoop of joy. "Congratulations Dad, we're delighted ..."

Jackie grabbed the receiver and gabbled, "That's really wonderful. We've hoped and hoped this would happen as she's perfect for you. I already feel she's like a mother, especially when she offered to help if we had a baby. This is the best Christmas present you both could have given us."

Becky, sharing the telephone, said "You're a sweetie, Jackie, I heard those lovely words and I feel like that about you both too. I'm sure we're going to be a happy family."

Promising to speak again in the morning, they wished each other "Good night".

"Well, there's no going back now, we've told 'em and they wouldn't let us."

"Going back, who's thinking of going back? You've not got cold feet already, my lad, have you?" she teased.

"No, darlin', but talkin' of cold feet, I 'ope y'don't 'ave cold'uns. If yer 'ave, it's single beds," he laughed.

"No, you're quite safe they're not too bad."

"Well, shall we go up. I think it's best if we sleep apart 'til we're married don't yer? I know people don't bother about such now-a-days but it's som'at to look forward to after we're wed. What d'yer think?"

"I'd love to say blow old-fashioned protocol but you're right. A wedding isn't the same when it's out of bed, wed and get back again. It loses some meaning. We'll wait, then it'll be perfect."

They stood inside her room, with their arms about each other for their last kiss of their first Christmas night.

CHAPTER 8
WINTER

D aylight crept in imperceptibly and, as the sky was so leaden, it seemed unchanged from night. Although there was not a breath of wind there was an atmosphere of deep foreboding. The birds felt it too and they hardly made a sound. Everything seemed to be listening and waiting as before the rising of the curtain at a stage performance.

There was a sense of relief when the action began. White snowflakes began to flutter and float downwards prompting the birds in the trees to begin moving about and give an occasional 'chirrup'. A duck quacked some way off and the cob stood on the water and flapped his wings shaking off his inertia. The cygnets stared with curiosity at the dancing snowflakes, their heads tilting one way and then the other trying to get a better view of these strange things. Pip snapped at one and, finding it was cold, shook his head and tried to throw it away but it had already melted.

As the temperature was just above freezing the snow melted as it landed then, later in the morning, the sun found a hole in the grey blanket of cloud and seemed to smile for a little while. It was certainly not a happy smile but rather a mournful one. It soon slid out of view again, this time behind a particularly dark monster of a cloud which hung like a black cloak over the hills. The rain began to fall from it remorselessly, before turning to sleet.

For several days the weather remained unchanged until, late one afternoon, the sky turned almost black and the wind began to blow in real earnest. That night, it moaned and screamed amongst the trees. The temperature dropped sharply to below zero.

The birds on the lake huddled together. Their heads beneath their wings for warmth and their feet, when not required to paddle, tucked up inside their feathers. It was warmer for them on the lake as the large mass of water was slower to cool than the surrounding land.

The following day dawned on a white scene. The snow continued to fall thickly, a strong wind driving it down at an angle of forty-five degrees gave it a hypnotic effect.

The birds pulled at any weed they could reach under the water, as most food was hidden beneath a white carpet. By the evening the wind had piled the snow up into drifts and the lake itself was beginning to freeze. At first it was only a thin layer of ice which was soon broken up by the movements of the birds. The snow stopped but the wind was merciless. For nearly a week the birds were able to keep part of the lake open, which looked like a black hole surrounded by a colossal white blanket.

Then, under cover of night, more snow fell and the temperature dropped still further, causing the lake to freeze hard and to close in on the group of water-birds. The majority of them did not move but sat there, cold and miserable, trying to keep their feet warm by tucking them up inside their plumage. By morning, however, only the swans were left as the others had flown onto the thick snow.

An RSPCA van with snow chains on its tyres, made its way slowly through the snow along an indentation which suggested where the field track would be. Eventually, the vehicle reached the lakeside and the two inspectors got out to study the bird situation. They noted the various water-fowl sheltering in snow hollows and the family of swans clustered in the closing hole. Returning to their vehicle they collected shovels and sacks of food. Having cleared an area of snow they heaped some grain there. One threw some bread towards the swans but, unfortunately, it fell short as they were too far out.

The men turned their attention to the deer and took some hay bales on foot to the wooded area for them. Leaving it in a pile they hoped that it would be found before the snow covered it.

Upon their return the men stood talking near to the swans. One man pointed to a cygnet who had not raised his head from under his wing, then they went back to the van and slowly drove off.

That night the swan family finally gave up as the ice and snow was threatening to enclose them in its deadly grip. It was a hard struggle to climb out onto the bank of slippery snow but they managed it. All, that is, but one cygnet. They settled down to eat the bread which they discovered partly hidden in the white larder.

It was a little male cygnet who was left behind and, lifting his head weakly, made some half-hearted attempts to follow them, but his feet slipped as he tried to clamber out. Calling pathetically to his family, he laid his neck flat along the snow trying to reach them, but as cold and hunger had weakened him he closed his eyes. After a few moments he lifted his head again, it swayed with the effort. Finally he pushed it under his wing and slipped into the sleep of hypothermia.

When morning came the wind had died away and the sun was shining. Birds were moving about desperately searching for food and occasionally calling. Some people were tempted out with cameras to record the beautiful scenery.

The snow was melting on the ice where it was at its thinnest leaving dark patches. When some ducks came flying in, thinking it was water they skidded into each other creating a heap of feathered confusion. As quickly as they could they flew up again and back to the snow.

A Canada goose, needing a drink, flew across to one larger patch of black ice. As he landed his feet shot forward throwing him back onto his tail and his wings flapped frantically to regain his balance. He stood up and looked about him in surprise. Although he poked at the ice with his bill it was too thick for him to penetrate. Cameras were clicking and people were talking and laughing, their voices loud in the still air.

The swans were preening and looking about them, all but the little cygnet who, by this time, was actually frozen in. When a man threw some bread to the swans he noticed that the cygnet did not even lift his head.

It was early afternoon when the blue van returned, this time with some long ladders strapped to the roof-rack. The man with the camera had reported the plight of the cygnet to the RSPCA but the inspectors had first to finish a rescue already in progress before going to the lake.

The men lifted the ladders off the vehicle and carried them to the lake-side, carefully testing the ground as they went. Then they returned for some sacks and a swan carrier. They laid the ladders down over the ice, pushing them slowly and carefully towards the cygnet. The swan family took fright and slithered out of their reach; as without a proper surface for take off they were unable to fly away.

The cygnet was quite a long way out. So, using the two ladders, the inspectors had to crawl along to the end pulling the rear ladder alongside then pushing it ahead of them to extend their path. The work was hard and slow but at last they managed to reach the cygnet. The nearest man touched the bird and was pleased to find him still alive. Next, they had to chop carefully at the ice with a fireman's axe to free him. The cygnet partly withdrew his head from his wing but put it back again — he was past caring.

Five minutes later the men had him free. They hauled him out onto the sacking beside them to absorb some of the water and help to warm the icy bird. Placing another sack in the opened carrier they lifted the sick bird onto it and buckled him safely inside. They lay the bird's head and neck carefully over the top of the carrier. It was a slow, difficult crawl back and the long neck kept flopping down and was in danger of being harmed. When not moving the ladders, one man carried the cygnet by the carrier-handles and draped the bird's neck across his own shoulders to keep it out of harm's way.

They eventually reached land. The cygnet was placed inside the vehicle, before they returned to collect the ladders and fasten them back onto the roof-rack. The two men stamped their feet and rubbed their hands to get some life back into those cold parts. Checking around the lake once more they climbed into the vanand drove away.

Travelling south on the Coniston road they reached the gateway of Birdholme Wild Bird Hospital where they turned in and drove up the gravel drive to stop by Reception. Steve heard them and went outside to see who had arrived.

"Hi there, Frank, got something for us?"

"Aye, it's a cygnet that was frozen int'e water at lower end of Windermere. It's pretty bad. Don't know if you'll save it. It was a ladder job."

"That's hard work. Like a cuppa?"

"Love one. Thanks."

"Jackie," Steve called "Can you put the kettle on? Frank and Bill are here, cold and thirsty after a cygnet rescue. I want to see to the bird."

"OK," came her voice from the kitchen "Send them in."

Steve picked up the swan carrier in one hand and the floppy neck with the other, and went into the hospital building. It was warm in there and the walls were lined with an assortment of boxes and cages. He opened the glass door of a large wooden cage and, gently lifting the cygnet from the carrier, he placed him inside onto a bed of clean newspapers, laying his limp neck over his back. He switched on the heater which warmed the floor of the cage. Going to the medicine cupboard he took out some homoeopathic Dulcamara†, their favourite remedy for any illness caused by the patient becoming cold and wet. He opened the unresisting bill, popped a tiny tablet at the back of the cygnet's tongue and closed the bill again. He stroked the miserable head as he laid it down onto the cold, grey feathers of his back, before closing the glass front and leaving the bird to sleep.

Steve then retired to the house for a chat with Frank and Bill. He wanted to hear what had happened to the cygnet, apart from having his own cup of tea.

The freeze stayed another two weeks, the birds and animals relying on people to bring them food and eating snow for water. At last the temperature began to rise slowly and the repenting sun melted the snow and ice, bringing an enthusiastic activity amongst all wild creatures.

The swans had been able to drink water from the hole left by the cygnet's body; frequent use had stopped it from freezing over. On this particular morning the cob waddled over to the hole and sat down on the edge before he pushed himself off and into the water. Joyfully he tried to bathe, and as there was so little room, the activity of his strong body broke off chunks of ice. This enlarged the hole until, eventually, he was able to bathe properly.

It was the beginning of a fast thaw and, more and more birds were able to get onto the water. There was great excitement as they drank, swam and bathed; their busy bodies helping to break up the remaining ice.

It was not until the lake had completely thawed that Steve's Ford estate came slowly along the lakeside track to stop where he could see the swan family across the open water. Two bright eyes were

---

† See homoeopathy at end of book.

watching through the back window and an eager voice greeted Steve when he opened the tail-gate. He lifted the swan carrier which was heavy with the now healthy bird strapped inside it, and carried it to the water's edge. The cygnet looked very different from the day he was rescued by the RSPCA. Bright and alert, he called excitedly the moment he saw his family and began to struggle for his release.

Steve unbuckled the straps allowing the cygnet to rush into the water. The young swan used both his wings and legs to propel himself as fast as possible towards the advancing party. Steve stood by, proudly watching the cygnet who, almost dead upon arrival at his hospital, was now hurrying towards his family and obviously so very pleased to be back 'home'.

January melted into February. The increasing hours of daylight encouraged snowdrops into flower, soon to be followed by wild daffodils waving their heads in the breeze. There was a stirring amongst the animals and birds as they sensed there would be an early spring. Much bird-song filled the air.

The pen and cob felt very attracted to each other and were courting frequently. Breast to breast and necks stretched up high, they slowly turned their heads first one way then the other, sometimes almost cheek to cheek before taking a sip of water, preening a feather or two, or having a bathe.

On one of these occasions Pip went over to see what was happening and his father turned angrily on him and sent him off. He was surprised and upset by this strange behaviour from his normally gentle father. The next time the adults started courting, the cob stopped suddenly and angrily swam at the cygnets scattering them before returning to his pen.

One morning just after daybreak, the cob was fussing round his pen when a Canada goose came too close. With a furious hiss and a well aimed blow from his wing butt, the swan left the goose in no doubt that he was unwelcome. When a duck came swimming idly by, the cob was getting more and more annoyed and grabbed her by the neck and pushed her under water in an effort to drown her. Fortunately for the duck another sound distracted him and he let her go. She flew off with a loud quacking.

He became more and more irritated at the presence of his own youngsters. They had become very wary of him and utterly bewildered by his change of attitude towards them. No longer was he their gentle guardian, but a very worrying threat.

One day, three young cygnets came flying towards the family from further up the lake. The moment they landed the cob hissed in anger and charged at them, causing the youngsters to take to their wings again. Still with arched wings and his head drawn back inside them, he charged his own youngsters. Their complacency turned to panic. He kept charging, not allowing them to settle, making it quite clear it was time they left.

The pen sat still, watching, as they were forced into the air. Her eyes following her young family as they left forever with Pip as their accepted new leader.

The cob shook himself and swam up to his pen. She answered his greeting but turned away to watch her babies becoming small dots in the distant sky, flying away to begin their new lives.

Flying in formation, the bewildered cygnets stayed close to Pip. He led them towards the river where he and his sister had spent time earlier in the winter. It was a perplexed little group, for their parents had been good to them and so this sudden rejection caused them to feel alone and vulnerable.

They flew on until they could see the river shimmering in the distance like a long, twisting ribbon. As he approached, Pip dropped low and flew over it looking down and around, searching for some signs of the other cygnets. Eventually he saw them, almost hidden amongst tall reeds in a backwater which ran between some fields. He called to them and then dropped down onto the water with the others following his example. Pip and his sister exchanged greetings with their friends, while the other three members of the family nervously nodded their heads in friendship.

Most of the cygnets in the group were drab brown with a little white showing here and there. A few were over a year old, dressed in white but still showing their dark bills. Two pure white ones, a pen and cob who had been together for a long time, had just got their red bills and would shortly leave to find their own first nesting site.

The flock was getting larger with groups of new cygnets continually arriving. Sometimes they divided, with some birds staying in favourite spots and the others wandering off. The river was both wide and very long, so there was plenty of room for them all. Pip and his family settled further up the river together with seven other cygnets. They were near to a reedy backwater, perhaps reminding them of their old home.

One sunny afternoon when they were sitting on the bank, a sound from above made Pip look up. Two grey cygnets were calling and preparing to land on the river. The group slithered into the water full of curiosity.

As the newcomers landed, Pip stretched his neck to full height and swam towards them, whilst the others stayed behind to watch. The newcomers were both female and 'pipped' a nervous greeting. Pip dipped his bill downwards to show non-aggression and answered 'Quoh quoh'.

He sailed forward with great dignity and one of the new females met him with her head turned sideways in submission. She had a clear white patch on her forehead. It was Star.

CHAPTER 9
SPRING

K en was standing by the window with a cup of coffee in one hand and a wad of house brochures in the other. He was not, however, taking any notice of the things in his hands but was gazing at the newly opening buds on the shrubs, the brilliant colours of the tulips and the remaining double daffodils. A blackbird flew down and began gathering dried grass for his nest.

"Yes, m' beauty," he said to the bird, "it's time for 'ouse buildin', for yer and me." With that he sat down at the table and spread out the brochures.

Becky glanced at the glistening surface of Derwentwater as she drove past with a feeling of elation, not only because of the brilliant light and colours of the natural world around her but because she was on the threshold of a new beginning. She switched on her car radio and pressed a few buttons until she found some music that she liked. Putting her foot down on the accelerator, she joyfully sped along.

As she rounded one corner, which was sharper than previous ones, she had to slam her foot down hard on her brake pedal as some sheep had strayed onto the road. She managed to stop just inches from the hind-most of the fleeing sheep, her heart pounded against her ribs with the shock. She remained stationary for a few moments to recover before starting off again and moving forward more slowly. It did not stop her enjoyment of the drive: rather it enhanced it, now she was more alert to the present instead of living in an imagined future.

The sign 'Ulverston' made her heart give a bounce and she hurried on towards Ken's house. The familiar sight of his drive brought a happy smile to her face. Immediately Bess was alerted and barked to tell Ken, who opened the door and stood waiting for her with a broad smile on his face.

She was just getting out of the car when she was nearly knocked back in again as Bess arrived and greeted her with enthusiasm. The big dog grabbed her handbag and, carrying it proudly with her head held high, trotted indoors with it.

"Ken, hello. It's a glorious day and you're looking great," she called happily to him.

"Mornin' lass, much more glorious now yer've arrived. Com'on in, kettle's singin'."

He held his arms out to her as she stepped into the hall. Her arms went round his neck and they stayed a few moments saying nothing but holding each other tight. They kissed lightly before turning and, hand in hand, went into the kitchen. The sunlight streamed in through the old sash window, spot-lighting the unruly heap of house brochures on the table.

"Bess, where's my bag?"

Obediently, the dog got up and walked to her blanket to pick up the bag and take it to her.

"Thank you darling. You're a very good girl. There might be something in it for you. Shall we look?" She opened the bag, holding it so that Bess could see what was happening. The big ears went forward in anticipation, but she waited patiently whilst the bonio was taken from its resting place and offered to her.

"Yer spoil 'er and, with two of us doin' it, she'll be 'opeless."

"Not her. She's too clever and, what's more, she deserves it."

"I agree with yer there, m'sweet. It looks as though I'm going to be busy with two of yer needin' spoilin'."

When their eyes met, they revealed a teasing gaiety re-emerging from their youth but tempered with the understanding of maturity.

"Now then, lass, enjoy yer coffee while it's 'ot an' I'll explain m' feelin's about this lot. Look at 'em for yersel' ... I'll tell yer what I

101

think. That pile," waving his hand "is of no value to us, but these three 'ave possibilities. One 'ouse is on the edge of Cartmel and with a reasonable bit of ground. Second one is a "lakeland stone cottage on the outskirts of Coniston" and third, "lakeland stone cottage on the edge of the fells" which sounds very nice but might be too far out when we're ol' even 'tho' it'd be quite near to Jackie an' Steve."

Becky took the discarded pile first and fingered through them before putting them down again and picking up the three places of interest. She read them carefully and looking up, she met his waiting gaze. "Let's go and look at them."

"Alright then, I'll 'phone the agent and see if we can go this mornin'."

He got up and went to the hall, leaving Becky to look dreamily out into the garden and listen to his voice on the telephone.

In a few minutes he came back into the kitchen and announced that the agent would ring them back as soon as he had made the appointments. "Which d'yer like the sound of best, Bec?"

"The one on the fells sounds glorious, although I appreciate what you mean about growing old. It seems funny, talking about getting old when we are feeling young again; as though we're back in our youth starting our lives together. It's a strange contradiction, love making us feel immortal and common sense making us think of our real age and what will happen."

"Love is quite right. We should feel immortal but still be sens'ble and make sure we don't 'ave problems when we're ol'," replied Ken sagely.

At the sound of the telephone in the hall he got up swiftly to answer it. Upon his return he said, "Right m' lass, coat on, we're off."

Ken backed the Rover out of his dilapidated garage and opened the back door for Bess whilst Becky sat in the passenger seat.

"Oh, lovey, I don't think I locked my car," she said.

"Give me yer key and I'll do it."

She watched his lively walk as he strode across to the Hillman.

"Yes, y'did. Yer only said that to wear m'out," he teased, as he got into the driving seat.

"Go on with you, you're as fit as a fiddle. All the walking you and Bess do you'll never grow old."

"Never grow ol'! With all the jobs that'll need doin' in the new place to keep yer and Bess 'appy, I'll need lots of tasty food to keep me goin'."

Becky leaned across the gear lever, and reached up to give him a kiss. "You'll get everything a man could ask."

He grinned at her as he set the car in motion and they talked happy nonsense before relapsing into a comfortable silence.

First, they went to the house on the outskirts of Cartmel. It was in good condition, the rooms were of a good size and the garden was nicely kept. It was not too close to the busy life of the town, but somehow they did not feel enthusiastic about it. They left, thanking the owners, and drove towards the "cottage on the edge of the fells".

As the sun shone from a cloudless sky the countryside looked inviting. "Walks up there would be lovely and fancy looking out of the windows and seeing those views!" commented Becky, wistfully.

They found the cottage easily and were shown over it. Although it needed quite a lot of work to make it comfortable, they liked the feel of this place.

Finally, they drove to Coniston and found the third cottage. They opened the gate and stood inside the front garden. It was crammed with beds of tulips and fading daffodils backed by mature shrubs in various states of bloom. Some had burst into flower, whilst some were in bud holding back their own show until the others had finished. Within the embrace of this display was a neatly mown lawn.

"The person who's laid out this garden knows plants. It's beautiful," said Becky with appreciation.

The front door opened and a lady in her seventies smiled a welcome. "Have you come from the agents?"

"Yes that's it. Can we 'ave a look over the cottage?"

"Certainly, dears, come in, come in."

Inside the house was warm with a cosy feeling about it. They wandered from room to room and when they looked out into the back garden found that to be as beautifully laid out as the front.

"Who's done the garden? It's perfect,"asked Becky.

"That's my husband. He's ever so sad to leave it but he's eighty now and we're going to live in sheltered accommodation. We feel that we'd do better to move now, while we're still mobile, and make the new place our home, rather than wait till one of us has gone, leaving the other all lonely."

"That sounds very sens'ble and I'm sure yer 'usband'll find 'e can do some gardenin' where yer're goin'."

"Oh yes, he can certainly do that. We're just hoping someone will come here who will love and care for it as he has done. It's sad to think it could be ruined, as so often happens when new people move into a home, not feeling the same way about certain things."

Becky and Ken closed the gate behind them and got back into the car. "Well Bec, what d' y' think?"

"I love it. What do you think?"

"Well, the same. There's one or two things that'll need attention, like some rotten wood on the back door-step which makes me want to look closer at other parts. I'll 'ave to get Steve to look in the roof as 'e's more agile than I am an' I don't fancy gettin' stuck! It's in easy reach of walks for ol' Bess into the barg'in. That big shed'll act as a workshop or a second garage so we can keep two cars if we want, 'tho we'll prob'ly only need one."

"It sounds as though you like it too." She turned hopeful eyes on his face.

"Yes, if yer like, we'll go into the agents and make an offer on our way 'ome."

"I'm really sure and there's nothing I'd like better."

He reached for her hand and gave it a squeeze before starting the car. There was a moan from the passenger on the back seat and a wet nose was thrust into his neck.

"Later Bess, yer'll have yer walk, but business first. For once y' come second."

The German shepherd flopped down and put her head on her paws in disgust.

Once inside the estate agents, business began in earnest. Ken made a firm offer and told the agent that he would like their Ulverston branch to take on the sale of his house.

Suddenly the shock of reality hit him. Until that moment everything seemed a happy game. He realised that the very act of putting his old home on the market meant that he really was going to leave it after all those years. It had been in the family for over sixty years as his parents had lived there before him. He jerked himself back from his thoughts as the agent was looking at him, waiting for a reply to something. Quickly he pulled himself together. "Eh-h sorry, what was that?"

"I think it best for me to contact my colleague and explain the urgency, due to the fact that you are interested in this cottage. He can come and see you to value yours and discuss the sale in detail," the man re-explained.

Ken agreed. He and Becky waited whilst arrangements were made for a visit by an agent from their Ulverston office later that afternoon.

It was a busy day and Bess demanded a walk when they got back — which she got. Then, after a quick sandwich, they scurried about tidying the house ready for the estate agent's visit.

The appointed hour arrived and Ken took the man round, answering questions and asking a few himself. The sun was still shining, so the agent was able to take some photographs before he left.

"Well, lass, we've got the wheels turnin'. Any cold feet? Are y'quite sure yer prepared to throw in everythin' an' live with me?"

"My dearest Ken, what have I to throw in? I have a rented place that isn't more than a temporary home. I live alone and, unless I'm with you, I'm pretty lonely. It's you, my darling, who will be selling the old home that has been your life."

"Yes, I must admit I felt funny in the estate agents, but I got over it."

"I thought you did, I felt your sense of shock after you asked them to sell your house. You don't have to sell, if you don't want to."

"Yes it's right to sell. We need a new place to begin our lives together, not one filled with all sorts of memories." He reached out and took hold of her hand. Just then the telephone rang.

" 'Ello. Jackie, lass, 'ow are yer? - Yer what? - No, I don't believe it - Are y'sure? - Well done, the pair of yer. Wait a tick while I tell Becky. Yes, that's right, she's 'ere. Becky, I'm goin' to be a grandfather! "

"Oh that's marvellous." She jumped to her feet and went to Ken's side, kissed his cheek, and took the receiver. "Well done Jackie, I'm so pleased. When will it be? - end of September, that's a good month. It'll be the makings of you both, even though it'll be hard work. Don't forget, I'll be around to help."

Ken took the phone back and told his daughter about the cottage and his intention to sell their old home.

Sitting down again with a very much needed cup of tea, Ken looked across at Becky and said. "We'd better get married. We can't leave it 'til we're movin' 'ouse as we'll be far too busy. Besides, the baby can't 'ave a grandfather and no grandmother, so what d' y' think?"

"I think it's a great idea. I must admit I wondered when you'd come round to it." she teased.

"Yer've got m' ring, gal. What else d' y' want?"

"Your body, of course." The happiness within her caused her face to have a radiant glow.

"My! yer forward, wicked woman. 'Ow delightful!" He jumped to his feet, and pulled her up and into his arms, then kissed her passionately. "Woman, yer bring out the beast in me." Before she could reply, he was kissing her again, becoming more gentle as the playfulness gave way to real love. One hand held her whilst the other read the contours of her body and approving the journey.

"Let's get married next week, then yer needn't keep goin' back to Portinscale and we can practice married life before we become grandparents."

Becky laughed. "I don't think either of us need practice at being married, besides we can't get married that fast, there's things to do and arrange."

"I don't see why not. All we need to do is see the Registry Office, tell Jackie an' Steve to keep a date clear an' that's that."

Becky looked into those eager eyes that she had grown to love. She considered for a moment about their wedding and decided that, apart from Jackie and Steve and perhaps a few of Ken's friends, there was no-one else to invite and nothing much to arrange. It was not like the first exciting church wedding of youth. "Go on then, I'll go along with that."

It was his turn to look stunned. "Yer mean that?"

"Yes Ken, I agree. Let's get married as soon as possible. We love each other and want to be together — that is the most important thing. Also, we are old enough not to put too much emphasis on an expensive wedding day."

"Stay the night, Becky, then we can go off tomorra' an' make the arrangements. This'll make Jackie an' Steve sit up. They're prob'ly wonderin' if we'll really get married."

"Alright love, I'll stay. Now, how about mundane things like food, shall I cook something?"

"No. Yer can put yer feet up. I'll cook. Make the most of it, yer'll get plenty of that that when we're married. Then I'll sit back an' become a lazy so-an'-so, enjoyin' bein' waited on."

"I think, my sweet, that we'll both enjoy spoiling each other."

CHAPTER 10
PREPARATIONS

The following morning Becky was downstairs before Ken. She had been awakened by Bess, to whom a closed door was no problem. At 5 a.m. the dog had come in, jumped onto the bed and snuggled down beside her. She dozed for about three-quarters-of-an-hour with one arm round the animal and her face resting between the tall ears before deciding to get up. She wanted time to be able to greet Ken with a nice, cooked breakfast.

It was the smell of bacon, toast and coffee drifting into his nostrils that woke him instead of Bess who normally called him from his bed. In happy anticipation he got up, washed, shaved and dressed, then went quietly into his kitchen.

A scene of homeliness greeted him after all his lonely years. Becky was standing at the old Aga turning the bacon in the frying pan. The coffee pot was standing by the side of one of the hot plates and toast was waiting in the rack on the properly set table. Bess was sitting by her side, watching her busy hands and hoping that something would fall onto the floor, needing her to tidy it up. The dog turned as she heard Ken. She flattened her ears in pleasure then, with a quick glance at the frying-pan, gave a little 'woof' and bounded to him. Becky turned round and smiled her welcome.

"What a lovely sight. Two of m'favourite gals. If it's goin' to go on like this I'll be the 'appiest man alive."

He walked across the room and placed his arm around Becky's shoulders and she, putting down her cooking fork, swivelled round within his embrace to face him and put her arms about his neck. They kissed gently, very aware of being two middle-aged people lucky enough to have a second chance at happiness and very much in love with each other. There was no youthful excitement, as life's lessons had broadened their outlook but taught them to value what they had found. The look that passed between them was almost one of incredulity. They treated each other with a sort of reverence in case it was all a dream and, with a blink of an eye, both would revert to their former existences.

Reading his mind, Becky touched his forehead with one finger and said, "It's true darling, we are here together. By the look on your face you were thinking the same as I was."

Ken gave her a hug, nearly squeezing the breath out of her and said, "Aye, an' it's great."

They stayed sitting at the breakfast table by the window, having finished their meal, watching Bess playing with a stick on the lawn. The dog was pouncing on it, picking it up and shaking it before tossing it away then charging after it and repeating the performance time and time again. She kept glancing up to make sure they were still watching her. Suddenly she grabbed her stick and bounded through the open kitchen door to present them with her gift. After placing it on the floor between them, she went to her water bowl for a drink. Most of it went down her throat but some squirted out through her jowls onto the floor then, turning her head to look at them, she forgot to swallow the last mouthful, which dribbled out in a stream as she made her way back across the kitchen.

"Yer mucky pup," admonished Ken.

"You're just like my Dusky, she used to do that."

The telephone rang, it was the estate agent who needed some extra information. They promised to have the details completed by the following day, so that he could sign the agreement for them to handle the sale.

"Shall we start sorting out some of your things, Ken? Say 'no' if you wish to do this alone as it can be a very painful thing, but if you don't mind about it I'd be very pleased to help. If this place is anything like mine was, where so many memories were stuffed away in boxes, in the roof, cupboards, and even outside in sheds, I hardly knew where to begin. I expect it will be the same for you."

"Yes Bec, it's like that 'ere an' quite possibly worse. The memories 'ere are un'appy. So I'd be pleased to 'ave yer 'elp."

"Supposing we tidy one bedroom and fill it with things from the roof that you want to keep. We can box up burnable stuff you want to scrap and have a big bonfire. Other stuff that is too good to burn can be taken to a jumble sale. The roof is so often the worst to sort out."

They spent the morning doing this and by midday had a large heap at the bottom of the garden ready to burn.

"Becky, d'yer fancy takin' this stuff for the Scouts Jumble Sale while I start the fire, then we can go for a walk with Bess?"

"Yes of course, if you can direct me."

Ken watched the departing car which was piled up with boxes and plastic bags then turned his attention to the fire. Soon flames were leaping up, consuming memories in a cleansing funeral pyre.

He stood back, momentarily mesmerised by the happening. An old photograph of Jennie before their marriage seemed to come to life as it danced in the flames. The hot air lifted it from its resting place and threw it about before the intense heat curled its edges and obliterated the picture forever. So fierce was the fire's heat that a smouldering white heap was all that remained when Becky returned. Ken was relieved to see her and leave his past in the embers. The three set off for their walk.

Bess squeezed round the wicket gate as Ken held it in the midway position for her, before she streaked off after a wood pigeon flying low over the field.

"Thanks for yer wonderful 'elp this mornin', love. It would 'ave driven me mad on m'own."

"Pleasure Ken — after all that's what a partner is for."

"Talkin' of partners, 'ow about m'suggestion of an early marriage? Are yer still 'appy with a simple Registry Office marriage or d'yer want a more posh affair?"

"I'm quite happy. I meant what I said last night, let's get married and spend our money on things for our new home. If we each keep the things most precious to us, we can buy whatever is missing."

"Right then lass, tomorra' we'll go to Cartmel an' make the arrangements, afterwards we'll go shoppin' for yer dress and then ..."

"Whoa there, not so fast. Firstly, it appears that I'm to stay overnight again ... "

"Of course, y' don't think I'm lettin' yer go yet, d' yer?"

Becky laughed. Ken thought it was a laugh which conjured up the sparkling water trickling over stones in the beck. She was aptly named.

"Alright then, for a while, until we've got things arranged. Now, as far as a dress is concerned, that's woman's work. I shall ask my future daughter if she'll come with me to help me choose one."

Ken was delighted at her wishing to involve Jackie and beamed at her as he heard the word 'daughter'. 'We're goin' to be a family again,' his heart seemed to shout.

He thought about Steve's parents and how they all used to be such good friends. It was his fault that they had drifted apart. He had felt so out-of-things when his wife left him that he had shunned the world, even his friends. "I'd like to invite Steve's parents to our weddin', they were always so nice. I'm afraid I dropped 'em, which was unkind."

"That's fine with me, and only right as they're your son-in-law's parents."

"Well lass, when's it to be?"

"Let's say ... three weeks," she stated, but looked at him questioningly.

A smile lit his dear, weather-beaten face and Becky reached up and kissed him. They strolled arm-in-arm following Bess, who was trotting ahead with the occasional glance over her shoulder to make sure they were still behind her.

The next morning Ken and Becky drove to Birdholme as there was so much they wanted to talk about. Ken had telephoned them after breakfast inviting them to a pub lunch. When they arrived however, they were greeted in a rather unusual fashion.

"Come in quietly and listen."

They all stood at the bottom of the stairs as instructed and waited, wondering what they were supposed to hear. Suddenly, a piercing scream broke the silence. "Kia, Kia, Kia."

"What on earth was that?" asked Becky, "It seemed to come from one of the bedrooms."

"Come and see," whispered Jackie and quietly led them upstairs where she opened the door of a guest bedroom. There, perched on the wardrobe, was a female kestrel, her black eyes fixed on them. Jackie walked slowly but deliberately into the centre of the room, watching the bird.

The kestrel stayed quite still, as Jackie talked soothingly to her. The bird's head began to bob up and down, then she leaned forward

110

and, opening her wings, floated gracefully down, to land on the girl's head. The bird began flapping her wings and uttering her familar call whilst at the same time gripping Jackie's thick hair in her tallons. It was as if she was trying to lift her. Abruptly, the kestrel released her grip and flew straight out through the open window. The family hurried to see where she had gone and were in time to see her land in an apple tree at the end of the lawn.

"What on earth was all that about?"asked Becky.

"Well, you remember the kestrel you found and brought us?"

"Yes, of course, how could I forget her, we called her Kessy, didn't we? That's not her, is it?"

"Yes Becky. We recognise her by a slight bump in the wing bone where it was broken. It doesn't inconvenience her, fortunately. She's been released for two months now and we thought we'd seen the last of her, until she arrived this morning. It's as though she's trying to tell us something. She keeps flying in through the window; coming to me as she did then and flying back into that apple tree."

"Jackie, look carefully amongst the branches." Steve, lined his head with hers and pointed. He had been watching the tree intently. "Can you see her?"

"Yes, I've not lost sight of her yet."

"Where is she then?"

"Three-quarters of the way up on the right."

"OK, what is that a quarter of the way up on the left and that, just below, a bit deeper into the tree, and again slightly below that?"

Jackie studied the areas. With a "whoop", she said — "More kestrels! Could they be her babies?"

Everyone craned their necks forward to look. The kestrel called to her fledglings and launched herself into the air to be followed by her three youngsters. Having not long been out of their nest they were making heavy work of the flight. She landed just inside the window, the young ones arranged themselves on the outer ledge. The family held its breath in wonderment as Jackie spoke to the bird in a continuous, calming monologue.

Once more the adult kestrel flew in and landed on the wardrobe, which had become her favourite spot, and called to her babies to follow. One by one they fluttered in and huddled against the wall; worried about the strangeness of the enclosing room. Again the bird flew to Jackie's head and leaned down to preen one of her curls, which hung over her forehead.

"What is it Kessy? What are you trying to tell me?"

111

The kestrel launched herself again into the air and flew off through the window, leaving the three babies on the wardrobe.

"I don't believe it. She's just left me to baby-sit."

"If we don't want to miss the next part of this, we'd better have our chat up here. There's a chair there for you Becky. I'll go and get three more and perhaps you'll bring up the coffee, love?"

"OK Steve, be back in a minute."

Soon they were all sitting in the corner of the room, leaving the window area clear. They had a lot of news to exchange and arrangements to agree. Jackie and Steve had enjoyed a few days in Sussex. They had visited the Arundel Wildfowl Trust and Jackie spoke of the friendly atmosphere, how the birds came to see if there was any food going and how she felt she wanted to cuddle one of the little Bewick swans — "They're such darlings". Steve said he thought the surrounding countryside quite breaktaking, especially the views from the top of Bury Hill with the river Arun winding over the Amberley Wild Brooks.

They went on to say they had had a telephone call from Emma and Jeff in Australia. Baby Tommy was well and toddling around now and the sheep farm was keeping them busy. Sometimes friends finding a bird in distress, having learnt about Emma's love for the feathered world, would bring it to her. She had a first year black cygnet with her at the time which had an injured wing but was now recovering. They loved to visit a nearby lake in the Swan Valley where a pair of black swans had nested and produced four cygnets. Tommy seemed to have inherited a love of birds. Last week, Emma had found him sitting on the floor next to the black cygnet.

The three kestrel fledglings suddenly began to make little welcoming noises in their throats. Mother arrived on the window-sill and, after looking around flew in to deliver a newly-killed mouse, amidst squeals of excitement from her youngsters.

"Charming bird, now I've not only got to clean up their droppings, but mess from their meal too."

"We could send them out," commented Steve, with a knowing wink at Ken.

Jackie looked at him and smiled, but just said, "A woman's work is never done."

When it was time for their trip to the pub the fledglings were still on the wardrobe, so they closed the bedroom door and left them on their own.

They all got into the Rover for the journey along the country lanes to the pub they had chosen in Cartmel.

Sitting at their table with drinks before them, Ken broached the subject that had been worrying him. "I know I'm to blame for not keeping in touch, son, but I'd like to ask y'parents o'er one evenin'. 'Ow d'yer think they'd react after all this time?"

"They'd be very pleased, Dad. They understood you better than you realised and knew you weren't really shunning them. Several times they wondered whether to try and reach out to you but were afraid of a rebuff."

" 'Ow awful. I'm sorry I was so blind. Would yer both come the same evenin' to 'elp out?"

"Yes, of course, we'd be delighted to. Supposing we ring from our place when we get back ? We'll be together and can arrange a date to suit us all"

"Thanks lad, that's taken a weight off me mind. I came to th'idea when thinkin' of our weddin' and, as I said to Becky, I'd like to invite 'em.

They ate home-made steak and kidney pie in silence as each thought about the year ahead. Knowing Jackie and Becky loved chocolate gateau and cream, Ken would not listen to their half-hearted protests of 'too fattening'.

"I suppose you're trying to make sure we both need the next size in clothes for the wedding?" Jackie teased her father.

"Becky's skinny enough an' needs a bit more weight. Shortly yer'll need the next size up any'ow, m'gal" he replied, pleased with his wit. After a while he got up, went to the bar and returned with a grin but said nothing. A few minutes later the barman arrived at their table with four coffees and liqueurs.

"Don't get the wrong idea, I don't intend splashin' out regularly but it's not often that we 'ave a weddin', a new 'ome, and a new baby to celebrate, all in one year."

Jackie leaned across to him and gave him a kiss on his cheek. "I'm so very pleased, Dad, about you and Becky." She glanced at her step-mum-to-be, as she spoke, "and, of course, Steve and I are thrilled to bits about the baby."

"What 'ave yer ordered, a boy or a girl?"

They laughed and Steve replied "We will love either. As far as I'm concerned, it would be nice to have a boy so I can guide him in life with things that I feel are important. If it's a girl, I'll have two lovely ladies to care for. Either one would give me the chance to do foolish things again, without looking as though I'm being childish. "

On returning to Birdholme, they went upstairs to see if the kestrels had gone. To their surprise they found they were all there. They had been dozing but awoke the instant they heard sounds. Four pairs of black eyes were fixed on the door as it opened. Jackie went in first and talked to the mother, whilst the others watched from the doorway. After a moment, the adult bird opened her wings and flew to Jackie's head giving her wing-flapping, tallon-gripping performance, screaming 'Kia, kia, kia'. Still perched there she preened a feather or two before lazily flying to the window-ledge, where she turned and called to the fledglings.

Hesitating a few moments, the youngsters flew rather nervously to her side, where they stayed looking at the outside world. At last, following mother, they all took off. She led them in a circle round the garden, getting higher and higher until, with a final shriek, she soared up into the sky and away into the distance. The family watched the four birds disappearing from view.

"How strange," commented Jackie. "She left them with us, as though they needed to rest for a bit longer and now she has taken them away."

"Probably they only left the nest early this morning and weren't strong enough for the flight. She left them with us where she knew they'd be safe, so she could feed them up a bit. After their doze, she must have sensed they had got that extra strength."

"Steve, you're a clever old stick."

"Not really sweetheart, but don't forget I was brought up amongst birds and animals. Dad passed on his love and understanding of birds to me, so I like to try to interpret their behaviour."

" 'Ow are yer folks?"

"Mum and Dad are keeping pretty well, thanks. Mum has had some ups and downs. She found that when she got a cold, it went down onto her chest and she got a bit breathless and was coughing a lot. Thank goodness, Jackie went to her rescue with homoeopathic Ammonium Carb. She says that Jackie's little tablets always cured her quickly."

"What about the ol' dog?"

"Old Shep died three years ago — purely old age. He'd had a good life and the folks were lucky as they didn't have that heart-rending job of having to have him put to sleep. He just went to sleep as normal one night, but didn't wake up in the morning. It was a perfect way to go. Come on, let's ring them up and arrange an evening together. Do you want to meet them here, Dad, or at your place?"

"Let's make it my place. It's nearer for 'em and makes it obvious I'm tryin' to make amends."

Steve's mother answered the telephone and was very pleased to hear from them. She said they would be delighted to see Ken again and arrangments were made for the following week.

Becky and Jackie decided to go shopping the next morning in Ulverston while Ken would go to the Registry Office to arrange a date for the wedding. They agreed it would be nice for the food to be laid on at the old house for the small number of guests. This would be its last important function before they sold up and moved.

The younger couple took Ken and Becky into their smallest bedroom before they left, to show them how they were going to decorate and furnish it for the baby.

"I'm glad you two are really getting married, and so quickly too, not only because I've been unhappy about Dad being on his own but also, now I'm carrying this baby, I know there're going to be many times *I'll* be wanting a mother." She glanced quickly from one to the other.

Becky's eyes filled with tears as she put her arms round Jackie. Holding her tight, she said softly, "My dear, I'll be here to help you any time and those words sounded lovely, making me feel really wanted. I shall do my best to be a good mother to you for I can't think of a nicer daughter." Tears were flowing down both faces as they embraced each other, and the men stood back feeling pleased, but a little awkward.

CHAPTER 11
"THE BEST LAID SCHEMES ..."

Becky called to Ken through the open kitchen window. Her hands were covered in suds as she washed the breakfast crockery and watched him throwing a ball for Bess. She had heard the postman drop some letters through the door and wondered if anything had arrived to further their plans. She felt so confident about life again, as though she had climbed out of the pit into which she had fallen after her husband's death.

"Yes Bec?" He stood still, holding the ball high above his head.

"The post has arrived, love, and I've got wet hands."

"Just comin'."

Bess chose that moment to leap for the ball and as gravity exerted its pull she caught her front dew-claw in his open cardigan neatly pulling it off his shoulder.

"Don't mind me, yer daft bitch. Look what yer've done. Yer've pulled a loop in the wool." Bess sniffed at the offending wool and lowered her ears as though saying. "Oh dear, I suppose I'd better look contrite but I don't know what the fuss is about". Her happy expression returned as she ran by his side and into the house.

Ken collected the mail and sat at the table to study it.

"The estate agents 'aven't wasted much time." He commented, " 'Ere's the write-up of this place. The photos look good, too."

"Let's see. Oh, yes, they look great. Let's hope we'll be lucky and soon find a buyer."

"We 'aven't 'ad a reply yet from the agents about our offer on the cottage, so we'll just 'ave to 'ope. We'd be silly to increase it, as there's quite a lot we must do t'make it right, and there's no way I'm goin' to run us short of money at our time o' life."

"Well if it's to be, it will happen. If not, there's something better round the corner. Although I must admit that seems impossible as it's so perfect."

The telephone interrupted their conversation and Ken got up to answer it. " 'Ello. Oh yes. What, this mornin'? My, that's fast. 'ow come?"

Becky, intrigued, was wondering what it was all about and she looked up with interest as he came back into the room.

"Well lass, it's all 'appenin'. Apparently a couple was askin' for an 'ouse like this'un before the details were finished. As they were only stayin' up 'ere for a short while, the agents told 'em where to find us and suggested they came to see it from th'outside. This they did and liked it, so 'ave asked to view this mornin'."

"Gosh, that's amazing. I'd better do a polish-up." She hurried off to do what she could in the short time available. Ken, watching her go, was thankful that she had stayed with him. He knew, if left to him, the house would not look its best. Jackie was always grumbling at him for not noticing a jumble here and there.

The hands of the clock seemed to fly round and in no time at all the front door bell rang. He opened it and there stood a couple in their thirties.

"Mornin'. Com'on in. Don't worry about the dog. Away Bess. Basket." Bess drooped her ears and trudged off, showing how hurt she was to be dismissed.

Ken took them through the various rooms, showing them into cupboards and explaining the workings of this and that. At one point, on looking out through a window, they said what a lovely garden it would be for their two young children.

"Yes, it's great for kids. M'daughter used to love playin' in and around all the shrubs and climbin' the trees."

"We live in a town and it is for the childrens' sake that we want to move. It is near enough to drive to and from my business, which is

117

one thing that has attracted us to this area. May we have another look round, please?"

"Yes, by all means. Would yer like a cup o' tea?"

"That would be welcome, thank you," the man replied.

When the visitors left Ken, Becky and Bess wandered out into the garden.

"It'll be a wrench 'avin' to leave. All my life 'as been spent 'ere, it was my parents' 'ome before mine but I'll be glad when it's all done with."

Becky put her arm round his waist and he put his arm across her shoulders. "I know the feeling, Ken. The sooner you can sign up a buyer and we are able to sign for our new home, the sooner we can begin to live in the present, instead of being reminded of our past."

Ken gave her a squeeze.

They had lunch in the garden, with Bess successfully cadging food from them, and were just settling back for some relaxation when the telephone rang again. The look that flashed between them was one of nervous anticipation.

Becky stayed outside wondering if it was the agent and whether it was about their offer or the couple who had just been round. Surely it could not be the latter so soon. Maybe, it was about their offer on the cottage near Coniston? She hoped it was.

When Ken returned he was smiling and Bess bounced up to him sensing his pleasure and was determined to share it. She made a flying leap at him, but he skilfully dodged the ninety pound missile and turned smartly to fend off the return attack. "Get yer ball, not me." Bess hurled herself at it, sending it shooting down the garden, then gave chase. "That's got 'er off m'back." He sat down. "Lovely day isn't it?" he smiled.

"Yes dear, never mind all that. What about the phone call?"

"Phone call, what phone call?" he teased.

Becky threw herself at him trying to tickle him into submission. He laughed and, grabbing hold of her, held her firmly at arm's length. "Now yer 're at my mercy, lass. Be'ave or I'll send yer to yer basket, too. Women! What am I to do?"

"Ken please don't keep me in suspense. What's happened?"

He relented and let her go. "The couple that's just bin round fell madly in love with the ol' 'ouse and 'ave made a very good offer, which I've accepted." He wore a very pleased and smug expression.

"Darling, that's fantastic. I've never heard of things happening so fast. There must be a snag."

"Well, nothin's certain 'til we've exchanged contracts, but it's a very good start any'ow."

"Now, all we need is to hear that the lady has accepted our offer. She must! She must! We'll be in a pickle if that goes wrong. Tho', I suppose, you could put your things into store and come and live with me."

"Don't talk like that, you'll put the mockers on it all. Com'on, let's go out with Bess. She needs 'er walk and if the agents want us, they'll ring 'til they get us."

They spent the afternoon walking on the hills and returned tired but contented. As Ken's key went into the lock he heard the telephone ringing. He rushed in to grab it. Becky stood by him, expectantly. "Oh, I see. No, that's it. No, definitely no more." There was some talk from the other end before Ken said "goodbye" and put the telephone down. He turned to Becky and said "Sorry lass, the lady's got a better offer than ours for the cottage."

"Oh, Ken! No!"

"I'm about to put the kettle on. Tomorra's another day. We'll let this sale go on — as yer say, we'll manage."

The house had lost its gaiety and even Bess sat silently in her basket.

"Robbie Burns was right with 'is poem 'To A Mouse' when 'e wrote -

> The best laid schemes o' mice an' men
> Gang aft a-gley,
> An' lea'e us nought but grief an' pain,
> For promised joy."

"I don't know that one."

"It's about the 'ard workin' little mouse, buildin' his 'ome in the fields, and then the reaper comes along and the little nest is ruined, the mouse 'as to start again. Well lass, we'll begin again, too."

After they had eaten, Becky said "I really ought to be going back to Portinscale. We're not married yet."

"Why? Where's the sense in it? We're busy an' there's so much to sort out. What d'yer propose to do, drive back at night an' to me again in the mornin'? We live in the seventies when no-one bothers about whether a couple are wed or not — it'll make it easier and we'd be spendin' time together."

"I suppose you're right. OK, if you're happy, I'll stay. What have you in mind for tomorrow then?"

119

" 'Ouse 'untin', of course. What else?" He smiled at her serious face and pulled her onto his lap. "We're not lettin' a little thing like this get us down now, are we?"

"Ken Mason, I love you." She took his face between her hands and kissed it. She kissed his eyes, his forehead, his nose, his cheeks, his chin and finally his mouth, eagerly seeking each others lips they went into a passionate embrace.

The evening passed peacefully with their disappointment slowly dissipating, so that by bedtime they were feeling fairly optimistic.

The following morning, after breakfast and a quick dog-walk, they set off to the estate agents in Ulverston. It was almost an hour later when they left with several brochures and two appointments for that morning. They drove to the first property and looked over it but it did not appeal to them.

"There was 'ardly room to swing a small cat, never mind a big dog," muttered Ken.

"Yes, it was rather pokey and so dark too. I didn't like the feel of it."

"Let's 'ope the next one'll be better. I thought our wants were simple but we soon threw out most of that pile of 'ouse details th'agent gave us."

After travelling for about half-an-hour towards Ambleside. they found the second house quite easily. Once again, it would not do. There was no privacy at all from neighbours or passers-by. Sadly, they returned to the car and sat there in silence. Suddenly, Ken sat up and started the engine.

"Are we going home?"

" 'Ome? 'Course not. We've not found our place yet."

Becky looked at him in surprise. His face was set in determined lines and his attention was fixed on the road ahead. She did not say anything but just sat watching the passing scenery, waiting to see what would happen next.

They drove on and on, turning into little roads here and there; down any tracks that might lead to human habitation. At mid-day, as they were passing a pub, Ken braked and turned into the car park. "We'll get som'at t'eat, then go on. OK, lass?"

"That'll be more than welcome."

They were eating toasted sandwiches when the barman passed their table and Ken asked him if he knew of any houses or cottages for sale. Unfortunately, he did not. So, after a short rest, they set off again.

They searched along as many roads as they could find in an area bordered by the Kendal–Bowness road to the south and as far as Kentmere to the north.

It was mid-afternoon and they had stopped to walk Bess, having parked on the steep road south of Crook. They walked in silence, neither having anything to say but finding comfort in holding hands. They stopped and stood looking at the beautiful scenery all around them most of which belonged to the National Trust.

Suddenly, Ken stiffened and, narrowing his eyes, stared hard into the distance. "Look over there at that little cottage down in the dip. There's som'at white and shiny. Could it be a "For Sale" notice?"

"That's wishful thinking, my dear. You can't tell at this distance."

"Com'on women, we're off," he called.

Bess was first to arrive at the car, happily wagging her tail as she waited to jump in. "There yer are," he said to Becky, "She knows."

Becky smiled at him, shaking her head in pretended dismay. However he would not be cast down.

He drove around, searching for a road that he hoped would lead to the cottage he had seen. It was not easy following winding roads that ran up hills and down again, round corners, twisting and turning until he did not know which way they were facing. He stopped the car and got out. "Right, the sun is there on our left, an' so the cottage should be over there ... so it means we must ...." His voice trailed off as he was talking to himself.

Once back in the car he drove on, turning one way and then the other. Finally, he stopped outside a cottage set back deep within a garden with a "For Sale" notice board inside the front hedge. He switched off the engine and sat back with a very satisfied look on his face. Becky was absolutely dumbfounded.

"Stay there an' mind the car, Bess," he instructed.

It was an old cottage built of solid lakeland stone. It looked as though it had been neglected in recent times. The lawn was mown but the borders were full of weeds. In days gone by it had certainly been cared for by a keen gardener. Ken pressed the door bell which rang distantly. After a few moments they were rewarded by the sound of footsteps. A man in his late fifties opened the door and Ken explained the reason for their unannounced visit.

"Come in — you're both welcome. I'm afraid I'm not set out for visitors, please excuse the mess.

The owner showed them over the cottage, which had a very peaceful, homely atmosphere. When they looked out through the back bedroom window, they saw what had been a beautiful garden.

It was well planted and had an interesting layout, using grass paths to join up various sections. Flowering shrubs bordered the main area which was a large lawn. By all appearances, it had not been tended for some time.

"I don't know if you're keen gardeners. All this was laid out by my wife whilst all I did was mow the lawns. Unfortunately, she's not here now so it's been left to me," he explained.

"Oh, I see. Er-r I'm sorry. I know what it's like, to be left on one's own," Becky sympathised.

"I may have given you the wrong impression. You see my wife has a sister in Canada. She's a bit younger than I am and has always wanted to be near her sister, especially as we're getting on a bit now. Neither of us have any family left here in England, so she persuaded me to buy a little place over there. She stayed there and I came back to sell up. I hope to join her soon, when the cottage is sold. Unfortunately, I've had no luck so far. Suppose it's too quiet for most young folk and too much garden for older ones."

"Too much garden? Well 'ow far does yer land go then?" asked Ken, craning his neck at the window to see where the boundaries were.

"You can't see the fences from here, they're hidden behind those trees at the bottom, and to your right the other side of that larch and down below that hillock on your left."

"We've no details, so we'd better visit yer estate agent and 'ave a think. Thank yer for lettin' us see over the cottage an' good luck to yer."

They got into the car and sat looking back at the cottage. "It's in quite good condition inside and its untidiness and the lack of attention outside backs up his story about his wife no longer being with him, " commented Becky.

"True. Roof looks OK an' so do the walls. No cracks in ceilin's but paintwork needs a splash or two. Yes," he said, still looking and thinking as he spoke, "Not bad, not bad."

"You sound more cautious now, love."

"Yes Bec. Once bit, twice shy. But I like it. What d' y' think?"

She smiled and leant across him to plant a little kiss on his cheek, "I love it."

Ken's serious face melted into a wide smile as he looked straight into her eyes. "Yer do, do yer? Well, we'll 'ave to see what the fellow wants for it." He squeezed her hand. The Rover bounced back onto the road from the grass where it had been parked and they drove straight to Kendal.

Finding a nearby car park, they left Bess in charge of the car once more, and walked to the agents to collect details of the cottage. Having noticed a cafe on the way, they retraced their footsteps to it and went in. Ken ordered a pot of tea and they studied the details as they drank.

" 'Ow's this Bec? 'Fantastic views, extensive grounds includin' copse which surrounds a small, artificial tarn. Main garden well designed and stocked. Cottage over 'undred years old with two-foot-thick walls. All in good condition. Within reasonable distance of Kendal for shoppin'. Offers around eighteen thousand pounds.' Shall we go back, m'sweet, and offer the agent fifteen thou. and see what 'appens, after all the man's desp'rate to move now?"

"What about a survey?"

"We can make an offer dependant on such. Any'ow I'd take Steve along to 'elp check it over".

They went back to the agents and Ken placed the details on the man's desk.

"Yes sir, would you like to view it? It is certainly worth a look, it's ..."

"No, thank yer. We'd just like t'make an offer of fifteen thousand for it."

"An offer - but you haven't seen it yet."

"Don't need to, just want t'make an offer," Ken continued with a straight face, revealing nothing.

The man looked at them, trying to decide if they were serious. He picked up the telephone and dialled. There was no reply. "Never mind, just keep tryin' and let us know." He gave the man his address and telephone number, then he and Becky left.

They both burst out laughing as soon as they were out of sight. "Poor man, he didn't know how to take you, you tease."

Back at the car, Bess greeted them with enthusiastic licks, as though they had been away for an age.

"Daft bitch, yer'll lick us away. Save yersel' for yer new 'ome. Yer'll be able to explore the 'uge garden an' never be bored again."

"Ken, do you think we'll get it?"

"Get it? I've already moved in! There's no problem this time, yer mark my words."

CHAPTER 12
"...SOMETIMES GO RIGHT"

Ken had been up since early light as there was so much to do. Becky had been back in Portinscale for the past week sorting out her own affairs. Bess, having had her walk at six o'clock, was contentedly wandering in the garden checking on the creatures that had visited her domain during the night.

Surrounded by boxes, one for "throw out", one for "don't-know-what-to-do-with-it", others for packed goods "definitely to be taken", Ken sat back on his heels, wondering if it would be better to call in a house clearance firm and start again. He looked at his watch. It was nearly ten o'clock and Becky would arrive shortly complete with sandwiches and a flask of coffee to take with them to the cottage.

He had been right in his hunch regarding their dream cottage. The poor man was so desperate to sell and join his wife in Canada. They had haggled a bit over the price and, by raising his offer price just five hundred pounds, Ken had clinched the deal. His own house sale was going through smoothly so he was confident that they could move within the next six weeks.

Bess's ears shot up as they perceived the familiar sound of Becky's car as it turned into the drive. With a joyful "woof" she bounded across the lawn and down the drive to greet her.

"Hello, my darling." Becky leaned down to hug the big dog who licked her face and nearly waved her shaggy tail right off. She took Becky's wrist gently in her mouth to lead her back across the garden and through the open kitchen door. "Hello — I'm here and being led in by Bess."

Ken stood up, extricating himself from his boxes, as they arrived at the living room doorway. Seeing them he laughed and said, "Put 'er down Bess, she's mine," then he took Becky into his arms and kissed her. "I've missed yer, m'sweet. It's a good job we're gettin' married next week. After that yer'll 'ave no more excuses to keep desertin' me."

"Oh, you poor old thing, how you suffer. How did you manage all those years on your own?"

"With difficulty. Now com'on, yer've got to 'elp me decide what to do with this lot."

Bess walked in amongst the boxes and began poking about in one of the unsorted piles. "Not yer! I mean Becky. Yer daft dog" Bess put on one of her really hurt and hard-done-by expressions that she was so good at. With a defiant rake at the pile with a fore paw, she unearthed one of her old balls. Picking it up she took it to Ken and dropped it at his feet. "Alright yer clever 'airey beast, yer win, my apologies. Off yer go with it."

Becky's gaze wandered around the room. "Do you want my opinion, love?"

"I do. I've got my thoughts but before I mention 'em I'd like yers."

"I was in this situation when I moved into my rented flat and you know what I did."

"That's what I thought too. We're movin' into a much smaller place and there's yer things as well as mine. If I clear out the sittin' room of anythin' I don't want and then put in everythin' I do want from other rooms, I can call in the 'ouse clearance blokes. If yer're stayin' tonight yer can take a look at some of the china and such-like to see what yer want us to keep, as that's in a woman's world."

They went back into the kitchen and had coffee and biscuits before setting out for the cottage. "I'll be staying over tonight, love, so I can help you sort some things out. It would be nice to call on Jackie and Steve on the way back this afternoon. I need to check on a few details for the wedding celebrations they're so kindly organising for us."

Ken backed his Rover out of the garage. Becky opened the rear door for Bess and then put the picnic into the boot. Ken left the engine ticking over and went to lock up the house, glancing at it wistfully before returning to the car.

"Now don't you go all soft on me. You must look forward not backward." Ken glanced at her with an embarrassed smile but said nothing. He slipped the car into reverse and let the familar whine of the gear-box soothe him. Once on the road, they left Ulverston behind and headed straight for the winding country lanes which would lead them to the cottage.

Both feeling a surge of excitement as they approached their new home area, they looked about them, avidly absorbing as much as possible of the atmosphere and views. The car boot was full of garden tools for, with the agreement of the owner, they were going to start some garden rescue work, as well as measuring up for curtains and mentally organising furniture.

"I'm looking forward to going down the garden to see what the tarn is like," Becky said, with an eagerness more usually associated with the young.

"We'll do that, lass. I'd like to see it, too. I must say, when Steve and I looked over the property we didn't bother goin' round the grounds. It was rainin' too 'ard and there was a cold north-westerly blowin'."

They turned into the cottage driveway. "Stay 'ere Bess, for a while."

When they went in, they found that the owner was in the same state of confusion as Ken had been back at Ulverston. There were boxes everywhere.

"You're welcome to wander as you please and measure up. Excuse the mess but as you can see, I'm not sure what I'm doing. I'm used to my wife seeing to this sort of thing. Although most stuff will be sold I'm just trying to find those special items to keep."

"I know exactly what you mean, we're in the same pickle," replied Becky, understandingly.

"If there's anything you fancy and would care to make me an offer, I'd be pleased to see it go."

"Thank yer, we'll bear that in mind."

Becky went round measuring up the windows for curtains, while Ken took other dimensions so they could plan the furniture.

"What do think about the curtains and carpets? They look fine to me. Was anything mentioned about them?"

"Oh yes, I forgot to tell yer, 'e's thrown 'em in the sale."

126

"That's good. What a shame I've wasted all that time measuring windows when I didn't need to."

"Becky I'm sorry. I didn't think. We've done everythin' so fast, I've not 'ad much time to remember what's 'appened."

She wandered around the cottage, trying to impress every detail on her mind to help her with furnishing ideas. At last she turned her attention to the garden. Looking out through an upstairs window she saw the overgrown lawns and borders full of weeds, backed by a tangle of unruly branches and brambles .

"Bec. Come and look at this," came Ken's voice from the downstairs hall.

He was standing before a very fine, old mahogany bookcase-cum-sideboard, with a marquetry bouquet of flowers on each of the doors. "It'll go well with my dinin' suite. Shall we make an offer?" he asked.

"You're right, it is rather lovely, and would fit in nicely. Whilst we're on the subject, upstairs in the guest bedroom is what looks like a new, or newish, double divan bed. We were thinking of getting one, weren't we?"

"I'll pop upstairs and take a look at it. If it seems OK, I'll make an offer for both of 'em. 'Ow about the 'fridge and washin' machine? The oven is built-in and included in the sale."

"I'd like my own washing machine as it's practically new and his is quite old — also I'm not keen on that type."

"That's a good reason for not buyin' it. Right I'll take a look at the 'fridge. If it seems in good nick, I'll include it in our offer for the furniture."

"Great! I'll go outside now and see what we can do today. Hurry up and keep me company so we can investigate our new garden together."

The owner invited them to let Bess join them. She was delighted and trotted about, nose to the ground and tail waving, following invisible trails all around the garden. All three of them walked through the copse pushing their way through the tangled undergrowth. Suddenly they came upon the peaceful little tarn, its surface so still it seemed unreal.

"If someone actually created this, then they did a superb job," breathed Becky.

"In days gone by, ponds and the like were often made by excavatin' the 'ole, then makin' a water-resistant base and sides with clay, mud and straw. When done prop'ly, it was very successful. I'm guessin', that if it is man-made, this'un was built the same.

"The beauty of this garden is that we can cultivate as much as we want and just leave the rest wild. We can walk where we want to, letting the wildlife and nature look after the rest. Oh Ken, isn't it a perfect place?" She rested her head against his shoulder, nestling into his encircling arm.

A splash disturbed them from their dreaming and, turning towards the sound, they were in time to see Bess's head ploughing its way through the water close to the bank. She was swimming towards an area of gently sloping land which was clear of nettles. When she reached this point her paws touched the ground. She bounded out of the water and shook herself vigorously, flinging a spray out in all directions. Seeing them standing watching her she raced up to them and shook again, obviously keen to share her experience. " 'Ey yer varmint, off with yer. If yer're daft enough to fall in and get wet don't include us." Ken admonished his beloved pet, who stood with her tongue hanging out of her mouth, as though grinning at him.

They wandered on until they could see the cottage through the trees whereupon Becky said, "What do you think about giving the cottage a new name, to go with our new lives together?"

"What d'yer 'ave in mind, lass?"

"Well, everything in the garden is badly overgrown. We're going to have to do a lot of cutting down and burning to make room for new growth. So, how about Phoenix Cottage? You know the legend of the mythical bird that, when it grew old, threw itself onto a pyre. But, instead of dying, it regained its youth to begin again." Ken pondered on this and agreed that he liked the idea.

First, they cleared an area that had obviously once been used for burning, but had been lost under the reclaiming brambles and stinging nettles. Then they found the old compost area and, after removing the invasive weeds, discovered a very well-rotted heap. Ken picked up a handful and let it run back through his hand. "My, that's great stuff. We'll soon 'ave this place in good 'eart, my gal."

The next few hours were spent chopping down and burning dead wood and clearing brambles. It was very pleasing as they felt they were doing something positive for their new home. By the time they left they had both derived a great deal of satisfaction from their exertions.

On the way home, they called in to see Jackie and Steve. They told them all about their day at the cottage, their decision to change its name, the purchase of the furniture, and the discovery of the lovely tarn. In turn, they learnt that Jackie, as her father wanted, had planned the wedding buffet in the old house. It was to be a very quiet wedding with just Jackie, Steve and his parents. Becky had not made any friends in the area and was a long way from people she used to know. She insisted that it was to be the beginning of a new life with opportunities for them to make new friends together. Ken, who had shut himself away from friends for so long, welcomed the idea. Jackie had been disappointed as she really wanted to give them a big celebration but she understood.

*

It seemed no time at all before their wedding day dawned. Becky was luxuriously soaking in a bubble bath, practically submerged by the scented foam. Relaxing amongst the bubbles, she let her mind drift back over the past years. She had married Charles when in her late teens and, as the wife of a diplomat, had always travelled with him. They had lived for many years in France before his return to London. Her secure and happy life had changed with the sudden death of her dear husband. Life had become meaningless and the predictable became unpredictable. If Becky's life had been empty at that point it was almost too much to bear when Dusky, too, reached the end of her years. She was at her lowest ebb, but had decided that she must make an effort to rebuild her life. Renewing her interest in fell-walking she found the fresh air and excercise made her feel better. She realised that by being more positive she had made things start to go right again. Granted, it had not happened overnight. Being very lonely she rented first one place then another, wandered and searched. She did not know what she was searching for. She had missed Charles so much that she had not contemplated looking for a husband.

She had already packed her suitcases and put them in the car, for from today she would be living with Ken. He was a dear, there was no doubt about that and he needed her as much as she needed him. How strange it was that a German shepherd dog had brought them together.

Ken had been up very early that morning and given Bess a long walk. She was lying on the hearthrug, panting. He was sitting in his old seat by the kitchen window with a mug of tea, looking out at his familiar garden. Now that the day had come to leave all this behind, he felt a little strange, although he had wanted to move for some time. He thought then of Becky and how warm and kind she was. He knew he really loved her even though he had said he

129

would never trust another woman. A wet nose was thrust under his hand, " 'Cept yer of course, my precious." He looked at the clock and, realising that time was getting on, decided he had better go upstairs and get ready.

It was 9.30 am as, closing the door behind her, Becky walked across to her beautifully polished car. She was dressed in a new pale-blue suit with a white silk blouse. The silver German shepherd brooch, which Ken had given her at Christmas, was pinned to the lapel of the jacket. As she drove along the narrow, winding lakeland roads her heart was singing with joy at the thought of leaving behind her solitary existence to become a married woman again. She had felt only half complete since being widowed and looked forward to regaining that sense of wholeness. She drove straight to Ken's house as Jackie and Steve would be already there, so that they could all go to the Registry Office together.

Leaving her car next to Ken's Rover, which was just as highly polished as her own, Becky walked towards the house.

"Becky, you look lovely" said Jackie, coming to greet her. "I'm so glad I persuaded you to buy that suit, it's perfect for you." She kissed her and the two women walked indoors hand in hand.

"Hello Becky. Feeling excited?" asked Steve, who was putting some drinks on a side table.

"I'm all of a twitter."

"Dad will be down in a moment, let's have some Dutch courage. What would you like, a sherry or something stronger?"

"A sherry would be nice. Thanks."

"Coming up, ladies."

Steve gave them both their glasses and said, "Here's to the future of our new Mum! May she find perfect happiness and contentment with Dad." Raising their glasses Jackie and Steve drank the toast.

"Oh, thank you both. You really are the nicest family I could ever wish to have." Her eyes glistened with tears of happiness.

"Come on, let's show you what we've done in the dining room."

Jackie led the way, Becky drew in her breath with surprise. The cardboard boxes had been pushed against one wall and in the middle of the room the table was laden with a variety of plates and dishes. Sandwiches, sausage rolls, vol-au-vents, and cheese cut into squares on sticks with cubes of pineapple, all visible through their plastic covering. There were dishes of trifles and other desserts. In pride of place, in the centre of the table, was a beautiful wedding cake. A banner with the words 'Congratulations to Dad and our new Mum' hung over the fire-place.

"Oh, What can I say? It's absolutely wonderful." She was quite lost for words and just took hold of their hands and squeezed them. After a pause she said, "You've done far more than I ever imagined. Thank you so very much for taking me to your hearts. I'll try not to let you down."

"You won't let us down, you couldn't," said Jackie. "We really feel this way about you, don't we, Steve?"

"Certainly, Becky. Ken has been alone far too long. Poor Jackie has been trying to keep an eye on him, as well as on me and the birds. We're not only relieved on that basis but its far nicer for Jackie to have a Dad and Mum and, for me, two in-laws are better than one." He put his arm around her shoulders and led her back to the kitchen.

Eager paws bounded down the stairs and Bess sprang into the room, to be intercepted by Steve. "Steady, big lump, she's got her pretties on and doesn't want you to spoil them." Cautiously he released Bess's collar and Becky leaned forward to greet her dear four-footed friend.

"Is she be'avin'?" asked the master of the house as he entered the room, all dressed up for the occasion.

"Perfectly. She knows when to keep her paws on the ground."

"Well, I've bin givin' 'er a lecture on weddin' manners," he said with a twinkle in his eyes. "Is that my glass, Steve lad?"

"Yes Dad.   May I wish you both all the luck in the world for the wedding and throughout all the many, many years after it." Steve raised his glass.

"I echo that wish," said Jackie and they drank a toast to the happy couple.

"Now, one more thing and then we must get moving. Wait there a minute, please," said Jackie as she and Steve disappeared into the dining room.

Becky did as she was told, looking at Ken with a questioning smile on her face, but he told her nothing. She could hear their voices whispering in the other room. At last they reappeared with their hands behind their backs. Jackie came forward first and presented her with a little spray of lily-of-the-valley, which she pinned on Becky's jacket. "There, the white looks lovely against the blue of your jacket." Steve came forward and presented her with a bouquet of freesias and roses. The perfumed blooms were nestling amidst gypsophilia, whose miriad of tiny white flowers appeared to dance around the ensemble as though they were without stems. "No bride is complete without flowers," he said.

131

"You two really have spoiled me. Dear Steve, dear Jackie how can I thank you?"

"Com'on now, time we were off," commanded the head of the family. "Bess, m'lovely, yer stay 'ere and wait for us."

As they walked to the Rover gleaming in the sunlight, Becky looked at the two young people who were about to become her family. Jackie looked so pretty in her new daffodil and white dress, made of such soft material that the skirt alternately swirled and clung to her as she moved. She looked up at Steve admiring his handsome features. His dark suit emphasized his imposing figure, erect and broad shouldered. She glanced at his hands as they opened the door for her; strong but sensitive.

When they arrived at the Registry Office car park Ken's legs felt wobbly and he was glad he did not have to walk far. Steve's parents were already there waiting for the others to arrive. They waved and called out their greetings.

"Hello everyone. Alright Ken?"

"Yes thanks. 'Ow are yer both?" he replied, feeling grateful that they had singled him out. He did not deserve such kindness but was determined to make it up to them.

As they all walked towards the Registry Office Ken asked, " 'Ows the pigeons, Tom?"

"Great, I've nearly a hundred now and doing fine. One cock bird in particular is a real little winner and has already given me several excellent squeakers this year."

"What about yer, Jill, still busy with the goats?"

"Yes, you must come over with Becky and have a bite to eat with us. We'll show you all our furry and feathery family. Bring Bess too, of course. I'm glad you still have her. We miss old Shep, although he'd had a good life. Pets leave such a great emptiness when they go."

They walked into the building and were ushered into the waiting room. Ken's inside was all a-quiver with nerves and he looked at his watch for about the tenth time. Five minutes to wait.

"Oh Becky, I nearly forgot," said Jackie, "As you're not wearing ear-rings, I wondered if you'd like to wear these? They belonged to my grandmother on Dad's side and would be the 'borrowed and old' bit. You're alright for the 'something blue and new' as your suit covers that one." She held out a pair of dainty gold clip-on ear-rings, shaped like flying birds, each with a tiny diamond for an eye.

"Jackie, they're exquisite. Thank you dear, I'd love to wear them. It's so sweet of you to think of it." She clipped them on and Jackie checked they were on right as Becky did not have a mirror.

Ken was very pleased at Jackie's gesture and held out his hands to them both. "What a gorgeous pair yer make, ain't I a lucky chap?" He kissed them both.

The marriage room was large and beautifully decorated with flowers of all colours. Although it was only a small group of people who entered the room, this did not concern them. They were all family and the only ones that mattered.

As the familar words of the wedding ceremony were uttered, Becky and Ken had both happy and sad feelings. Happy at being joined to each other but sad as they recalled their past lives.

"You may kiss the bride."

Ken jerked himself out of his reverie, turned to Becky and kissed her.

Once outside, the fresh air broke over them and suddenly everyone was laughing and chattering. They walked together to the cars and, as Ken opened the passenger door for Becky, Steve and Jackie threw confetti over them.

"Look at my car!" Ken pretended to moan, "I've spent all that time cleanin' it and now it looks like ..."

"... there's been a new bride and groom in it." interrupted Steve, laughing. He shut the door on the newly-weds and sat with Jackie in his parents' car.

When they arrived at the old family house Jackie and Jill whisked off all the plastic coverings. Steve opened Asti Spumanti which had been cooling in the fridge and, filling the waiting glasses, handed them out, saying "Let's toast the bride and groom, Ken and Becky, our Dad and new Mum." A nicely timed 'woof' of approval made them all laugh.

Ken smiled at Becky, put down his glass and excused himself. Bess looked up and hurried after her master. After a few minutes he returned carrying a very large parcel covered in wrapping paper. Bess walked behind him carrying another colourful parcel. Ken placed his on the floor in front of Becky, "This I made for my bride in the 'opes that I'll not 'ave to sew on any more buttons."

Before Becky could open the parcel Bess pushed her way in and thrust her own present into her new mistress's hands.

"Aren't I the lucky one?" said Becky, overwhelmed with happiness, "Thanks, Bess." She stroked the soft fur and took her parcel. "Thank you, my dear Ken. This looks fascinating."

133

"Yer'd better open Bess' first or yer'll get no peace.

The family watched as Becky unwrapped the small parcel to discover a box of liqueur chocolates. Bess sniffed it, accepted her thanks and walked away. Becky removed the wrapping paper from Ken's present to discover a beautiful needlework cabinet. The top was decorated with marquetry and opened to reveal a work-box lined with quilted pink satin. Underneath was a shallow drawer to take sewing cottons. The cabinet was French polished in a satin finish.

"Ken, this is exquisite! You really are a craftsman", she breathed. "My dear, thank you so very much." Her eyes shone with love as she got up to kiss him.

After the buffet lunch Steve and Tom went out of the room, to return carrying another very large parcel between them. This too was wrapped in colourful paper.

"We decided that, as you have all you need for the house, the four of us should buy you this. We felt it was so perfect and hope you think so too."

Becky and Ken looked amazed as the parcel stood on the ground at their feet to a height of about thirty inches. "G'on love, yer open it. I'm cowardly, it might bite." Becky opened it to find a mass of tissue paper. Removing this from the top she discovered a beautifully modelled head of a German shepherd. She gasped. Ken's eyes widened in surprise. Pulling away the rest of the packing she revealed a full-sized porcelain dog. Bess got up and went across to sniff it with great interest, looked up at Ken and Becky for reassurance and offered them her paw.

"It's amazin' an' very much appreciated," said Ken.

"It's absolutely beautiful," said Becky, almost overcome with gratitude, "Thank you all, so very much. It will have place of honour in our new home, not only to remember the wonderful wedding day you have given us, but also to remind us of how we met — brought together by dear Bess." There were kisses all round, and then Jackie went into the kitchen to make a pot of tea.

Everyone was chatting happily when Jackie suggested it was time to cut the cake. Steve fetched his camera and took a photo of the cake and another of Ken and Becky making the first cut.

Later that afternoon, Ken announced that it was time he took his new bride on their honeymoon. Becky looked at him in surprise as she knew nothing about it. "We'll be away for a week. I've booked in for two people and one dog."

Becky, recovering from her surprise remembered that she would need some clothes. "Don't worry, Bec. Jackie 'as done a little work for yer. She's already sorted out som'at yer might need from the cases that were in yer car. Will that be alright?"

"What a conniving family I've joined," she laughed, "and what a fun one too. As long as I'll be respectable then I'll accept whatever is there. Thank you. Where are we going?"

"Wait and see, Mrs Mason," he smiled, enjoying the mystery.

"Leave us to clear away and lock up, Dad."

"Thank yer love, that'll be nice. We can 'ave a pleasant drive and not arrive too late."

They went to the car and let Bess into the back, then he opened the boot so that Becky could have a quick look in her suitcase before she settled in her seat.

"I suppose that's why you borrowed my car key on the pretence of moving it 'out of the way', as you said."

"That's right, was it worth it, Mum?" said Jackie, smiling.

Becky's eyes filled with emotion and she leaned out of the car to hug Jackie. "Thanks darling, in every way."

Ken started the engine. "Goodbyes" were called and Mr and Mrs Mason set off for their honeymoon, accompanied by their own cupid in the form of a German shepherd dog.

CHAPTER 13
ON THE RIVER

The cygnets still had drab grey colouring and, until they reached adulthood, would continue to live in groups. Pairs usually go off to find their first nesting site in their fourth year. Towards the end of the first year their plumage begins to show white feathering but it is not until their third birthday that all the browny patches and feather tips disappear and their grey bills become pinkish. The deep orange bill comes only with complete maturity.

Pip and Star behaved like old friends from the moment of her arrival and were never far away from each other. The other sister had joined the rest of Pip's family and all formed part of a large group, sometimes swelling to thirty or forty swans and cygnets. At other times it divided into many smaller groups occupying different parts of Rusland Pool, which runs down to Morecombe Bay.

There were many ducks, geese, moorhens, coots, divers and, of course, seagulls of different species. A pair of shelducks had arrived; they are one of the largest members of the duck family, resembling small geese. Their bodies are coloured in strong bands of brown and white with black wing coverts and tails. Their scarlet bills with fleshy knobs present a strong contrast to their heads and wing-flashes which are green shot with black. They tend to be rather argumentative and sometimes even confront cygnets.

Another duck with a red bill flew in: all her plumage was black except for some small white patches. She was a muscovy and had red skin round her eyes matching her bill. Hissing as they do instead of quacking, she was continually being chased off as the other wildfowl could not relate to her. From time to time she would fly onto the land where, as she walked, she hissed and moved her neck backwards and forewards in rhythm with the movement of her very short legs — the motion was reminiscent of the tye-bars across the wheels of an old steam engine.

After a while the muscovy became accepted, although she continued to keep a little apart from the others. Her mate had died and she had left her domestic home to try and find him. It was loneliness and hunger which forced her to join the group. Never having had to look for her own food before, she needed the guidance of others to find it.

One morning, a man and woman were walking along the bank. They stopped to look at the birds and the woman noticed a movement in the reeds. When the muscovy swam slowly out she grabbed her husband's arm in excitement. "That's our Covy. Surely it is." The man agreed it certainly looked like her and he began calling, "Covy, Covy come here."

The duck started to move towards them but the nervousness of the other birds affected her and she stopped, darting her head backwards and forewards, hissing. It was enough to convince the people that she was their lost bird but both agreed it would be difficult to catch her. They returned each day with food and Covy got used to pushing her way in with the others to feed. She gradually gained confidence. Once she was very near the bank, eating hungrily, when the man made a grab for her. She was too fast for him and thrashing wings and hurrying legs soon had her safely out in mid-water. All he got was two feathers. She was free, had company and was getting regular feeds, so she intended to stay that way!

July was hot and the cygnets were lazily paddling up-river with the incoming tide. They passed fishermen spaced out along the bank taking part in a fishing competition, which lasted for most of the day. Pip kept well clear of the floats and made sure that Star did too. He did not know why but he remembered his father's stern hiss when he had gone near a float when he was still young.

The birds continued along the river to where a reedy backwater led them to a shallow, muddy area where they could poke about for worms and anything else that moved. Some clambered up onto the bank to preen or sit and doze in the sun.

By late afternoon the fishing contest ended and, after the weighing of the fish and returning them to the river, the contestants gathered up their belongings and departed.

The tide was on the ebb and the river looked like a huge conveyer belt returning to the sea, carrying with it all sorts of things; floating vegetation, branches, a bit of a broken plank. The water-birds, too, were enjoying the easy swim back to their various quarters.

The cygnets swam through the reed-beds of the backwater in single file, like an undulating ribbon threading its way to the river. The bank was deserted and the birds emerged into the ebbing water and found themselves gathering speed as they were swept into the flow. Sailing past a shallow bay they noticed some bits of bread caught round a tree root and turned in to investigate. They searched under water and found some tasty maggots — left-over bait thrown away by a fisherman. When they could find nothing more they all moved off again.

Further down-river was another little bay with some reeds growing beneath an overhanging crack willow and, remembering their earlier success, the cygnets turned in to investigate. One bird found the remains of a sandwich amongst the reeds and several others went in to help clear it up.

Another cygnet, pushing her way through a particularly thick patch, unknowingly caught a fish-hook in her wing feathers. The hook was attached to a length of broken nylon line hanging from a branch above her. As she felt the pull she paddled more strongly and turned to see what it was. The hook then embedded itself firmly and the line became twisted around her neck. She lifted her leg to try and scratch it away but that, too, became entangled. There was a second hook along the line which found a hold half way along her neck. The more she struggled the worse she became ensnared. Every time she tried to paddle, the line pulled at her neck and in turn at her wing. By this time she found herself being carried along by the tide so, sitting quietly she let the water take her home, steering by angling her webbed feet. Finally, she managed to hide in the reeds by the bank near the place where the other birds had congregated.

The next day the muscovy's owners returned with some food and their duck eagerly rushed forward for it, but kept a very wary eye open for any repeated effort to catch her. Her people, however, just wanted to regain her confidence and so did not try to touch her. As the other birds also surged forward to get the food some jostled the hooked cygnet close by, who did not even try to lift her head, as the line and hooks hurt too much.

On seeing her the man realised that something was wrong, so he threw food directly to her to see what would happen. She still did not move. Fortunately the bird was within arms reach so he quickly made a grab for her neck. She cried out in fear and pain, at the same time the man saw the line. He reached down with his other hand and gathered the bird into his arms lifting her bodily, water pouring down his clothes. Setting her down on the ground he kept a hand on her to prevent a possible escape. Then he and his wife searched amongst her feathers to see the extent of the problem.

"Have you some scissors in your bag?" he asked his wife.

The woman searched and found some which she handed to her husband. He cut the line, freeing the bird's limbs then found the two hooks, which were deeply embedded in her flesh and sealed in with dried blood. Blood began to seep from the wound again as the hooks were disturbed. He also discovered that the line he removed had cut into her neck which was bleeding badly.

"We'll have to take this poor youngster to that bird hospital near Cartmel. It's not that far. We can't put her back like this. Even if I could get the hooks out without hurting her the wounds could go septic."

Fortunately, their car was nearby and soon the cygnet was on her way to be released from her misery.

About a week later, the man and woman brought a large wicker basket to the river. It was partitioned inside and, although the front half was empty, in the back half was a muscovy drake who was puffing and hissing. He took a great interest in his surroundings when the basket was placed on the ground facing the water-birds with the front half opened. The man fastened a long piece of string to the door, threaded the other end through the side and walked away onto higher ground with it. His wife threw quite a lot of food onto the water and the river bank before joining her husband to wait.

The birds obligingly scrambled up to get it. The muscovy duck, however, watched from the water. The people began to despair as

139

all the food had gone and still their duck would not leave the river. All they could do was sit and hope.

It was a long time before the duck's curiosity overcame her fear of being caught. Eventually, the puffing and hissing drake broke through her reserve. She suddenly spread her wings and left the water, landing right by the basket. The people held their breath, knowing that one false move would ruin their chances completely. The duck walked round the basket and then walked back the other way, repeating this several times, puffing as she walked. Finally, she sat down with her head inside the basket and the two muscovys had a long, wheezy conversation.

The man longed to pull the string to try and push the bird into the basket but knew it would send her back into the river at high speed. The duck withdrew her head to look about her then stood up, turned round and began to walk back to the river. Suddenly she turned around again and walked straight back into the basket.

The man jerked the string, snapping the door shut behind her and raced down to the basket. He was just in time to prevent her bulk from forcing the door open and shot the bolt home, securely. Their great patience had been rewarded as had the determination of the duck for she had shown her human friends that she was lonely and needed another mate.

Ten days later Steve arrived with the cygnet in his arms. He had removed the hooks, stitched a bad tear and cleaned the wounds. She had fully recovered and was eager to be free. He placed her on the ground at his feet and held her a moment as he talked to her to stop her rushing away. As he gently released his hold she stepped free and slid into the water. She called eagerly to the others, who swam towards her answering her call.

A passer-by stopped to watch and asked Steve what had happened. He was always glad to talk about his work and about the problems that birds came up against. It made people more aware of the dangers and, consequently more able to avoid creating them. He explained about hooks, lines and the dreaded lead, which is so easily lost from sinkers. He also explained about lead shot from wildfowlers' guns, which water-birds swallow as stones to grind up food in their gizzards. Some men stick to the rules and shoot only legal game, others do not believe in this, but happily blast away killing anything that comes into their sights.

Later, the cygnets were searching the bays again for food. Boys with home-made fishing tackle had been casting with very light weights on fine nylon. The lines had become snagged on a clump of reeds and snapped as the boys tried to free them. Some weights had been pulled off and had sunk into the mud. The previous autumn wildfowlers had used the same area and shot had fallen into the little bay. As the cygnets foraged for food, churning up the mud in their search, some discovered and swallowed the long-lost shot.

It takes only a short time for the lead to poison the birds depending on how much is swallowed. One of the first signs is tiredness; the bird sleeps a lot, then the lower part of its neck weakens and slowly becomes paralysed. This shows as a kink, but as far as the bird is concerned it gets harder to swallow food and can cause a blockage and the bird starves. Finally, if enough lead becomes seated in the liver it can actually destroy that organ.

A passerby saw one of the cygnets sleeping in the reeds; it did not seem inclined to move. Luckily the person felt concerned and reported it to the RSPCA. Shortly afterwards their van arrived and the inspectors walked along the banks studying the birds until they found the sleeping one. At first they were unable to reach it. Inspection of the rest of the group showed that two others were not looking well, one showing signs of the 'kinky' neck. They fetched a swan hook on a telescopic pole from the van. It was just long enough to hook over the cygnet's neck and pull it towards them. All they needed to do was lean down and lift it from the water. The other two cygnets were swimming and much harder to catch. The sick one was put in the van on some sacking and driven off to the bird hospital.

The following day Steve arrived with the inspectors. They launched an inflatable dingy with a Seagull outboard motor. One of the men climbed in and pulled the starter cord. The engine burst into life and the light craft shot away to round-up the cygnets. Steve and the other inspector waited in pre-arranged spots with the swan hooks. Men have the ability to plan and liaise but swans have the agility on water to avoid capture. They seemed to be staying back watching in amusement, letting their would-be captors get near and then, with a quick kick of powerful webbed feet, they were neatly out of reach. During the day, two or three of the fit cygnets had been caught accidently and then released again, but the two they wanted kept well clear until, at last, perseverence was rewarded. It had taken the entire working day before the two poisoned birds were eventually caught.

Steve took the birds home to begin treatment. The one brought in by the inspectors the previous day was already on a course of daily injections to try to neutralise the effect of the lead. If the cygnet became stronger Steve was considering the surgical removal of the lead. He had taken an X-ray and located the evil substance. He hoped the other two cygnets were much less affected but he would begin their injections as soon as they settled down. It would be many weeks before the birds would be fit enough to return to the river.

Pip and Star often went for short flights together, sometimes alone, at other times with a group, and were getting to know the area very well. Occasionally they flew out to sea, to return along the coast then circle back home. After one such flight they noticed Steve releasing two of the cygnets back onto the river. Pip and Star flew low overhead but did not land as they were wary of being caught. The cygnets were the two stronger ones lucky enough to have been caught and treated in time. The third one had been too sick and had died as its liver had been destroyed.

The pair of shelducks had nested and eleven fluffy ducklings covered in greyish brown and white down, bobbed along between their proud parents. Each cheeky little face had a slightly turned up bill. Even the cygnets did not venture too close as the drake was so fiercely protective.

Over the next few weeks, Jackie made final preparations for the birth of their first baby. Steve had arranged for some extra volunteers as she would not be able to help in the bird hospital for quite a while. He hoped he would not be out on call when Jackie needed him to take her to the hospital.

Autumn painted the trees in brilliant colours and all the russet tones competed with each other for the best display, as if to provide a great welcome for the baby.

Baby Monica arrived in the early morning of the third of October. She had big blue eyes, a head of very fair hair and, if the noise she was making was anything to go by, powerful lungs. Steve had been present throughout the birth and four anxious grandparents had waited in the waiting room. At last all the family was together, congratulating the new parents and admiring their tiny granddaughter. Becky held her and she and Ken gazed at the little red face with a slightly turned-up nose, smiling as two perfect little hands waved about. Ken put a big finger into the tiny hand.

"She's a determined little mite, just like 'er mother." He looked at Jackie and grinned. "Well done, my lass. Yer an' Steve 'ave got a daughter to be proud of, and yer've given us a lovely granddaughter. We must leave yer to rest now, dear. We'll see yer tomorrow."

142

The four grand-parents chatted happily for a while in the car park before driving off their separate ways, Tom and Jill to Ulverston, Ken and Becky to Phoenix Cottage into which they had finally moved during the summer.

CHAPTER 14
THE STORM

Autumn softly merged into winter. It seemed that after the severity of the previous year Mother Nature was giving her 'children' an easier time. With winter's arrival came migrating geese and huge flocks of oystercatchers which found their way to the estuary, some making their way to Rusland Pool. Snow, always a familiar visitor, made only a light powdering this year. There was no danger of the waters freezing. Being a tidal river, both seawater and always on the move, it rarely froze. Only the very coldest weather caused ice to form on it.

Late winter and early spring brought the new influx of cygnets chased away from their family units by their fathers as the urge for nesting was felt. The new youngsters had that lost, bewildered look and drifted about like rudderless ships.

Pip and Star soon learned to check carefully before landing on strange waters as the danger of attack by a resident cob swan was considerable. He was likely to sail towards them like a 'frigate with all guns firing'. On occasions they were caught out but they never stayed for the battle; preferring to retreat into the air as quickly as possible.

It was a softly lit, hazy spring morning, with the dew-covered grass sparkling and a lacework of cobwebs festooning the lower branches of the trees. Necklaces, that joined together the early spring plants on the banks, appeared to be made of a myriad of diamonds as the sun backlit the tiny specks of dew on the fine silken webs.

On this particular May morning Pip and Star were flying in a north-easterly arc from Rusland Pool towards Windermere. As the haze dissipated the colours around them took on the clarity of spring. The waters of the huge lake glinted in the distance, gradually filling more of the scenery as they approached. There were water-birds scattered over much of the surface, either in pairs or groups of non-breeders. At the northern end they dropped low over the water and, finding it clear of swans, landed on the cool, inviting surface. They spent the remainder of the morning and part of the afternoon lazily investigating the river entrances around Pull Wyke, gliding on to Wray Bay where bits of bread were thrown to them from people on board a cruiser anchored there.

After preening and dozing in the warmth of the sun, Pip suddenly felt restless again and, looking up into the sky, signalled to Star that he was going. Their webbed feet pattered on the water and with powerfully beating wings their white bodies, mottled with grey, lifted into the air. They flew down the middle of the lake, so low that they could almost have dipped their heads down into the water. The lake was widest at Belle Grange although it was not as deep as outside Wray Bay, where it goes down to a depth of 178 feet.

Flying on to the area of little islands they passed Lady Holme, Hen Holme, Thompson's Holme and the beautifully wooded Belle Isle with its spectacular rhododendrons which reach right down to the water's edge. Further south they flew higher to miss the ferry boat which ran between the east and west banks. They continued to fly the full length of the lake until Pip realised he was over familiar water, where he was born. They were flying low again as they passed Silver Holme. Pip's feet came forward ready to land on the water, when he noticed a pair of white swans ahead. So he lifted again circling them, closely followed by Star.

The cob had moved out into a position under the circling cygnets and was watching them with arched wings as he hissed, threateningly, several times. The pen was swimming up slowly and Pip noticed that she had six very young babies with her, bobbing about in her wake. She, too, was watching the circling cygnets but she had recognised Pip and answered his call. His father was getting anxious and arched his wings higher and hissed more meaningfully. Pip knew he was not welcome and led Star up into the safety of the sky. As he did so, one grey-tipped white feather went spiralling down.

The pen, her head tilting to one side, watched as it fluttered and danced slowly downwards until finally coming to rest so lightly on the water that it was barely wet. A kick from her webbed feet sent her skimming across to where it lay. She picked it up and, with it in her bill, raised her head and watched her son fly away with his chosen mate.

*

Back on the river there was great excitement as a pair of mallards had arrived with their twelve babies. The duck was quacking very loudly as though showing off. Meanwhile the drake, calling in his husky voice, was desperately trying to keep his family together. At the same moment another family with seven ducklings waddled down to the water's edge, having just walked across the field from their nesting site. The babies fell from the bank one by one to drop, unharmed, into the water. Their quacking mother was fussing around them, her head bobbing about in excitement. The drake was so happy that, confused, he could not make up his mind whether to guard the babies or mate with his duck. However, she firmly made up his mind for him; his duty was caring for the babies.

The two families became dangerously close, the ducklings all merging together, causing great consternation amongst their parents. Skirmishes broke out between the drakes and ducks, whilst the ducklings retired to a safe distance all in one group. Suddenly the adults stopped fighting and called to their off-spring, at the same time swimming away; each pair in the opposite direction. Instead of twelve babies only ten went to one pair and the remaining nine babies went to the other pair. The two ducklings who had gone to the wrong parents tried to leave and go after their departing family but the drake, thinking they were his own, stopped them. The babies had picked up the same scent whilst they had been huddled together during the disagreement. The two families went their separate ways not realising what had happened and two the ducklings, soon forgetting their own parents, followed unaware that they had a new family.

146

It was the cygnets' third summer and their plumage was white. Their bills were still grey but much lighter and with a pink tinge. The flock of cygnets had dwindled as the older ones had flown off in pairs; some to nest, others to wander about for another year. Pip and Star spent much of their time flying and visiting different lakes, ponds and waterways. As they were capable of flying at forty miles per hour, they could cover quite a distance.

On one occasion, they chanced to find a small lake totally hidden within a wooded area. The trees were perfectly reflected round the edge, making it like a framed mirror. There were some ducks and moorhens but no swans, so they circled before gliding in for a perfect landing. Gracefully closing their wings they flicked them neatly into position and swam side by side down the centre of the lake. It was a delightful place — quiet and peaceful. The water was so still that the movement of the swans sent widening ripples out to the water's edge, causing it to lap gently on the sandy shore, disturbing the reflection of the trees. Pip and Star found such contentment there that they stayed for nearly two weeks. At last, Pip's urge to wander returned and, speaking quietly to Star, the two left without a backward glance.

The year drifted on and the soft summer colours became the brilliant hues of autumn. It was still calm and balmy but the vegetation was vibrant with reds, oranges, yellows, ochres and siennas; vying for predominance. A last glorious fling before the trees cast their leaves off like an old coat, to lie in a deep, colourful heap on the ground.

November came in with a vengence. A storm had broken out at sea and it rushed in to disturb the peace that had reigned for so long inland. The wind howled and tall, graceful trees swayed and waved their branches like over-enthusiastic ballerinas. The surface of the water became alive and moved in confused deep ripples.

Pip and Star were quite tense, sensing the severity of the storm. Suddenly a large branch snapped with a crack like gun-fire to crash down into the river. This was enough to send both birds up into the sky.

As usual, Pip took the lead with Star flying closely behind. Flying in the high wind was difficult so they dropped down low over a wood for shelter. A sudden gust caught Star and sent her into a waving branch. She called out desperately as she fell but the wind stole her voice away and Pip flew on as before not realising that he was alone.

Star was knocked down through the tree, her huge wings becoming hooked on the twiggy branches. She landed heavily on the ground underneath and lay full length, her long neck stretched out in front of her and her wings spread out on either side. She had banged her head and was semi-conscious.

Eventually she came round and lifted her head a little to look around her. Her long neck waved about, weak from shock as she tried to lift her wings tidily over her back. One settled in place but the other flopped about with blood seeping from a gaping wound, showing the jagged ends of bone. Both the bones in the forearm, the radius and ulna were broken and in moving the broken wing it had twisted, so that the primary wing feathers lay pointing forwards and upwards instead of backwards.

Star tried to stand but fell down again as one leg was useless. She tried again, putting her weight mainly on her good side but it was no use as she did not have enough strength. Her injured leg was badly bruised and beginning to swell. By this time the rain was pouring down and the wind continued to howl and buffet the trees. There was nothing poor Star could do but put her head under her good wing and try to shut out her misery.

After another day the storm blew itself out. Star still lay there cold, wet and drifting in and out of consciousness. Unless help came soon she would have no hope of survival. She would die from either cold and wet as she could not cover her back properly, from infection from her wounds or, if she survived all that, from starvation. Sleep was her only respite.

Meanwhile, Pip had flown on for quite a distance before he looked over his shoulder and realised that Star was missing. He circled and flew back calling, although flying over where she lay the tree hid her from view and his wind-blown voice did not penetrate her dazed state; so he flew on. Finding a river, he dropped down onto it and sat looking around in sad bewilderment. He took a drink and swam off searching little creeks and among reeds. He kept looking up into the sky hoping to see her coming to him. Worried and restless he took to his wings again and flew on over fields and woods — unfortunately, going further away from her.

At the estuary a terrible result of the storm could be seen. The master of a ship had, illegally, cleaned out the oil tanks at sea to save time and money whilst in dock. He had sailed on undetected. The storm had swept the long oil slick near to the shore. Guillemots and razorbills had swum into this evil, sticky mess and the tide had swept the birds inshore and up the estuary. The stronger ones had

148

begun preening, trying desperately to clean their feathers. This was the worst thing they could do as they were swallowing the insiduous poison. Others huddled together on land, cold and miserable, their feathers stuck together, losing all insulation.

Once again RSPCA inspectors were out, this time with boxes, searching for the little victims which were placed together four or five to a box. Cramped conditions were good for them as they gave each other warmth and comfort. Also there was no room to preen. Many of the birds that came ashore later, died where they landed, just pathetic lumps of black tar. The masters of ships such as this do not seem to care about the suffering they cause. Cleaning oiled birds is a difficult process because it must be done in a particular manner to get their natural waterproofing back.

Whilst flying over a field, Pip thought he saw Star and eagerly dropped down to investigate. He was disappointed to find it was a large polythene box, so he opened his wings again and flew on. The heavy rain had stopped and the sun was trying to shine, when he noticed what seemed to be a river. It was gleaming, as though lit by a spotlight, where the surrounding heavy clouds focussed a sunbeam. He went down, legs forward, wing feathers opened, spilling air. Unfortunately, it was a wet road and in landing he jarred his legs and fell forward.

It was not a busy road but Pip had to dodge out of the way of cars. He tried to take off again, but the road was bordered by high hedges and the wind was blowing across it instead of along it. He needed to take off into the wind and therefore found it impossible.

A car stopped and a man and woman came towards him. He tried to run to keep away from them but could not move very fast as his legs were painful. There was a field gate nearby and the man was able to get beyond him to open it, whilst the woman stayed back to keep Pip between them. The man walked back to Pip who, seeing the open gate, hurried through it into the field. Closing it again, they got into their car and drove off, leaving him alone. Exhausted, Pip sat down to recover from the shock and rest his jarred legs. He pulled a few blades of grass but felt too miserable to eat.

The weather had taken a lot of his energy, flying under such conditions was gruelling and the upset of losing Star magnified his dismal situation. To make matters worse, he had eaten very little, having spent most of his time searching for her.

Looking about him and staring hopefully into the distant sky, he managed to get up. Shaking himself and opening his wings, he ran

149

into wind and took off. He flew on, not knowing where he was going until he saw below him their river. Tilting his wings to lose air he went in to ski-land. Tired and miserable he paddled into the reeds and put his head under his wing.

CHAPTER 15
RESCUE

When the telephone rang Jackie was cleaning a guillemot. She wrapped the wet bird in a towel before she went to answer it.

"Hello, yes. Have you picked it up? Oh, I see. Well, thank you for telling us. Good bye."

She returned to where Steve was washing another oiled guillemot. It was trying to stab his hands with its sharp bill in spite of the elastic band keeping it closed.

"Who was it?" he asked.

"A man reporting a swan with a smashed wing in Burn Barrow Wood. Unfortunately, he didn't pick it up as it hissed at him," she explained.

"Oh, dear, that means we must collect it. We can hardly spare the time as we're stretched to the limit with all these birds to wash. Our helpers are busy dealing with our other patients."

"I wonder if Dad and Becky would go and take a look. They certainly wouldn't worry about it hissing at them. Bess's nose would be useful in finding it, too."

"You could try, love, but don't forget he's hoping to get help to move that larch that's come down in front of his garage. He might not be able to get his car out."

"I'll ring and see."

After Jackie had put the guillemot in the warmed hospital cage she dialled her father's number. Her step-mother answered.

"Hello, Becky, any luck with that tree?"

"There's a farmer and his tractor out there now. They're pulling it clear so we will be able to get out soon. Your dad says he'll cut the tree up later, with his chain-saw. Are you needing us dear? I hope there's nothing wrong with little Monica?"

"No, don't worry, she's fine; in fact, she's asleep, thank goodness. I'm so busy helping Steve clean these oiled birds. I wonder if you could help us, though. There's a poor swan with a broken wing, lying helpless, just off the main track in Burn Barrow Wood. The man who found it wouldn't pick it up and bring it here as it hissed at him. Is there any chance ?"

"I'm sure we can, dear. Now don't you worry any more. If they find a problem to delay moving the tree I'll ring you back and let you know, otherwise we'll be off. Bess'll be delighted for a run, at least. That poor bird — fancy just having to lie there injured and in pain. It must be cold and wet too."

Jackie felt relieved. After explaining the arrangement to Steve, she picked up a razorbill, expertly dodged the snap of its so aptly named weapon, and began to work washing-up liquid into the mess of thick, sticky tar.

Steve was working at the other sink, rinsing against the lie of the feathers, with a hair-washing attachment. This had to be done until every drop of the cleanser was washed away. He continued rinsing until the water droplets began to roll off the birds plumage, proving that their own waterproofing was beginning to return. Without this long exhaustive process, it could take months of care before the bird's own natural oil could protect it. This is why the cleaning process is best carried out by experts, for many well-meaning people do not realise how thoroughly the job must be done. They need to know when it is safe to release the bird. Often birds are given their freedom too soon with tragic results. The birds swim happily out to sea, only to sink and drown.

*

In Burn Barrow Wood, Star had tried to move several times causing her wing to seep blood again. The rain and her struggles had created mud around her, which had become caked around the wound. Tired out, she lay still; her head and neck lying on the ground in front of her in the shape of a question mark. She was too weak to lift it. Her blood-stained wing was in a twisted heap and she drifted into semi-consciousness where time and pain were lost. A 'question mark' was certainly hanging over her life.

After many hours she felt something warm by her head. She opened her bleary eyes to take a look. It was a dog's nose. Star pulled back instinctively and gave a half-hearted hiss. Her neck swayed with weakness and when the dog backed away she closed her eyes again letting her head sink onto her back.

Bess raced back to Ken and Becky barking excitedly at them.

"I wonder if she's found the swan? Bess, where is it? Show us," urged Ken.

The dog raced off a short distance, then stood waiting for them to catch up before trotting on again. Eventually, she disappeared behind a bush leaving only her tail in view. She had found Star.

Becky bent down and gently touched the swan. Star raised her head slightly, this time only half opening her eyes and gave a little hiss before dropping it down again.

"Oh, you poor darling," she whispered to the bird. Looking at her husband she said, "At least she's still alive, love."

Ken had brought an old blanket with him and he laid it on the driest bit of ground he could find, saying "I'll lift 'er. Yer take the weight of that injured wing, so we don't cause more damage or pain."

"It's all twisted. Just a minute, let me try and put it right." She looked carefully at it and was able to see by the twists of the flesh, which way it was lying. Carefully she rotated it so that it could be laid correctly over the bird's back.

"Well done Bec. Yer support it now. Ready? ... Lift."

Together they lifted Star and placed her on the blanket, wrapped her body up but left her neck out. Ken tucked the bundle under his arm and they set off with Bess trotting along beside them. She repeatedly looked up into her master's face and at the bird, obviously very pleased with herself.

Star's neck kept hanging down and was in danger of being knocked as they walked, Becky took hold of it, nestling it in the crook of her arm. Talking soothingly and stroking the swan's pathetic head she tried to calm the frightened eyes.

Ken was very relieved when they reached his Rover as the bundle seemed to get heavier with every step. He did not want to have to put it down to rest as the swan had become used to being carried and seemed more settled.

"Shall I have her on my knees, Ken?"

"Yes, that's a good idea."

As they set off for the hospital the big dog sat bolt upright on the back seat looking out of the windows, like an important, chauffeur-driven executive.

Turning in through the hospital gates they stopped by the reception door. Jackie heard the car and, carrying Monica, came out to greet them. As Ken opened the passenger door and took the swan from Becky's lap, Bess gave a frustrated 'woof'.

"Alright Bessie, I'll let you out." Jackie opened the back door and the dog leapt out, gave Monica's little hand a quick lick, before rushing to Ken to see 'her' swan, She also licked the bird's white head. Star hissed at the wet tongue and jerked her head out of reach hiding it inside the back of Ken's coat collar.

They all went inside where the swan was placed on the table and her blanket carefully unwrapped. Steve looked at the broken wing, covered with congealed blood mixed with mud, then felt along the length of bone on either side to find out the extent of the injury. "Oh, you poor thing," he muttered. "Jackie if you take Dad and Mum indoors I'll get one of the lads to help me with this swan."

Monica stretched out her hand towards Star. "It's a poorly swan, Daddy's going to make it better." Monica reached forward again, so Jackie let the child touch the soft, white feathers of its neck.

Once in the kitchen, Bess settled herself on the hearthrug to enjoy the warmth of the open fire. Becky, sitting down on a fireside chair, held out her arms for Monica who toddled across the room to her. Jackie put the kettle on and got out the mugs.

"What happened about the tree, Dad?"

"We were lucky. The farmer came straight over with chains to put round the tree trunk. We dragged it to one side. We'd 'ave been in a proper mess otherwise as the garage doors were jammed shut and 'eld tight by branches. Luckily, we've only 'ad a bit of damage to one corner of the brickwork. It's sad, though, the tree was a bigg'un and 'ad bin standin' a long while. Still, I s'pose th'end of life comes to us all in different ways."

"I understand you've been very busy here with all those poor oiled-up birds. I heard about it on the news," said Becky.

"Yes, they've been coming in from the coast and the estuary round here. Walkers, as well as the RSPCA have been bringing them. Little Moni keeps me busy of course, so I can't do as much in the hospital as I used to. Thank goodness for our willing helpers or Steve would have more to do than would be good for him."

The child looked at her mother when she heard her name.

"You're a bright little button. Aren't you darling? You don't miss much." Monica turned her blue eyes up to Becky, holding out her favourite toy duck.

Ken smiled as he remembered Jackie at that age and said, "Just like 'er mother, a real 'andful. Mark my words, when she's bigger she'll try to boss us all around."

"Dad!" Jackie admonished.

"Never mind "Dad", in that tone of voice, as though butter wouldn't melt in yer mouth. Where's my tea? You've no excuse now, yer mother's looking' after 'er fav'rite granddaughter."

"You're a bully." A loving look shot between them belying their teasing words and she went back to pouring out the tea.

At that moment Steve came in and concerned faces turned, questioningly, in his direction.

"How's the swan?" asked Jackie.

"Resting," he replied. "She's exhausted. I've cleaned the wound and tied up the wing. She's had a Penbriton penicillin injection and I've left her in the warm cage to sleep. Tomorrow, when she's rested, I may have to pin it but I'll consider that in the morning. As you know I don't like pinning if I can avoid it. It means a double danger from anaesthetic, once to insert the pin and again to remove it."

They sat talking in the warm farmhouse kitchen until Monica's tea-time approached. Ken and Becky said their "good-byes", woke Bess from her slumbers and left for home.

The following morning Steve set up the surgery and Star was carried in and laid on the table. He had decided to risk an anaesthetic to enable him to repair the wing. He set up the anaesthetic cone over the swans head. Jackie had already put Monica in the travel cot to sleep so that she could help Steve.

"I'll go and scrub up, Jackie, keep an eye on our patient, please. The stethoscope's on the side, there."

Jackie found it and, listening to the swan's heart beat, was assured that the bird was going under satisfactorily. She then checked on the anaesthetic vapour flow. Star moved her head, necessitating the repositioning of the cone. "Alright, sweetie, just you go to sleep," she murmured soothingly. It was not long before the swan was safely in an induced sleep and, after checking the bird's heart beat again, Jackie turned down the vapour flow rate.

"How's she doing?" Steve asked.

"OK. She's there. Her heart's steady and there was no reaction when I pinched her web."

By this time, Steve had collected the instruments from the steriliser and was ready to operate. He removed feathers from the wound site, cleaned it and the bone ends, then puffed antiseptic powder inside and around the exposed bone and the surrounding flesh. Bringing the broken, jagged ends together, he was pleased to see that, in spite of a few missing fragments, they seemed quite ready to stay in position. The jagged ends actually helping in this instance.

Next, he stitched together the torn flesh, scraping the edges of the skin a little, to make them bleed and facilitate better healing. After puffing in more antiseptic powder he bandaged the wound and bound the broken wing with a six-inch splint. He secured the folded wing to prevent the bird from moving the joint and so disturbing the set. This gave extra splint-power by using the good bones of the folded wing.

Jackie turned off the anaesthetic machine as Steve gave the patient another Penbriton injection. "All yours, Jackie." He turned away from the table and flexed his shoulders to relax the muscles. His neck and shoulders were both stiff as he had been leaning over his patient doing intense work for more than half-an-hour.

She laid the floppy head and neck over the bird's back. Then, cradling the unconscious patient in her arms, carried her to her warm cage and laid her down, arranging her neck comfortably before leaving her. Steve was clearing away after the operation when she returned, and he smiled at her with love and appreciation. She went into the reception area to check on the travel cot with its peacefully sleeping occupant.

"Darling," Jackie said, "I'm going back to sit with our patient until she's conscious. After all, she might thrash about whilst she's coming round and need to be held to prevent her doing herself a mischief. We don't want her to cause herself any more trouble."

Steve came across the room to her and put his hands on her shoulders, then slid them slowly up her neck to stop when he was cupping her head. He stood for a moment looking deeply into her eyes before dismissing her with a kiss.

CHAPTER 16
CONVALESCENCE

Star slowly began to open her eyes. Through blurred vision she looked around her and found that everything was strange. She listened anxiously to the unfamiliar sounds. There was no lapping water, splattering rain or howling wind, no sound of Pip's voice or other bird noises. She was only partially conscious and did not flap as Jackie had feared but raised her head and neck, which swayed with weakness before sinking down again onto her back, this time scribing a graceful curve. She tucked her bill into her feathers and closed her eyes again, shutting out her misery.

"Come on pretty girl, wake up. You're going to be alright." Jackie's voice seemed to hover in the air around Star's brain and she felt something gently stroking her head. Her mind floated back to the lake and she thought it was Pip's bill. She opened her eyes for a moment but, being unable to take in where she was and what had happened to her, she slipped away again into semi-consciousness.

Jackie stayed with Star for about half-an-hour, talking to her and stroking her to help bring her round. Eventually, she became fully conscious and, as her vision cleared, looked around her with her neck held high and rigid. She turned her head sharply one way and another, fear filling her eyes.

"It's alright, sweetie, no-one's going to hurt you," Jackie's voice murmured again and again until gradually Star's fear lessened and the tension went from her neck.

Slowly and steadily Jackie moved her hand towards the bowl of water placed in the corner of the cage and splashed her fingers in it. Hearing the familiar sound the swan realised that she was thirsty and lowered her head to the bottom of the cage, where water ought to be. Puzzled, she looked about her and searched with her bill for the water that she could hear but not find. Jackie's fingers kept splashing and as soon as the searching bill was near enough she splashed it. Star snapped her mandibles together in eager anticipation as though smacking her lips. Jackie persevered, hopeful that Star would accidently find the water without having to be helped further. However, although she found the edge of the bowl, she did not realise she had to lift her bill up and over that obstacle. Normally, she would find water at the lowest level and here it was in the wrong place and quite a puzzle. Jackie leaned over Star, gently took her bill and pressed it into the water. The bird drank eagerly as Jackie closed the cage top and left.

It was a week before Star tried to stand. The swelling had left her leg and it was no longer painful but very weak and she kept getting up and flopping down again. As the weak leg was on the same side as the broken and bound wing, this exacerbated the problem of keeping her balance. Steve was cleaning out some cages when he heard her struggles so, after finishing that particular cage, he went over to her and opened the top. "Come on, poppet," he whispered and, standing in front of her, he slid his arms beneath her from each side and lifted her a little. Star was startled but no longer afraid as these people had only shown her kindness. Her feet immediately went into action and, as well as taking her weight, they tried to walk. Steve could feel that all the strength was on one side and he also noted that the webs on her weak foot were only partially spread. "You're doing fine, little-one, but you'll have to rest a bit more." He let Star sink back onto her pile of wood shavings and she nuzzled his neck before he withdrew his arms and stood up.

The following day Steve was delighted to find Star standing, although with most of her weight on her good leg, so he decided it was time to put her with the other swans. Opening her cage-top he leaned in and picked her up. She struggled, but he had his arm around her good wing so she could not open it. Also he held her kicking legs away from him. "There little girl, you're going to be with friends now that you're able to stand, so you won't be lonely anymore." He carried her out, across the yard into another building which housed several open-topped stalls. Each stall had a small sliding door which allowed the occupants to go outside. Some of these enclosures had water in their outer runs.

In the larger stall there were three young swans and one adult. Star called as she saw them from her elevated position in Steve's arms. The others turned to watch and some answered her. She was carefully deposited near to bowls of food and water. Standing well back from them, Steve watched for a while to make sure that they all settled happily together. There was one young male who was inclined to be domineering and he soon waddled over to Star and began to bully her. He hissed and grabbed her by her neck. She called in distress and turned her head away. Steve shouted sharply to the bully and told him to leave her alone. The young cob looked sulkily at Steve and turned his head away. The door of the building had quietly opened a moment before but Steve was concentrating on the birds and had not noticed. It was Bill the RSPCA inspector and speaking softly, he said "It's quite amazing how swans seem to understand, isn't it?"

Steve turned at the voice and smiled at his friend. "Hi there, Bill. Yes, it's an amazing thing and I'm often surprised and pleased when I'm able to communicate with them. If I tell this to people who have had nothing to do with swans, they just think I'm daft."

"Is that the one you told me was brought down in the storm?"

"Yes, that's her. She's doing fine; a bit weak still on her bad side, but that's to be expected."

"Just look at that. Old Bully-boy is sitting down with Storm and preening himself as though he'd never been any different."

"Storm! that's a good name for her. You're good at names, you are," he laughed. "Well now she's settled let's go and have a cuppa. If Jackie's not seen you and put the kettle on, I'll do it."

"She saw me and waved. In fact, she pointed to this building so I could find you."

"Is this just a social visit or have you got something for me?"

"Always social when I come here but I have some patients too; a couple of herring gulls that can't stand."

"Right I'll take a look first, as they often need swift attention."

Bill went to his van and returned with a cardboard carrier. He followed Steve into the hospital. Carefully, Bill opened the top and let Steve take over. The two birds were sitting side-by-side and looked up at him. One opened his bill ready to make a defensive peck, the other remained still with its eyes partially shut. Both birds were wet. Steve moved his hand in close to them and one gull grabbed his finger.

"What did you do that for, Steve?"

"I wanted to find out how weak he is. The power of his snap is very telling." He picked up the quieter bird and felt its legs to see if there were any breaks. They had some movement but no strength. Steve checked the other one and found it to be the same except that it was a little stronger, as demonstrated by its attempt to peck. Closing the box he picked up the internal telephone and buzzed for Jackie. "Sweetie, we have two gulls that would do best on your homoeopathic treatment. Can you come over?"

"What's all this about?" asked Bill

"We find that these gulls have a much better recovery rate when dosed with homoeopathic remedies, Jackie is much more experienced in that subject than I am. It appears that these two have been weakened by the stormy weather."

Just then the door opened. Jackie smiled at them in turn and said "Where're my patients then?" Without waiting for an answer she lifted the lid and peered over the top of the box. "What's the matter?" The threatening hooked bill aimed for her fingers. "Naughty bird," she scolded, carefully edging her hand under first one then the other, feeling their degree of warmth and whether the wetness had penetrated their plumage. She needed to assess how strongly their hearts were beating.

Steve explained his diagnosis. Jackie nodded and went to her cabinet where she kept these remedies. She took out two vials and returned to the birds. "I'm giving the quiet one, which is cold, one dose of Carbo veg. 200 and the other one Arsenicum alb. 30." Whilst speaking, she took out a Carbo veg. tablet in one hand and, opening the quiet bill with the other, pushed the remedy down the open throat. Next she took an Arsenicum tablet and the other waiting bill grabbed her finger, so it was an easy job to push the remedy down. Steve took the birds and placed them side-by-side in a warmed cage to dry off and warm up.

"Why did you give them different medicines Jackie?" asked Bill in a puzzled voice. "After all they're both suffering from the same thing."

"True Bill, but they have reacted differently to it, one bird is colder and weaker and inclined to give up. Did you notice that its eyes were partially closed? It wouldn't be seeing clearly. That one isn't going to give us much time to save it. The other one is more of a fighter. It is much warmer and rather anxious, that's why it's attacking. I gave that one the Arsenicum because the symptoms fitted. The cold one needed a deep fast action, hence the 200 potency Carbo veg. Possibly it will not be necessary to repeat that high potency again but I shall judge what to give next by how the bird's symptoms change."

"Goodness lass, I'm out of my depth. Let's go an' have that cuppa."

*

Bill had just left when the telephone rang and Jackie went to answer it. Her voice sounded serious so Steve listened. As soon as he could he asked what was wrong. "Just a minute," Jackie said to the caller, "Steve wants to know what's wrong." Turning to Steve, she said "It's Becky, saying that Dad has gone down with 'flu and won't have the doctor. You know what he's like." She carried on talking into the telephone and Steve, with a shake of his head, turned away.

Suddenly there was a howl from the kitchen - it was Monica. Jackie excused herself momentarily from Becky and rushed to her. She was sitting in her playpen waving her hand in the air clutching a plastic ball and screaming.

"Moni, Moni what's the matter?" Suddenly Jackie realised that she was not clutching the ball at all but had her finger caught inside it. She took the child's hand and squeezed the ball to release it.. "Oh darling, what a naughty ball. Did it bite Moni's finger, come on, Mummy kiss it better." Like magic the child stopped crying and smiled up at her mother's face. Jackie gave her the furry duck and hurried back to the telephone. "Sorry Becky, but Moni had somehow found a hole in her plastic ball and got her finger stuck inside it. She's OK now. So what are we going to do about Dad?" She listened for a while then said "Alright, I won't worry, unless you call me."

Steve came back to see if anything had to be done. "Becky says he's not too bad but, as usual, rather awkward when he's ill. I feel he must have got cold looking for the swan in all that rain. She'll ring me if he gets worse. If he still won't see a doctor — which I very much doubt he will — I'll go over and dose him homoeopathically. We know he responds well to that."

As the day came to a close husband and wife were very tired. It continued to be cold and miserable outside and therefore many patients were being brought to them for help. Steve had developed a cough during the last few days and Jackie was living on her nerves. Looking after Monica, giving her husband remedies to stop his cough from worsening, keeping her mind alert for the birds in her care, trying to supply the family with cooked meals, keeping the house clean, doing the shopping... and now the worry of her father too . . .

Suddenly she sat down and burst into tears. Steve went to her chair and, dropping to his knees, put his arms around her. He said nothing but held her until gradually her sobs subsided and she rested with her head against him and her eyes closed. They had that very special relationship that few people are lucky enough to know. Rising to his feet he pushed a cushion under her head and, giving her a light kiss, left her side. He did not go far, merely to the cupboard for a piece of chocolate which he brought to her and popped into her mouth. She opened her tear-reddened eyes and smiled at him before closing them again and falling asleep. Steve made up the fire in the grate and sat down with a cup of tea and a piece of cake. At half-past ten he gently woke her to take her up to bed, saying "You're trying to do too much, love."

The following morning, Steve was sitting at the breakfast table reading a letter when Jackie entered with their coffee. Noticing the Australian stamp on the envelope, she said "Is that from Emma?"

Steve looked up, smiling, "Yes, as a matter of fact, it could be a god-send".

"What do you mean?" asked Jackie as she helped Monica dip bread into her boiled egg."Emma has a friend whose daughter desperately wants to come to England for a few months and wonders if we know of anyone who needs an au pair."

"I can't think of anyone".

"Jackie, love. Don't you see? She could come here, not as an au pair, we couldn't pay her anything, but she could live here in exchange for some domestic work, as long as she has some money of her own. I was thinking when you were so tired last night how much we need some help. She could have the spare bedroom and help look after Monica. What do you think?"

"It sounds a wonderful idea. How old is she?"

Steve looked at the letter. "She's nineteen, lives in the country outside Perth, up in the hills, near to Mandaring where there is the only 'bird hospital' in Australia. Her name is Sarah."

"Well, if Emma knows her and she doesn't mind living in the country ... I agree, it is a god-send!"

"I'll phone Emma this afternoon, so as to catch her before they go to bed and say Sarah can come as soon as she likes. Now, I must go and check on those gulls." He gave Monica a kiss as he passed the high chair and Jackie a hug as she rose to clear the table.

It was arranged that Sarah would come to England at the end of the month. She would fly to Heathrow and catch the flight up to Manchester, where Steve would meet her.

*

During the next few days Jackie made sure the spare bedroom was comfortable. She realised the girl would be feeling tired after her long journey and wanted to make her feel as 'at home' as possible. She hoped that Sarah and Monica would take to each other and was feeling quite elated at the thought of having help to look after the child who was now getting around a lot quicker. Another pair of eyes to keep watch and to occupy her for part of the day would allow Jackie respite, enabling her to give more help in the hospital.

*

After several days it was apparent that Star was not progressing as she should. She sat apart from the others and had not been seen eating. They had seen her drink but that was all.

"I'm worried about Storm, perhaps you can spend a little time with her." suggested Steve

That afternoon Jackie took Monica with her and sat by the swans to observe them. Storm certainly did not seem to care for anything, in fact, all she wanted was to be left alone and to sleep. She could stand but did not want to be bothered. Jackie fingered her legs and her broken wing to see if there was any tell-tale heat indicating something was going wrong, but there was none. When Steve came in she told him that she thought the swan was missing a friend.

"She's too young for a mate."

"For a mated mate yes, but not too young for a boyfriend."

"Yes, I suppose you're right. She's certainly behaving like an adult bereaved swan. Any ideas as to what we should do?"

"Yes, I'll dose her with some Ignatia. Will you take care of Moni for a minute?"

Jackie collected a tablet from her cupboard and, standing astride Star, lifted the bird's head, opened the bill and dropped the tablet inside. She stroked the resigned face before letting go her hold. The

163

droopy head made Jackie sad and, impulsively, she bent and kissed it. "Get better, darling, then you can go and find him," she whispered. Star's head sank to her chest where it stayed a while immobile.

"You feel helpless, just watching her fade away. The pair-bonding is so strong that separated swans can lose the will to live. It is very sad."

"Steve, you must be positive, we know about it in time. Let Ignatia do its work. She's got some company even if they're the wrong ones."

They left the building and went about tending all the other birds. Monica played with a feather in her pushchair as Jackie pushed it with one hand and carried a bucket of dead poults for the various birds of prey with the other. Steve had taken a supply of food to the main lake for the birds who were fit enough to be allowed to fly away. This lake was also used for disabled ones who needed a permanent home.

Star and Pip had already visited that water from the freedom of the air some time ago.

CHAPTER 17
HELP FOR PIP

Bill called to Steve as he saw him down by the pond. "Coming — one minute."

Bill returned to his van and, opening the back, lifted out a swan with its head tucked under its wing. As he carried it to the hospital door the bird made no effort to remove its head nor did it attempt to defend itself.

Steve came hurrying towards them, studying the swan's attitude as he did so. "Doesn't look too good. Doesn't seem to care any more," he commented. "Let's take it inside."

Bill put the bird down on the floor; it still did not move. Steve bent down beside it and ran his hand over the body and along the neck and gently withdrew the head from under the wing. Two sad, bleary eyes looked back at him.

Jackie saw the swan arrive. Sarah was already at Birdholme and Monica was enjoying the company of her new 'auntie'.

Feeling relieved that she could leave the two together, she hurried over to find out what was wrong. "Oh, the poor thing." She dropped down on her knees beside the miserable bird and ran her hands over the soft white feathers with their tell-tale brown tips. She, too, took the sad face in her hands. "He's cold and starving. Let's get him into a warm cage quickly."

"You said 'he' how do you know? I appreciate that the knob on the bill is beginning to grow but that isn't always conclusive."

"I just feel it's a male, there's something about him that tells me so."

"You can't argue with that," commented her husband as he looked at Bill, with a grin.

"Let's call it woman's logic," he replied.

"No, Bill, let's call it 'Jackie's instinct' it's more difficult still to understand but more likely to be right."

Ignoring them, she busily filled a hot-water bottle for the swan. Steve placed him in a cosy, wooden-sided enclosure and switched on the overhead infra-red lamp. Jackie brought the hot-water bottle and, lifting one wing, she leaned it against his side letting the wing return to hold it in position. She went to the homoeopathic medicine cupboard and, taking out the Dulcamara vial, dropped a tablet down the unresisting swan's throat.

"What's that you've given him?"

"Dulcamara, Steve, to combat problems caused by his being thoroughly wet. I think there's far more to it than that, but at least it's a starting point."

"I'll give him some oral vitamins too. I feel he needs some sustenance urgently."

"Yes, but wait half-an-hour for the Dulcamara to start its action."

The three left the hospital and Bill told them his next call was in Bowness. With a wave, he jumped into the van and drove away.

Half-an-hour later Steve and Jackie went back to see the new swan. As they approached, he lifted his head a little and gave a weak hiss.

"That's something. Do you want to give him some Visorbin now?"

Steve sucked up some of the pleasant-tasting multi-vitamins into a syringe, without the needle attached. Taking it to the patient he raised the limp head and neck before dripping the liquid very slowly down his throat. "We'll leave him another thirty minutes and then, if there's no improvement, I'll give him glucose saline."

It was over four hours before Pip opened his eyes and tried to see where he was through his confused, misty vision. It felt as though the sun was shining as his back was pleasantly warm but, on looking up, it did not look like the sun. He felt the ground around him with his bill, which was a strange substance, neither earth nor grass. There was something white sticking up in front of him and he grabbed at it. It was the paper that he was sitting on, he tore a bit off only to toss it away in disgust. The door opened and Jackie walked in.

"Hello sweetheart. You're awake. That's good." Pip gave a feeble hiss and turned his head away.

"Here you are. Some water for you." Jackie steadily leaned over the open top and placed the bowl in the corner of the cage, well within his reach. She splashed her fingers in it to help him recognise it. Pip listened, longing for a drink and dipped his head to the paper expecting to find it there. She wet his face with the water and he searched more intently all around his body with his bill, swallowing in anticipation. As Star's had done before him, his bill kept coming up against the side of the bowl. Jackie waited until his bill was there again and with one hand well placed to get under his bill she pushed it up and over the edge of the bowl. With the other hand she reached over to stop him pulling back his head. She guided his bill into the water and he had his first drink in captivity. As he was beginning to look more relaxed, Jackie slowly opened the door of his cage and knelt on the floor beside him. She continued lightly splashing her fingers in the water. He withdrew his head into its restful curve and looked from Jackie's face to her fingers. She kept murmuring to him so that he learnt to recognise her and realise she was not a threat. Withdrawing her hand a little from the bowl, she let it remain on the floor of the cage. Pip smacked his mandibles together in anticipation of another drink. Then, with a look into Jackie's face, he unhesitatingly pushed his bill into the water and drank.

Steve came in and saw them. Jackie smiled at him and told him of the new success.

"Well done, love, now we can give him vitamins in his water and you will be able to sprinkle some Vitalyn in it too, so he gets the flavour. This dog food is very useful and nourishing for our sick water-birds, isn't it? "

Jackie nodded in agreement but at the sound of a vehicle outside Steve left her and strolled out to meet it. Meanwhile, she walked round the various other cages in her particular care.

Next time the door opened, Steve was carrying a fully-adult male swan with an injured leg. He took him to a large open-topped pen and set him down on the bed of newspapers. The cob hissed defiantly and made several mock attacks with his bill as Steve moved about, settling him in and seeing that food and water were within reach. "Alright, old fella, no need for that. I'm your friend." He offered the bird a bit of brown bread as something he was likely to recognise. It was snatched from his hand but dropped.

Steve was satisfied that the cob knew food and water were there and would have some when more at ease. In his water bowl was a little Vitalyn to get him accustomed to the taste before making it his main meal. Steve decided to return later to check on the bird's damaged leg. Apparently, he had been taking off in open country, alongside a road. Unfortunately, a car had come round a bend at that moment. The swan had not been quite high enough and his leg had been hit by the roof of the car. Shocked, the swan had dropped onto the verge. The driver, being a kind man and able to stop safely, went to his rescue. The man told Steve that the cob had hissed and tried to hit him but, being ready for the possible attack, he grabbed the wing and quickly folded it into place before taking the big, white bird in his arms.

"The biggest problem," he told Steve, "was trying to open the car door with two arms full of swan." He had managed it, however, and put him in the rear foot-well facing into a corner, hoping to keep him still. Fortunately, it had worked and he was able to drive to the hospital without difficulty.

Steve smiled to himself as he remembered his own first attempt at catching a swan and how his heart pounded, until he felt the great white body in his arms and realised what a truly magnificent creature he was privileged to be holding.

Pip called to him across the room and the cob answered, shuffling his snow-white feathers. The new-comer felt disgust at being carried about like a parcel.

Later that afternoon, they were doing the hospital rounds when Jackie stopped by Pip. As she poured some more water into his bowl she noted that the Vitalyn was uneaten. Next, she went to see the new cob and opened his enclosure to be greeted by a fierce hiss. She was carrying a tube of Arnica ointment, which the swan smartly knocked out of her hand with a well-aimed blow from his wing. "Steady now, lad. That won't do. We've got to be friends if you want to go free again." She put a restraining hand on his wing and reached over him with the other to retrieve the ointment.

Steve came across to see how the new cob was doing. "His leg seems to be just bruised," he said, "There's plenty of movement in it but it won't bear his weight. I'll hold him if you can apply some Arnica." He put his arms around the bird and lifted him, leaving his

168

kicking legs to be dealt with by Jackie. She felt the leg and, satisfied that the blood supply was keeping it warm but not hot, she applied the ointment. Steve put him down again, only to receive a half-hearted blow on his leg at the same time.

"I'm going to give him a 200 potency Arnica tablet as well, then we needn't keep having to medicate him and upset him."

"Alright, can you manage if I carry on with the duck pen?"

"Yes, no problem."

Returning with her tablets, she kept well clear of that wing whilst getting a tablet out of the vial. "Come on, old fella." She stood astride his back, keeping control of his wings with her legs and, taking hold of his head with her free hand, slid a finger into his bill. Before he realised what was happening the tablet was inside and she had closed the bill again and was stroking his neck to make him swallow. He hissed at her but when she let go he allowed her to leave without further defensive action.

"When you're clear Jackie, could you take a look at the young pen with the broken wing. She's still very mopey and I don't think she's eaten anything yet."

"Yes, I'll go in a minute. She's certainly a worry. It would be extra sad to lose her because she's given up, rather than due to her injuries. I'll sit near her for a while and see what I can learn."

"Where's Moni, having a rest?"

"Yes, Sarah is looking after her. I'll take a look at her on my way to the other building. In fact, I may put her in her pushchair to take her with me."

Jackie went indoors and could hear her baby prattling happily to herself. On her way upstairs she nodded to Sarah and smiled with pleasure thinking how lucky they were to have such a lovely contented child. "Hello darling, how's Mummy's girl then?" She bent over the cot, picked her up and kissed her. Cuddling the infant in her arms she crooned to her a few words from the Walt Disney film 'Pinocchio' —

> "When you wish upon a star,
> Makes no difference who you are
> Anything your heart desires will come to you ..."

Jackie wrapped a blanket around Monica, carried her downstairs and sat her in the pushchair, placing the favourite toy duck into her outstretched arms. Mother and child went off to the convalescent building to sit and observe.

All the swans, except Star, were outside enjoying the water, splashing themselves and preening. Star was still indoors in a corner with her head under her wing, taking no notice of anything that was going on. Jackie left the pushchair in the reception area, where she could still keep an eye on Monica, and went into the stall with Star. She bent down and gently stroked the bird. After a while the swan wearily lifted her head a little from its feathery bed. Jackie's fingers felt round the broken wing to make sure it was not showing any signs of overheating due to infection. She knelt in front of the bird and drew the sad head into her lap and caressed it, gradually she slid her arms beneath the body, one on each side, and pressured the bird into standing. Star relied on the supporting arms as she was too weary of life to bother any more and draped her long neck over Jackie's shoulder. Loving concern for the bird flowed from the young woman as she pressed her face into the soft, warm, downy breast and kept whispering to her patient. Slowly, the bird sank down until she was sitting on Jackie's knee, her head slipping down and resting under her chin. Jackie kept up voice and body contact with Star until her arms ached and she had to move. Finally, she guided the unresisting head into the water bowl for a drink of the water and vitamins. Before leaving, she took a vial of Ignatia 200 from her pocket and gave another dose. 'It's marvellous for all types of bereavement, whether human, animal or bird,' she thought. From experience she was confident in giving the higher potency. Although, when she recommended a remedy for others to use, she always suggested either 6, 12 or 30 potency at the most.

"Tomorrow, beautiful girl, I'm going to give you a little swim." She stood up and was pleased to see the white head turn to watch her leave.

That evening Steve and Jackie were sitting on either side of the fire in the kitchen, relaxing after the birds were all shut down for the night. Sarah was up in her room writing some letters and Monica was asleep. Steve's mind wandered back to his patients and he said, "That young cob in the hospital is trying to stand up now but he won't eat, perhaps you can give him a bit of your magic treatment."

Jackie sat in silence staring into the flames and Steve turned his head to look at her. "Penny for them, sweetheart, are you thinking what I'm thinking?"

She looked into his eyes for a moment and said, "Yes, I could be. You're thinking of putting the two sad ones together aren't you?"

"Yes that's right. One might help the other."

"True, but there might be more to it than that."

170

"What do you mean?"

"Well, the broken-winged female that Bill called Storm hasn't responded to the company of the others, has she?"

"No, she hasn't, you're right. What are you suggesting, then?"

"Suppose they both just happen to be pining for each other. Suppose she broke her wing and he has been looking for her and tired himself out."

"Now then, sweetheart, you really are being a romantic this time. Aren't you letting your imagination run away with you? Coincidences like that just don't happen." He smiled lovingly at her to soften his words.

"I suppose you're right." She looked sadly back into the fire feeling that her bright idea had been dashed. Steve picked up his book and opened it at the book mark. "Still, I think we must try, after all we can't lose." She smiled at her husband as he spoke. He returned her look, but warned "As long as you don't build up too much hope."

CHAPTER 18
MIRACLES DO HAPPEN

The following morning Jackie went in early to see Star and was greeted as a friend with "Que que que." She returned the greeting and, leaning over the top of the stall, ran her hand down the long neck. As she stood back to watch, Star turned her head to the open sky and looked up with a deep longing in her eyes. Jackie called Steve to tell him that Storm was getting back her desire to live, even though her eyes showed the sadness in her heart. Then Jackie went to collect Pip from the hospital. He hissed a little as she opened his cage but gave very little resistance to being picked up.

"I'm taking you to see a lovely little girl, who needs your help," she told the swan, "so you've got to be a kind and considerate boy and see what you can do."

Pip held his long neck out in front of them as he was carried into the convalescent building.

Star, who was sitting in her usual corner, lifted her head as she heard Jackie's voice and watched as the new swan was carried in. Stopping by the stall, Jackie placed Pip down by Star's side and stood back. The two birds, however, looked away from each other not wanting to be bothered by another bird. Jackie's heart sank.

Star was the first to turn her head and take a look at her new neighbour. All of a sudden she seemed to come to life. A tremor shot through her long neck, then she pushed her bill into the back feathers of the swan next to her with an excited call. Pip's head shot up at her voice and touch and he eagerly staggered to his feet. He pressed his own bill onto her back and called, and called. Star struggled to get to her feet but fell back down again. Her weakened leg had not yet had enough exercise to regain full strength. Jackie stood as though transfixed, then tears started to stream down her face and she ran to Steve calling his name.

The couple stood watching, arms around each other, as Star and Pip preened each other, nuzzled their heads against the other's body and ate hungrily from the bowl of water and food. Jackie hurried to get some more Vitalyn which she poured into the bowl, adding more water. The two white heads hardly left the food. Together they ate and drank until there was nothing left. At last they laid their heads down on each other's back and slept.

"Well, my girl, I must admit you're a wonder, a real wonder. How on earth did you know that they were a pair?"

"I didn't. I just felt it a possibility. After all, I've spent hours with each one and they both seemed so much alike, and we know we tend to grow like those we love, be it animal, bird or human." Steve took her in his arms. Husband and wife kissed with deep understanding and love.

The ringing of the telephone pulled them both up with a jerk and Steve went to answer it. He called to Jackie that Bill was coming over with some more oiled birds. Apparently a patch of oil entering the estuary had claimed three cygnets and about a dozen mallards. This time someone had already cleaned them but they needed after-care. One cygnet and four mallards were not eating, so they would need individual attention. Jackie busied herself getting places ready for them. Steve was coming and going, taking out dirty bedding and bringing in fresh.

"You know, it's typical of this work; as soon as something good happens, something else comes along to give us concern again," he observed.

"Just imagine though, if those good things didn't happen."

"If we didn't care for each other as much as we care for our patients and always remember the good things that happen, we would crack up under the strain," said Jackie.

"We've got the best chance of standing the pace as when either of us are unhappy we both feel it. Unfortunately, many partners seem unaware of each other's moods and are unable to help."

"I know what you mean, Steve. I feel the same. Look at our two 'lover' swans. They were both ready to die until they found each other, now I know that mutual love will speed their recovery."

"Talking of the 'lovers'. Look Jackie, they're out on the pond."

"Oh, that's wonderful."

The arrival of the RSPCA van interrupted their conversation and Steve went out to meet it. Bill jumped out of the driver's seat as Steve was already opening the back door of the vehicle. Between them they carried the baskets of ducks and the three cygnets into the hospital.

"This one is very light in weight and looks quite sick," Steve said as he placed the cygnet under the infra-red lamp. "I have a nasty feeling that she might already have been suffering from lead, but it took the oil to bring her in."

"Poor little creature", said Bill. She's not getting a good start in life, is she?"

"No. I wouldn't be surprised if her short life is about to end before it's properly begun. I'll get Jackie to see if she can work a bit of magic."

They settled the birds and Steve began to decide what medications to give them. Bill asked if he could use their telephone to report in. His next call out was to investigate a reported case of an illtreated dog.

The new birds were checked and sorted into groups depending on their state of health. Some of the ducks were given homoeopathic Petroleum 30 as an antidote to the oil, this is effective providing it is taken in time, before there is any irreversible harm to their internal organs. Jackie decided to begin with Carbo veg. 200 for the cygnet, as it was already near to death. After this, she left the hospital to go and finish her work in the house.

Steve heard her footsteps hurrying away across the yard as he looked around at the various cages and stalls. He thought back to the early days of their marriage when they had plenty of spare time and compared it to their present desperately busy days. He realised that, with the constant tension, they could easily be at each other's throats or perhaps feel disillusioned with life. They saw and worked with so much suffering and most of it caused by humanity. Some they could help, some they could not, others that flew away cured would possibly fall prey to another disaster. Was it all a waste of time? Were they wasting the money that so many kind people gave them to continue this work? Could they be spending their lives in a more fruitful way? He walked across to the new, sick cygnet whose head was resting on its back. Putting his hand on her head, his fingers caressed her soft brown plumage. She lifted her head and looked at him through partly opened eyes and gave a faint "twee,twee,twee," in her high-pitched baby voice. "You're safe now, sweetheart, even if you are going to die, you've nothing more to fear." He withdrew his hand and the weary, black eyes closed. His attention was attracted by Jackie's returning footsteps.

"Steve, the 'phone's rung again, there's a tawny owl being brought from Grange-over-Sands, apparently it was stuck in a chimney and is covered in soot. The lady was so relieved to know we'd take it. She couldn't say enough nice things about our work. It was quite embarrassing, as well as pleasing."

"Soot eh-m-m, — let's see — Fuller's earth. That's the ticket, as it'll clean without getting the feathers wet. Let's hope he's not inhaled too much. Do we know if it's soot from coal or tar from burning wood?"

"No, but I'll ask when I take the bird in.

*

Late that afternoon Ken and Becky turned up with a panting Bess sitting in state on the back seat.

"Hello Dad, Mum, it's lovely to see you both. How are you, Dad?"

"Fine lass, fine," but a fit of coughing betrayed his true condition.

"Dad, you're not, and what's more you've been out walking with that cough," admonished his daughter.

"Nonsense child, that's nothin'; just a tickle. Now don't yer start a-fussin' or I'm back into that car and away."

"Come on in anyway and I'll put the kettle on. Becky, I did warn you, he's a demon when he's ill."

"That's alright, love. It's better to have a demon for a husband than not have one at all. He's not so bad really," she whispered, as they moved out of his hearing, "He's got over the worst. His temperature's down and that's the important thing. Don't worry, I've got my eye on him." She squeezed Jackie's hand reassuringly.

"Where's our lovely Bess?"

"She's wet so I left 'er in the car," said Ken as he followed them indoors.

"I've got a towel here Dad, she can come in, surely."

175

"Right y'are lass, I'll fetch 'er."

Ken was soon back, holding Bess by the collar. "Go to Jackie and get those paws dried."

She was on her knees waiting with a towel. Bess trotted straight to her and lifted a front paw in readiness. "What a good girl my Bessie is." Jackie rubbed the wet paws and legs, whilst a pink tongue washed her face. "Hey you, I'm getting wet as you're getting dry." The long tail swished about in reply.

"Where's our grand-daughter?"

"Darling, give poor Jackie a chance, she's only got one pair of legs and hands."

At that moment the tawny owl was brought in. Steve, intercepting the lady to guide her away from the house, left Jackie free to be with the family.

"We've been so busy since that storm. Thank goodness we have Andy who has recently started helping us. We've hardly been able to breathe, never mind rest. We even fall asleep at night worrying about a particular patient that's near to death. I'm so relieved, Dad, that you're on the mend. I couldn't stand it if you were seriously ill as well." Tears were filling her eyes but they did not overflow. She turned away to try and hide them.

"Now then my lass, yer can stop a-worryin'. I'll make ol' bones, 'specially with Becky 'ere a-fussin' over me. We've got that grand cottage and grounds and I couldn't be 'appier." Jackie turned to face him and the tears finally fell. "Com'ere yer daft creature, come to yer ol' dad." He held out his arms and enfolded her as he used to when she was young. Becky left them and went to make a cup of tea, then went upstairs to fetch Monica. Jackie had recovered by the time she returned with the child in her arms.

"There, Moni darling. Look there's Mummy with your Grandad."

Monica laughed excitedly, clapped her tiny hands and looked straight at her mother.

"Isn't she a clever little thing, she understands everything, doesn't she?" Jackie exclaimed happily, holding out her arms. "Who's my clever girl?"

"Com'on wonder-child, come to Grandad or Mummy'll never get me that tea Grannie 'as brewed." Ken teased.

"Dad, the most important thing in your life is your cup of tea. Really you're like a sponge!"

"Too true, m'gal, but someone 'as to clip yer wings or yer get so excited yer're likely to do som'at daft," he grinned. "Yer go up and down like a wind-blown sparra'."

Steve joined them in time for a drink and a chat. They had been discussing all the usual family things, when Ken asked after the cygnet that he and Becky had rescued. They told him the full story and when they had finished, Ken looked across at Becky as though in silent conversation. "Yer know we've got a bit of water down at bottom end. Well, we were a-thinkin' that we could give a safe 'ome to some water-birds. There's ducks and moorhens there but no swans or geese. If that wing don't mend, 'ow about bringin' 'em to us? If she can't fly maybe 'e'd stay with 'er too."

"That sounds lovely, Dad. Even if the wing does mend she won't be able to fly yet. By the time she is able to fly they'd be used to your water and, hopefully, made it their home. I'm not saying they won't fly away but they may well come back if they like it."

"Well then, think on it both of yer, and we'll come and collect 'em when yer call us."

Jackie and Monica stood beside Steve watching the Rover leave. All waved as the car turned onto the road. Steve went straight to the bird kitchen to prepare the evening meals, Jackie returned to the house to ask Sarah to give Monica her tea and get her ready for a bath before bedtime. Then she went to the hospital for her final jobs of the day.

First she looked at the new ducks. There was something wrong with one of them and she touched it. It was hard and unyielding. It had died peacefully while asleep — its head still under its wing. The body was put where such cases had to go. She checked the others and took out dirty papers and gave them fresh water. Going round from pen to cage until she reached the cygnet under the infra-red lamp Jackie prepared herself for another death. She had left this one until the end, not feeling mentally strong enough for another sorrow straight away. The cygnet appeared to be asleep but so had the duck. Jackie drew in a deep breath and reached in to touch the cygnet. Immediately, the brown head shot up and two fully-focused black eyes stared at her.

"Hello sweetie. You feeling better?"

"Twee-twee-twee." A much stronger voice replied.

After adding some vitamins to the water in the bowl she dabbled her fingers in it. Very soon the cygnet found the water and drank, lifting her long neck to let the refreshing water run down inside her. She looked at Jackie and snapped her mandibles together in anticipation of more water. The young swan searched the papers on which she was sitting trying to find the water, but it seemed to have disappeared. Jackie chuckled in delight and put her hand in the

177

water to splash it about. Again, the cygnet copied her and thirstily pushed her bill under the water and drank. Jackie went to get some Vitalyn and sprinkled some on the surface of the water. She managed to persuade the cygnet to take another drink. Whilst doing so it took in some of the flakes of dog food, which the cygnet shook out of its mouth in disgust. The bits flew everywhere. However after a few more attempts, the cygnet ate some and this time did not try to throw it away. Before she left, Jackie filled two bowls, one with water and vitamins and the other with very soggy Vitalyn. It was getting late by the time she went back to the house to prepare their evening meal. Sarah had been invited to go out later that evening to meet some of Andy's friends.

On the stove the pans were merrily bubbling, the table was set and Jackie was putting Monica into her night clothes, when Steve walked in looking tired and grubby. He went up for a bath and fresh clothes. When he came down he found the pans still bubbling with only just enough water left in them and his wife and baby asleep by the fire. He rescued their meal before gently waking his wife.

"Oh dear, I must have fallen asleep."

"I think you must, love," he smiled, "Never mind, I'll put Moni to bed. Come and eat, then you'll feel more your old self."

They ate in a companionable silence. Suddenly Steve said "Oh, by the way, that cygnet is a lot better. Your magic medicine's done the trick again so I've given her some Vitalyn and more water. Don't know if she'll eat it or not but we can try. Funny though, there were two bowls there, one dirty one and one with just a little water in the bottom. Looks as though she's drunk the water, but I don't know how the dirty one got there."

"Darling, that's wonderful. That dirty one was clean and filled with Vitalyn when I left it."

"That means she's eaten a bowlful. Great! If she keeps this up she'll pull through and put some weight on her bones."

"Funny isn't it? Some that we think will live – die. Others that we think have no chance – live!"

"That's life, my little sparrow — always unpredictable."

CHAPTER 19
WATER AT LAST

One morning, nearly four weeks after Star's wing had been set, Steve caught her and carried her to a nearby table.

"Will you hold her a moment, my scissors don't seem to be in my pocket where they should be. Must be in the hospital."

Jackie stood with a restraining arm over Star's back, her free hand gently stroking the long white neck. She talked soothingly to keep her calm. "Well Storm, soon we'll know if your wing's set properly and whether you'll to be able to fly free or have to go to live on my Dad's pond and be 'spoilt rotten'. We'll take your boyfriend too, of course, and you'll have plenty of good food and no-one'll harm you."

The door opened and Steve came back waving his scissors and said, "Right now, let's learn the worst." Carefully he cut through the various layers of binding and examined the wound site. "That's great, the wound has healed beautifully. Now let's see about the bone." He gently opened the wing. It was necessary to hold Star very firmly as the swan tried to open the other one, too, and would have knocked things off the table. He felt, with practiced fingers along the alignment of the bones and round the actual break point. "It's quite solid, as I hoped. I s'pose you dosed him with Symphytum; your favourite homoeopathic 'knit-bone'."

"Yes, I did. It really is incredible stuff, as we've proved time and time again, for any broken bone. It speeds up the mending time and reduces the risk of complications. Remember when Bill had his finger broken by that ram and I recommended Symphytum? It took a third of the expected mending time and the doctor couldn't believe how fast it had set!"

"Yes, that was rather amusing and old Bill was delighted, of course. I think that's why he's so intrigued by your various treatments," he replied.

Steve continued to feel along the wing. "As to be expected, it's rather stiff from being in the closed position for so long." He closed it again and let it go. Star's weakened muscles were unable to hold the limb up and it dropped down to her side. "I hope she won't be trailing the wing in any mud and ruin her flight feathers. It would be a shame if we have to resort to trimming short her primaries to reduce the weight. Although this would help her muscles, she'd be grounded 'til next summer moult. Still, I suppose if she's on Dad and Mum's pond with her boyfriend it won't matter. We'll give her a few days and see how she goes." As he spoke, he lifted Star up into his arms. "Jackie, if you come with me and collect her boyfriend we can put them together on the main pond. She can't fly and I'm sure he won't leave her."

"No, I'm sure he won't either, not after nearly dying when he was separated from her! I'll watch them anyway. If he starts flight runs and looking into the sky we can catch him again and wing-brail him. That'll put him temporarily in the same situation as she is."

Star and Pip found themselves being carried side-by-side to the main pond. Their long necks, which were held high and rigid, turning this way and that as they observed the large number of birds of so many different varieties. Steve and Jackie placed them at the edge of the water then stood back to watch.

Both birds lurched forward a few paces then stood stiffly looking about them until, with a shake to settle their disturbed feathers, they relaxed. Pip gave a long, relieved snort and looked about him with interest. Slowly he walked forward with the typical waddle of a swan. He placed each of his big, flat feet methodically one in front of the other, swinging his body rhythmically as he did so, until he stood in the shallows. Star followed closely behind him with the same unhurried dignity. It was as though they were savouring the first feeling of freedom after being so long in captivity. They stood together for a moment, looking about them. At last they pushed off and sat on the water waggling their tails with pleasure.

Suddenly, they launched themselves into wild, ecstatic bathing, rushing around in circles and beating the water with first one wing and then the other. Star's weak wing was trailing a bit but was supported by the water. Such activity would help the strength return to her muscles. After surging about, they suddenly stopped and faced each other. Pointing their bills down they turned away then, with courting movements, turned them in the opposite direction. Their heads were almost touching and their necks were held up high and erect. After a few minutes they relaxed and began to preen.

Steve placed his arm across his wife's shoulders which were conveniently at a comfortable height for him, and she snuggled up to him as they stood and watched. They said nothing for some time as words were unnecessary. After a while they smiled at each other, both feeling that little lump inside which comes when something beautiful takes the place of misery and pain. Again, it was like the phoenix rising from the ashes.

Their attention was drawn to the sound of a car in the yard. Jackie went to check that all was well with Monica and Sarah whilst Steve greeted the newcomers. They were two men whose arms, legs and clothing were covered in mud. They had been walking down by the estuary when they spotted a cob caught up in the reeds. It had a smashed wing. The men had waded into the shallow water, their feet finding it hard work on the thick muddy bottom. One had grabbed the cob by his neck and good wing, whilst the other man had disentangled the smashed wing. The swan had thrashed about trying to free himself but had only succeeded in rotating the damaged wing back on itself and entangling it amongst the tall reed stems. As they scrambled out, the men put the swan down on the steep muddy bank, whilst still holding him safely captive by his neck. No easy task in such slippery conditions and they, too, had become covered in mud.

The men held the big bird on the reception table so that Steve could examine the wing. He had to rotate it several times with great care to return it to the proper position. Then he studied the mess. There was mud everywhere and, on cleaning it off, he found the skin was infected. It was coloured with dark blue and red patches.

"What do you reckon, Mr Brough?"

"He's certainly made a mess of himself and without your catching him the infection growing in that wound would eventually have killed him. I can't say a lot more until after we've had him in surgery but, with an enlightened guess, I'd say that he'll make it. Whether he'll ever fly again, that I can't say."

"Can we leave 'im with you?"

"Yes, of course, thank you for helping him and bringing him to us — if you want to clean up a bit before you go, there's a sink in the corner."

"Thanks very much. Must say, we're only too relieved to 'ave somewhere like this to bring the poor beggar. I mean what could we 'ave done? Some vets'll tackle a bird but others say no, they're not trained in birds."

"That's true. They're trained for domestic animals. As far as birds are concerned it's usually farm birds with something like a general infection where they can mass medicate. The problem is, as I see it, that there are so many varieties of birds each reacting differently to disease and medicine. They would need a much longer and wider-ranging training. Vets are for the public and farms where people can pay them to care for their pets or livestock. We can legally treat wild birds as they're not owned by anyone. However, we do come up against the problem of drugs. By law these have to be administered by a vet and each hospital has a vet they can call on. Now, as we advise a vet what we want and how much to give for a particular specie, it does become rather ridiculous. Also, we need to medicate them quickly as a sick bird doesn't give us much time to act. Still, I suppose it stops well-meaning but uninformed people misusing drugs. This is why Jackie became interested in homoeopathic remedies, which she uses in preference to others. They have no side-effects; their effectiveness is very fast, which suits our patients, and we can purchase them by post directly from a pharmacy. We find that by using homoeopathic Aconite when a bird comes in terrified, it prevents the fear from killing it. No allopathic drugs will do this."

Jackie returned at that moment and pulled a face at the mess which should have been a swan's wing. "It looks as though I've come at the right moment," she said.

"We're just off," said the two men and stuffed a pound note into the collecting box. "Good luck with 'im."

"Goodbye and thanks for the donation."

"Pleasure. You deserve it and no doubt need it."

"I'll take him into surgery and start the anaesthetic machine. Can you take over whilst I scrub up and get ready?"

Jackie got the stethoscope then took over from Steve. She had difficulty in holding the swan still and keeping the mask on his head. He did not like the smell of the vapours. At one time she had to lean her body right over him and grab both his wings. The good one was sending things flying off the table and the injured one was in danger of being damaged beyond repair. The struggling slowly subsided and Jackie was able to release her hold and check his breathing. By the time Steve was ready and had the instruments laid out, she had been able to turn down the anaesthetic flow. "He's ready. I've tested him."

He worked for a while in silence, clearing dirt and feathers from the injury then cleansing the area and once again, himself. "This is a mess. It's broken in several places and there are bits of bone missing. I'm going to have to pin it. If he pulls through the surgery he'll need all your magic treatment if this wing's to stand a chance of healing."

"He'll get that, of course. I'll give him Arnica 200 when he comes round, for traumatic shock. Then I'll either give Bella Perennis 30 for after-surgical shock, or I may go straight on to Symphytum."

Steve was only partly listening as he was probing inside the wound with forceps, then he swore. Jackie looked at him in surprise, as it was something he rarely did. "What's up love?"

"Look." He held up his forceps which clasped lead shot. He dived into the wound by the other break and found some more. "Some bugger's shot him!" he exploded with fury. Jackie said nothing, seeing his intensely angry expression. She felt as angry as he and very sorry for the bird, but knew she would help most by saying nothing.

Steve selected a steel pin of the correct thickness and length. With great care he cut his way into the bone at one end and pushed the pin down its length. He left the screw-threaded end sticking out ready for attaching a handle which would be needed for the pin's eventual withdrawal. The bone should be set four weeks later when the pin would be removed, with the bird again under anaesthetic. He puffed antiseptic powder into and around the wounds and stitched them up. Jackie then switched off the anaesthetic machine as Steve gave the bird a Penbriton injection against infection and said "He's all yours."

She laid the cob's neck over his back and gathered him into her arms. "Can you manage, love?" He realised he had asked her to take a rather heavy bird. "When unconscious they always seem heavier."

"Yes, just about. If you'll open doors for me."

She laid the big bird in a pen under an infra-red lamp in the recovery room and sat down by her patient to wait for him to regain consciousness.

He was rather slow and Jackie was getting anxious. At last, he began to open his eyes and she breathed a sigh of relief. After a little while he opened his good wing fully and flapped it wildly. Jackie was up in a moment and, leaning over him, gathered up the wing. Only partly conscious, the cob did not know what he was doing. In his effort to stand up, being unbalanced by the bound wing, he threw himself over on his back. Jackie grabbed at him and fought to gather him into her arms as he thrashed desperately about hitting on her head with his good wing. She managed to get an arm over the top of him, trapping the active wing between their bodies. Putting her other arm underneath him, she picked him up, holding the injured side away from her.

Jackie sat down and placed the cob on her knee. His long neck was waving about and knocked itself on the chair leg, so she placed it over his back but it snaked out again and, once more, she had to grab hold of the neck. Acting quickly she pushed the swan's head inside her cardigan where the warmth and dark gave him peace. At last he lay still. She had been nursing him for about a quarter-of-an-hour when he withdrew his head and looked about him. Seeing clearly this time and noting his strange position, he raised his head and stared down into Jackie's face hissing defiantly at her. "Alright, old chap, you can go down now as you've come round." He struggled as she got up and carried him to his large pen. As she put him down he attempted to strike her with his good wing but she dodged and he missed. "It's no good," she told him, "You've got to get used to me. I don't like rude words and the sooner you learn it the better." She reached up to switch off the lamp and he hissed again.

Sarah brought Monica along in her pushchair to meet Jackie and to see the birds.

"Come on Moni, we'll leave him to settle down." They all went out into the weak sunlight of a rather pleasant December afternoon. Sarah was looking forward to the coming festivities and hoped it would be a 'white' Christmas. Jackie explained to her some of the old yuletide and New Year customs and, bending down said "It'll

184

soon be Christmas, Moni. We'll have to see what Father Christmas brings you. I hope he'll bring some peace for your Mum and Dad for a change."

Christmas Day arrived with watery sunshine after a night of heavy rain. Steve rose early to light the living room fire before taking a cup of tea up to Jackie, "Happy Christmas, darling". He smiled as he noticed that Monica was sitting in their bed with a stocking bulging with parcels.

They all sat in the comfortable double bed helping the child to open the packages. Father Christmas had left some wooden farm animals, bubble bath, a handkerchief with Pinnochio on it, a tube of chocolate drops, as well as an orange in the toe.

After breakfast Steve fed and watered the patients whilst Jackie started the lunch preparations. She was grateful that Becky had insisted on bringing with her most of the food, already cooked.

As the clock struck ten the Rover drew up outside the front door and all three got out. The four-legged one, beautifully brushed, bounded up to greet Jackie and Steve and give them Christmas kisses. "Where's Moni?" called Becky as she unloaded colourful parcels from the boot. "She's asleep. She has had a busy day already, so I thought a rest would be good for her." Jackie held the door open as Ken carried a cardboard box filled with food into the kitchen.

"Can yer get th'other one, Steve?"

"Right you are, Dad. What about this bag — want that too?"

"Yes, anythin' that looks likely, son. Thanks".

On entering the warm living-room they were handed a glass of sherry by Steve. " 'Ere's to us all," called out Ken raising his glass, "Includin' our little granddaughter that gives us so much 'appiness, bless 'er".

"Delicious. I might have guessed," commented Becky, noticing the label on the bottle, "Harvey's Bristol Cream, my favourite".

Steve smiled at Jackie and said "Bristol is quite a favourite with us, too. We spent a few days of our honeymoon there and visited the Wildfowl and Wetlands Centre at Slimbridge. It hardly seems possible that we've been married ten years."

Sarah came in and they were talking about Monica and her Christmas stocking when the telephone rang.

It was Sarah's parents in Australia, they had spent the day with Emma and Jeff enjoying a barbecue on the beach. "You lucky things", laughed Sarah, "It's been pouring cats and dogs here."

Sarah told her parents what she had been doing and that Andy had asked her out for the evening. Then she told them of some of the traditional Christmas food she would be eating. Before saying "Goodbye" she promised to write again soon. Greetings were passed between everyone and up-to-date news of Monica and Tommy exchanged. "We must 'phone Emma and Jeff on New Year's Day", said Steve as he put the receiver down.

Sarah ran upstairs to see if Monica was awake, while Steve and Ken went out to clean the cages in the hospital and check that all was well. Becky and Jackie carried the tray of glasses into the kitchen and began to lay the table.

"That was a first-class meal, m'dears", said Ken as they returned to the living room to open their presents. "It was a joint effort", smiled Jackie as she opened the radiogram and put on a record of carols from King's College, Cambridge. "And it's really wonderful having three generations together at Christmas. I'm sure Sarah is enjoying herself at Andy's house. It was nice of him to invite her over to meet his family". There were happy exchanges as each untied his or her presents. Jackie helped Monica to open her gifts from Becky and Ken, one was a cuddly teddy bear with a pink ribbon round his neck. "Oh, he's lovely," she pressed the toy to Monica's stomach and made her laugh. "Thank you so much".

Another parcel contained clothes including a prettily smocked dress which Becky had made. The last present left under the tree was given to Monica by Ken. "This one's for yer, m'dear. I 'ope yer like it." It was a wooden duck on wheels with a length of string on the front. "Now she's walkin' I made this to keep 'er company." The little girl took the duck into both hands and could not be parted from it for the rest of the day.

The afternoon passed pleasantly, Jackie and Steve were granted the peace they so well deserved as not one bird was found and brought in.

It was late in the evening when Jackie and Steve stood watching the red tail lights of the car leaving the drive. They turned to go back indoors. Suddenly, Jackie stopped, "Look!" She pointed into the

186

sky, "Wish! There's a shooting star." They both wished and turned towards each other with a loving smile. Each knew the innermost thoughts of the other — no wish could be secret. They joined hands and went indoors to the glow from both the lights and the fire. Turning the lights out, they sat together peacefully in the firelight enjoying their warm living room, so prettily decorated with greenery. Later, when they went upstairs to bed, they entered her bedroom and stood looking at their beautiful sleeping child.

*

The New Year came and went. Inside, the decorations had been taken down and outside cold, dreary January was darkening the countryside. After the merriment of the festivities, the arrival of dusk before the afternoon had finished accentuated the discouraging conditions where icy rain and cutting wind combined to cause as much misery as possible. Ice had to be broken on water bowls for outdoor birds and any weak ones had to be brought in again. Pip and Star stayed outside as they were progressing very well. The pen's wing was still slightly droopy but definitely improving.

By the end of January, Jackie noticed Pip making little runs on the water, wings flapping as though about to take off. Star had sat watching him but had not attempted to follow. Jackie rang Ken and Becky and told them they would need to take the birds to their pond quickly if they were not going to miss the chance of having them. They arranged to come and collect them the next day. That evening Steve enticed the swans, with food, into a special catching enclosure and shut the wire gate to keep them safe.

A deep, low pressure developed bringing in more gales. The wind howled through the night but by morning became calmer. Steve busied himself with the inside birds and asked Andy, who was doing the outside feeds, to make sure the cygnets that were to leave that morning were alright. On his return, he reported that all was well, although the water on the pond was very choppy and it was churning up the inner runs that went through the convalescent enclosures.

Pip was feeling restless as he did not like being enclosed. He saw a gap between the wire gate and the wire fence as the water swung it about and swam over to take a look. As it opened he pushed and, with a struggle, got through. Star was beside herself with anxiety and swam about by the gate, calling. The gate had returned to the

187

closed position and she could not see how he had escaped. Pip was on one side and Star on the other, both swans calling to each other in distress. This is how the family found them when they arrived, complete with swan-carriers and swan-hooks to catch them.

"Oh no! Now what do we do? If we're not careful we could spook the male into lifting, especially with this wind. He's upset already," wailed Jackie.

"I think our best hope is to open the gate and, if we position ourselves on the river side of it, he will go away from us and into our enclosure," suggested Steve, after some thought.

It seemed a sensible thing to do, so they quietly arranged themselves along the bank. Steve pulled on the opening gear creating a gap between gate and fence at the moment that both birds were near it.

Star made a quick dart and was through before any of them could react. Both birds, using wings and legs, hurried past the family. The wind was with them and before anyone realised what was happening they were air-borne.

The family watched with a deep feeling of sadness and loss. However, as they saw the two swans circle the hospital together before flying away, their feelings changed to delight in the knowledge that the two birds had cheated death and could now live together.

"Apart they die but together they fly" murmured Becky.

They strained their eyes to catch the last view of the beautiful white swans before they were swallowed up by the January gloom. Both human couples stood in silence, each considering how all creatures need loving companions to make their lives complete. The devotion shown by the birds reinforced the mutual love felt by the four people.

Seeing the empty swan-carriers that Ken had left by the water, Steve said "We've got a single cob with a badly broken wing which we've had to pin. I'm pretty certain he'll never fly again. In fact it's quite possible that the bones won't knit and he may have to have the wing off. It'd be nice if you'd give him a home 'though it'll be some weeks before we can discharge him."

"Steve, I think his wing will heal," said Jackie, "I caught him up this morning and ran my hands over it. I had a good feeling about it. True, he may never fly but I'm as certain as I can be that he'll keep his wing."

"That's my gal; she's in'erited my intuition," said Ken proudly.

188

"Yes, Dad, never a truer word. If our Jackie says a bird will or won't do something I don't argue with her."

Picking up the swan-carriers they walked through the convalescent house where Ken and Becky were introduced to 'Bolshy', as they had called him. The swan pulled himself up tall and hissed at them.

"Um-m-m I wonder what ol' Bess'd make of 'im. Still, I s'pose with a bit of freedom 'e'd settle, 'specially when 'e found we brought 'im food."

Pip and Star flew on until Star's wing began to ache and she dropped behind. Pip was alert to her every move and slackened his pace to match hers. Looking about him he saw a river and, after circling it to be sure it was safe, he led Star down to land on the surface.

They spent the next few weeks in a nomadic way. Until early one February afternoon, they were flying in a calm sky when Pip saw some water glinting in the hazy light. As usual, he circled to check it over and noted some ducks and a pair of moorhens. Dropping lower and satisfying himself that there was no danger, he and his mate flew down on to the water. They skied to a stop, sending ripples out all the way to the banks, disturbing the reflected landscape of their new home.

CHAPTER 20
HIDDEN BEAUTY

Completely hidden from casual view and approached only through surrounding woodlands, lay this beautiful and peaceful pond. Maybe it could be called a small lake since choking weed, encroaching scrub and dead branches had recently been removed. It was like an oval picture with irregular borders, set in a frame of delicate tracery. In spring the frame would become green and leafy. The picture itself being the reflected image of surrounding trees and the pale grey clouds that were giving way to white ones in a blue sky. Movement was added as water-birds caused little ripples to break up the image here and there.

The woodlands consisted of silver birch, aspen and weeping willows interspersed by the occasional oak. Soon the small leaves of the aspen, forever moving even in the lightest breeze, would be giving shelter to life on the ground beneath them. Early wild flowers were waiting in the earth to poke their heads through the rotting leaves when encouraged by the warmer weather and longer hours of daylight. Willows stood in groups at the water's edge, some leaning over as though studying their own reflections. Rushes seemed to be paddling in the shallows as ripples made them appear to be on the move. Various water plants patterned the surface and gave shelter to fish and other aquatic creatures. Adding to the beauty were our two regal swans who moved slowly across the lake causing their own wakes to spread out over the picture. Here, reality was suspended and an image of paradise glimpsed.

Bess was nosing about in the garden sniffing where various creatures had wandered. She always knew where each one had been during the night and made a daily routine of checking their tracks. She may even have known each as an individual, without ever meeting them face to face. Her wanderings took her into the wood and, with a happy tail, she followed her nose which led her down to the lake. There she stopped and stared.

As she watched, Pip and Star sailed out from behind the rushes and Bess's body stiffened. She had not seen them there before and wondered what they were doing on 'her' lake. She raised her nose to the air to appraise their scents which drifted to her across the water. One seemed familar and she flared her nostrils to evaluate it, whilst her eyes never left the birds. The scent brought an image to her mind of the white bird she had found in the woods some time ago. She remembered her master had carried it home. Spinning round she streaked away through the wood, by the garden and up to the cottage where she barked urgently at the back door.

"Hello Bess, come in love."

Bess whirled round and ran away a few steps before stopping to look back at Becky, then rounded to face her and barked again, bouncing on her front legs as though she was stamping her feet.

"What is it, girl?"

Bess gave another bark, turned and trotted a few feet and stood looking back over her shoulder.

"Just a minute, love, we'll come with you." She called to Ken who came to the door and was given the same demonstration.

Bess raced ahead of her master and mistress who, intrigued, followed as quickly as they could.

"Well, I don't know what she's found, but she's 'appy about it, any'ow."

They hurried along the path they had recently cleared, down to the water's edge, where they found Bess with a waving tail and pink tongue lolling over her white teeth. She turned to look at them, as if to say "See what I've found."

Becky hooked her hand under Ken's arm, pulled him close and whispered "I don't believe it. It's the 'lovers' ".

"It's two swans I grant yer, but 'ow d' y' know it's them? G'on with yer, that's wishful thinkin'."

" 'Course it's them, silly. Why else do you think Bess is so excited?"

Ken looked at the woman smiling up at him and grinned back at her. "I'm always bein' outdone by my three women, if it's not Jackie, it's m'dear wife or ol' Bess." As he spoke her name a wet nose was pushed into his hand.

The weeks passed. February melted unnoticed into March, which made as much noise and nuisance as possible. April began to weep and smile in turn. The smiles became broader as they welcomed May, whose flowers were soon to colour the lower lands.

Feeling the magical atmosphere, Pip and Star stopped and faced one another. They began the lovely head movements of swan courtship. Slowly and with great dignity, they turned their heads this way and that as they had done so often before, but this time there was an unusual feeling coursing through their bodies. They were feeling more and more aroused. Suddenly Pip gripped the back of Star's neck and mounted her back, their long necks laid out over the water. Then he slid off into the water and both birds dived and bathed happily before taking a final drink.

Under a hanging curtain created by a weeping willow was a small shallow bay with a hole in the bank leading to the home of a female water vole. This small creature peeped cautiously out. Her tiny eyes and flattened ears were dominated by her long whiskers. These were of great importance underground, enabling her to feel vibrations through them when they touched the sides of her tunnels. Some tiny shrews scuttled about amongst the grass searching for worms and other tasty morsels, occasionally they ran down into the water to search the sandy bottom for aquatic insects. Having to eat one-half to three-quarters of their body-weight each day, they were always busy. A movement further along the bank revealed a rabbit bobbing along, its slender ears attentive, before going down for a drink.

Blackbirds were flying around with beaks full of grass which made them look as though they had grown moustaches. A pair were building in suckers growing at the base of a nearby aspen. The cock bird spent a great deal of time singing from the top of the tree, declaring not only what a lucky chap he was, but that this was his tree and any interloper had better watch out. Meanwhile, his mate was weaving twigs and anything else that attracted her into that chosen site. Every now and then he would fly down to her with a leaf or some similar offering. They mated frequently, which not only fertilised her eggs, but was important to pair-bonding. When the nest was completed the hen bird settled herself comfortably and laid her first egg. Other birds were also building in various places in this delightful woodland, little realising how lucky they were to be in such a haven.

During April the gentle showers and warm sunshine had accentuated the beauty of the two swans, whose bills had turned a deep orange. Pip's knob had swelled so that it wobbled as he shook his head. Star had a smaller one, indicative of a pen.

They chose a narrow spur of land jutting out amongst the reeds for their first nest, and Pip began searching for sticks which he took to Star for her to place on their site. After some days of work she sat in the middle of the growing pile arranging the sticks around her, pushing in rushes and grass to fill holes and make it solid. Daily the nest grew until it was about six feet in diameter. When she sat on it she was almost hidden within the encircling embrace. By the second week of building, the swan's nest was complete and in it lay the first greeny-grey egg.

Pip swam to greet Star who stood up on her nest to welcome him. They both saw the egg and stared at it as if to say 'where on earth did that come from?' Star turned it over carefully with her bill and sat down again, experiencing the peace of her growing broodiness. Later, she moved off to have a bathe, pulling up and eating some water-weed, before returning to her nest with more grass to weave into it. After four eggs were laid she began sitting on them in earnest, to begin their incubation. A fifth one arrived shortly afterwards. She dozed most of the time with her head under her wing keeping the precious eggs warm. Pip was never far away.

The peace of the lake and the contentment of the two birds were complimentary. Even the weather was kind for there were only short, light showers of rain rather than heavy downpours.

Throughout the time of incubation Star did most of the sitting with Pip taking over for short spells whilst she had a bathe, a preen and some food. Each day when she returned to her nest, Star turned her eggs carefully with her bill. Placing her big, flat feet on either side of them, she lowered her soft warm body into a comfortable position, tucked her head under her wing and dozed. Pip swam a short distance away and placed himself on guard.

*

Thirty-six days had elapsed and a faint sound came from beneath her. Lowering her head and tilting it to one side to listen more directly, she located the sound "twee-twee." Star replied with soft grunt-like notes, "Quoh, quoh, quoh." Pip missed nothing and came round the reeds to find out what was happening. He also heard the tiny voice. The pen got up and momentarily left her nest in the cob's care so that she could have a quick bathe and a drink. Soon, she was back and urged him to let her onto the nest. Instinct told her not to turn the eggs at this stage, so she carefully sat back down without disturbing them.

The following day there were more tapping sounds coming from the shells. One determined inhabitant, impatient with his cramped quarters, was working hard! Soon a fine crack appeared round the outside of his shell. Even so, it was a few hours before a hole opened up, showing movement inside. Another little voice was calling steadily, punctuated by more tapping sounds. Star dozed a little with a feeling of tranquility. Pip was always close by, watching and waiting.

Through the haze of sleep Star felt a movement beneath her and, shifting her weight a little, looked to see what it was. The shell had broken in two and a wet, bedraggled little creature had emerged and was lying beneath her. She picked up the bits of shell and tossed them away, then settled down again.

The afternoon drifted on and Pip swam close to see if she was going for a bathe. She greeted him but did not move.

Evening arrived, encouraging the songs of the retiring birds as they gathered in the trees and bushes before roosting for the night. Bats dived over the water hunting for insects. A little owl twittered

194

a few plaintive notes, the 'morning alarm' for night creatures to wake up. Pip dozed with his head under his wing. He slept only lightly so that the slightest sound would rouse him.

Night passed and the eastern sky began to lighten, showing the trees in silhouette. Dawn was breaking. The blue, hazy light woke the birds encouraging them to join the chorus, welcoming the new day. The colours changed as creamy-gold clouds floated in the palest of blue skies. It was truly a new beginning, not only for that day but for the new family.

Star was discarding the other shells as tiny 'pipping' sounds now came from within her plumage. Four babies had hatched and were warm and snug under her wings. Pip was there continually poking about in her feathers to find out what was making the noise. He swam off to return with some water-weed for his mate. She accepted his gift, which was borne of devotion.

High above, a skylark warbled his lovely song. A robin sang in one of the birches and other birds joined in from further parts of the wood. It seemed as though they were all happy about the new babies.

To these accompanying sounds, Ken quietly led his family in single file along the narrow winding path towards the lake. Jackie, holding Monica by the hand, was close behind him, followed by Steve and Becky. For once Bess was in the rear, keeping everyone within her view. Ken took them to a spot where they could see the swans without disturbing them. Eagerly, they watched, passing a pair of binoculars between them, and soon were rewarded by the sight of a little grey head appearing in front of Star's white breast feathers, it looked around, then disappeared again.

"Oh! it's so wonderful. The 'lovers' have not only survived their ordeal but come to live here of their own accord," whispered Jackie. "This really makes our work worthwhile. "

"And we're all happy as well," said Becky with a misty look in her eyes, "As your Dad and I, having found each other, are no longer lonely. You two, not only do this wonderful work, but have given us a beautiful granddaughter as well."

Steve glanced from his parents-in-law to his pretty wife and little girl and, being full of emotion at that moment, his look to Jackie asked her to tell them their news.

She smiled from her husband to parents and announced·"Dad and Mum, in a few months you can expect a grandson."

"Grand*son*! Did you say? How do you know it's a boy at this early stage?" Steve was astounded.

Jackie laughed happily and said, "How do I know anything? I just *know* it is."

"Well, well, well. We can't argue with that, my gal," said her father proudly.

"Jackie, Steve, that's wonderful news. We're absolutely delighted."

"Well done, the pair of yer, and at nestin' time too! All I can add, as the ol' cob of this fam'ly, is — let's go 'ome and get a cup o' tea, I'm parched." Ken grinned as he put a hand on Steve's shoulder and patted his daughter's head.

It was the following day before Star got to her feet and stared down at the four fluffy creatures beneath her. They did not need to eat during their first day, as their egg-sacs were still inside their tiny bodies and being absorbed. There was an unhatched egg lying in the nest. Star rolled it about and listened. There was no sign of life and instinct told her to get rid of it. Putting her bill beneath it, she pushed it out and watched it roll into the water and sink.

Pip swam to her side and watched as she slid carefully into the water, leaving the cygnets to struggle over the edge of the nest to drop down beside her. Very slowly, Pip lead the way to some soft vegetation where he and Star broke up some small pieces for the babies. The cygnets picked the bits up and threw them about, perhaps a little going down inside them. It was not long before they scrambled up onto Star's back to snuggle down under her wings. The proud parents swam lazily around. Suddenly, Star realised how hungry she was because she had not eaten much during the last few days. Avidly she pulled up some nourishing roots from floating weed.

The new mother, feeling her babies moving about on her back, eased her wings a little and a grey head appeared. Bright black eyes stared at the handsome white swan ahead which was his father. Star returned to her nest feeling tired due to her long inactivity. She stepped up without shaking off her precious load and settled down feeling as though she had been for a very long swim.

Pip moved a little way from the nest for a bathe. He opened both wings and enthusiatically splashed and flapped. Making use of his wings, he rolled first to one side and then to the other until he was thoroughly wet. When he was satisfied he pushed himself upright and shook, sending sprays of water back into the lake.

At this point a moorhen came swimming by and was startled when Pip charged at him, hissing angrily. The moorhen flew off quickly as this had not happened before. The new father had his responsibilities. In the distance Pip heard a familiar swishing sound and lifted his head to locate it more accurately. As he waited and watched, three swans came flying into view and Pip's wings rose in readiness to defend his territory. However, the three flew on ignoring the little lake beneath them.

Another evening came and dissolved into night, with Pip sleeping near to his family. The full moon came out beaming benignly down onto the little community.

As the dawn light signalled daybreak, Star called to Pip, who swam majestically towards her. The pure white swan sat on her nest amongst the green rushes with the dainty leaves of a weeping willow hanging down — forming a curtain behind her. Together they made a picture of timeless beauty.

The light slowly brightened and colour flooded into the picture. A little head emerged from the white plumage. He had a small light patch on his grey forehead; just as his mother and grandmother before him. Pip watched and grunted a soft greeting. The newcomer put one of his feet on top of the other and, before Star could stop him, fell over and splashed into the water. Immediately, he turned towards Pip and swam as fast as his young legs would allow.

The tiny, dark grey bill stretched up and the huge orange one reached down to meet it. Little son nibbled his father's bill. Pip glanced across to Star, who was watching, and softly called "Quoh quoh, quoh."

197

HOMOEOPATHY

Homoeopathy is an holistic approach to medicine seeking to treat both the physical symptoms and the emotional stresses suffered by the patient.

The author has found homoeopathy particularly effective when treating sick and frightened birds.

Her book "Homoeopathic Treatment for Birds" is available from C.W.Daniel & Co.Ltd., 1 Church Path, Saffron Waldon, CB10 1JP, England.

The source of the preparations used in the text and application to birds in this story:

Aconite is Aconitum napelus, a variety of monks hood, which is picked in August towards the end of its flowing season. It is found in the Voges Mountains of France.
Used to treat birds suffering from an injury and shock such as when caught by a cat.

Arnica Montana is a perennial herb also known as leopard's bane and sneezewort. The whole plant (root, leaves and flowers) is commonly used in homoeopathy.
A first-aid treatment for birds suffering bruising or concussion.

Arsenicum Album is white oxide of arsenic, a greyish-white metallic element. Prepared by roasting natural arsenic of iron, nickel and cobalt.
Increases resistance to infection and fights food poisoning.

Bellis Perennis is the English garden daisy, which is recorded as having been used by Pliny in Roman times.
After the fresh plant has been chopped and pounded the juices are extracted for use.
Aids the clearing of bumps resulting from knocks. Can be used following Arnica if the lump remains after bruising has cleared.

(continued overleaf)

Carbo Vegetabilis is wood charcoal. The homoeopathic preparation uses beechwood burnt in the absence of air.
Used to treat cold and weakness when the bird is close to death.

Dulcamara is derived from woody nightshade which is a perenial plant commonly found in hedgerows and well-known for its poisonous bright red berries.
The homoeopathic treatment is derived from the green, pliant stems and leaves.
Used to treat conditions resulting from the bird being cold and wet.

Ignatia Amara is also called St. Ignatius' bean and was brought to Europe from China in the seventeenth century.
The bean is powdered before being prepared.
This is often prescribed for birds who have suffered an emotional shock, such as loss of a mate.

Symphytum has many common names including comfrey, knitbone, boneset, bruisewort and healing plant. All these confirm that the healing powers of this plant have long been well-known by country folk.
The root is chopped and pounded into pulp ready for homoeopathic preparation.
"Sympho" in Greek means "to unite" as this is used to aid the knitting of bones and flesh.

The above source materials are usually diluted for use by a factor of 10 or 100. The potency commonly recommended for beginners is 6c, which means the remedy has been diluted 6 times by a factor of 100.
THE USE OF HIGHER POTENCIES SHOULD BE LEFT TO AN EXPERIENCED PRACTITIONER.

The study of homoeopathy is a demanding and stimulating one. It is a vast subject on which many books have been written with humans in mind.

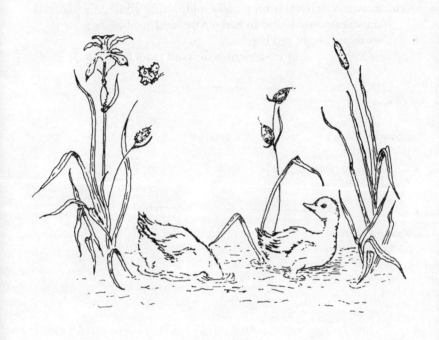